The Penny Court Enquirers

One Clue at a Time
A Victorian Mystery

Raymond Buckland

Queen Victoria Press

The Penny Court Enquirers Mysteries:

THE PENNY COURT ENQUIRERS:

ONE CLUE AT A TIME

ISBN 978-0-9794560-4-6

Queen Victoria Press

P.O. Box 892, Wooster, OH 44691-0892

www.raymondbucklandbooks.com

For Tara and in memory of Tish

ONE CLUE AT A TIME

London, 1886

Chapter One

Israel Rosenthal opened his mouth wide in a yawn as he dipped the oars of the wherry into the dark murky waters of the River Thames and propelled the heavy craft forwards, downstream. It was a late April morning, with the sun barely up, and the fog still lay thick and heavy on top of the water. A gritty, dirty wetness sprinkled the scene; neither an honest rain nor even a genuine drizzle. Israel glanced around at his brother Jakob in the stern, who was busy untangling a rough hemp line, and then faced forward again toward the bow. He pushed the boat along, letting the first ebbing tide of the day do most of the work.

"Fog is na' going to let up till midday at least, I reckon," he said, through another yawn.

"Look out for the bridge up ahead," responded Jakob, his head down as he concentrated on what he was doing.

"Aye. Aye."

They both heard the creak of a barge's sail, off to starboard, invisible in the fog. "And for other craft," Jakob muttered. But they were both accustomed to working their way up and down stream and avoiding other bigger, heavier craft on this much traveled stretch of the river.

Israel peered through the murky gloom, over the bow of the boat. Suddenly he laid down the oars and half rose in his seat.

"Steady as she goes, Jakob," he muttered. "Steady as she goes. I think we've got us a floater."

Jakob put aside the mess of tangled rope and moved forward alongside his brother, his hand automatically taking up the boathook that lay along the gunwale. "You see to the oars, 'rael," he said. "I'll fetch him in."

Israel turned around on his seat so that he could put his back into the rowing. With repeated looks over his shoulder, he pushed the boat on toward the huge, dark shape of London Bridge that oozed out of the gloom ahead of them.

"He's caught in some sort of tangled mess at the foot of the pier," said Jakob, steadying himself with a foot on the bow. As Israel brought the wherry around broadside to the bridge's footing, Jakob stuck out the boat hook and snagged the bundle half submerged in the water. He struggled briefly then was able to pull it free and towards the side of the boat. Israel dropped the oars into the boat and helped his brother pull the body in over the side. Water poured into the bottom of the boat.

Israel rolled the figure onto its back and pulled aside the cloth covering the face.

"*Oy gevalt!* It's a woman!" said Jakob.

Israel leaned forward. "More than that," he said. "She's alive!"

"It just doesn't *feel* right," said Bertie.

"Wouldn't bother me." Arnold, Bertie's brother-in-law, sipped on his cup of tea, his eyes still glued to the newspaper in front of him.

"Twenty-three years at *The Chronicle*," continued Bertie. "Twenty-three years! Fifteen as pressman and the last eight as foreman."

"Don't let it get to you," said Nellie his wife, as she and Isobel Wilson, their carrot-top, freckle-faced, fifteen year old maid-of-all-work, folded sheets and other linen.

Bertie Hawkins sat at the kitchen table, a sad look on his usually cheerful face. He chewed on his walrus mustache, a good indication to Nellie that he was truly upset.

"Drink your tea, Bertram, and you'll feel better. We'll look at the whole situation together after dinner this evening." Nellie was seldom unsettled by any of the vicissitudes of life, even those directly affecting her family. All that was ever needed was to put things into perspective, with due regard to the positive and the possible negative results of the situation. From there it should be possible to plan a route out of the mire and back onto solid footing. Or so she believed.

But she allowed herself a sigh. Bertie – he of the dark, wavy hair and the sparkling brown eyes; her childhood sweetheart, now for twenty years her dearly beloved husband – deserved better than this. He had started as a young boy, selling *The Daily Chronicle* on street corners and badgering the office to give him a "proper" job. Eventually, when he was fifteen, they had; cleaning out the ink troughs for the big Walter rotary web press that spun out the newspapers every morning. From there he had learned, in his own time from one of the friendlier pressmen, how to mount the plates and work with the printing and impression cylinders. He had eventually been rewarded with a job as a pressman's assistant. Bertie loved the newspaper business. It later took him years to remove the printer's ink from his fingers and from under his nails. But he was fascinated by the stories, especially the headlines that often featured robberies and even murders.

Time runs on regardless, mused Nellie. The giant newspaper *The Morning Post* had just swallowed up *The Daily Chronicle*. With no longer the need for so many presses, Bertie and his fellow pressmen had been let go. He had been given a small sum as severance pay, but with no prospects for future employment it was little wonder that he sat so sadly staring into his cup of rapidly cooling tea.

"You can do anything you want to now, Bertie," said Arnold, finally putting down his newspaper and taking up his tea-cup in both hands.

Arnold was nothing like his younger sister. Nellie was short and stocky . . . "buxom" people called her. She had blonde hair in ringlets that poked out of her frilled and beribboned cap. She was always cheerful and optimistic. And she was an excellent cook. Arnold Middleton, on the other hand, was a big man with a completely bald head. He wore large "mutton-chop" sideboards (Nellie said it was to compensate for his lack of hair on top). This hair was salt-and-pepper. Arnold was always very serious, having little sense of humor. Nellie admitted that he was – or seemed to be – very slow at grasping things. Yet she had to admit that he was thorough. Although a pessimist, he was full of good intentions and as honest as anyone could be. He worked at odd jobs around Covent Garden market. He used to work at the Newgate Market before it closed. He was unmarried and lodged with Mrs. Westbury on Old Fish Street, though spent all of his spare time with Bertie and Nellie.

"That's right, Bertram," said Nellie. "You can do anything your heart desires . . . within reason, of course."

Bertie gave a long, long sigh and drank deeply his now almost cold tea. He put down the cup and looked around at the others. Isobel, the dowdy housemaid with – it seemed to Bertie – a perpetually runny nose, busied herself with the linens. She placed them in piles and then, after wiping her nose on her sleeve, bore them away to the various rooms where they were needed. Nellie smiled at her husband, sensing that his perpetual optimism was about to resurface.

"You're absolutely right, Arnold," he said.

"I am?" Arnold sounded surprised.

"Yes. I can do what I like but, obviously, it must be something to advance the family fortunes."

"What would you truly *like* to do, Bertie?"

He didn't have to think about it. "I've always looked at those stories in *The Chronicle*; those robberies and even the murders. I always got very annoyed at the poor performance of the police in most of them. They don't seem to know what they are doing half the time. It takes them a month of Sundays to solve even the smallest of crimes."

"So what are you saying?" asked Nellie, now at work at the kitchen stove, seeing to the upcoming dinner.

"I'm saying that I believe I could do a whole lot better. No! I *know* I could do a whole lot better. If I was in their place and had all the facts that they have, I bet I could solve the crimes in less than half the time."

"So you want to be a policemen, Bertie?" Arnold sounded puzzled.

His brother-in-law shook his head. Nellie looked over her shoulder at her husband, waiting on his next words. "No, it's not that. Besides I'm too old now. But I bet I could solve any of their crimes in a much shorter time."

"Don't they have detective policemen?" asked Nellie, lifting a saucepan lid and stirring the contents of the pan with a large wooden spoon.

Bertie nodded. "Yes. They *detect* things . . . or are supposed to. I don't know that I could guarantee detecting everything, but I could make the right sort of enquiries that would lead to the best results."

"So . . . you'd be what? An 'enquirer'?" asked Arnold, the puzzlement still on his face.

Bertie thought for a moment, then smiled and nodded. "Yes. Yes, Arnold. I like that." Arnold beamed. "I'll be an Enquirer. No guarantees, but I bet my enquiries would bring results."

Nellie put the lid back on the saucepan and came to the table. "Are we talking about what you would really like to do, Bertram, or just dreaming?" Her voice was soft and serious.

He looked at her, his eyes unblinking. "We've said I can do anything I like. I think I would like to try my hand at this, Nell. Just to see if I could do it. Perhaps just to pass the time while I look for another job, anyway?"

She smiled at him. "I think you *could* do it, Bertie," she said. Then she turned back to the stove and continued in a more certain voice. "Well, we have this money the *Chronicle*, in its beneficence, gave you on parting. And we also have the small legacy that aunt Eleanor left me at the beginning of the year. Together I think we would have enough to set you up in business."

Bertie came to his feet and moved around to face his wife. He took her hands in his. "Nell . . ." he said.

She put a finger to his lips. "Ssh!" she said. "It's all settled. Though I will handle the money, and I will want a correct accounting of all expenses."

"What – what's going on?" asked Arnold.

Nellie glanced at him and smiled. She turned back to her husband. "There's just one thing," she said. "You will need an assistant – someone to help you do some of the legwork. I think maybe, Arnold . . ."

Bertie's eyes rose to look at the ceiling, as though appealing to a higher authority, but quickly returned to meet Nellie's smiling face. "Of course," he said. "Of course."

"So what do we call ourselves?" asked Arnold later, as they sat over dinner. He had finally absorbed the full gist of what was planned and was very excited to be a part of it.

When younger, and first working for *The Chronicle*, Bertie had saved his money towards the time he could marry his sweetheart. They had bought a nice house at 27 Penny Court, off Paternoster Row, near St. Paul's Cathedral. It had been convenient for Bertie working in Fleet Street. Bertie had said to his bride that she was the queen of his court. Nellie had said, in jest, that unfortunately her court was only worth a penny. Bertie had immediately replied that, with Nellie as queen, it was actually worth a sovereign.

"I know!" announced Nellie. "We'll call you The Penny Court Enquirers."

They all laughed and thought it an excellent name.

"And here's your – our – first job," said Arnold. He pulled the discarded newspaper to him and, folding it back, pointed to the headlines.

Young wife mysteriously disappears into thin air at pawnbrokers.

Chapter Two

Bertie glanced at the piece of paper he had pulled from his overcoat pocket, read the address he had scribbled down, and thrust it back into his pocket.

"Should be the next street over, Arnold," he said.

The two men turned down a narrow, cobblestone street, carefully picking their way through piles of rubbish, horse dung, and other detritus, and stepping between puddles of thrown-out household slops and urine. Bertie silently pointed to the traditional three brass balls projecting from the wall above the entrance to a small shop. The sign was showing wear and hung at a rakish angle, threatening to drop the balls on those who entered and exited. Bertie led the way, opening the shop door and entering with Arnold on his heels.

It was dark and gloomy in the shop, despite the sun struggling through low clouds outside. Bertie noticed a strong musty odor. A solitary oil lamp burned on the counter beside a pile of cheap jewelry, household items, and assorted bric-a-brac. An old man in ancient clothing peered at Bertie through bottle-lens, pince-nez glasses perched on the end of his bulbous, rubicund nose. His teeth were the color of old ivory. A greasy smoker's hat sat on his head, allowing wispy strands of grey hair to escape in an untidy tangle.

"What you got?" The voice was as wizened and cracked as its owner.

"I beg your pardon?" said Bertie.

"What you bringin' in? How much you need?"

"Oh! No, no I'm not here to pawn anything."

"Then what you wasting m'time for?" The old man snorted and looked around as though he'd like to spit somewhere.

"I – I just wanted to ask you one or two questions," said Bertie, feeling very uncomfortable. This wasn't the way he had seen things going. After all, he was one of The Penny Court Enquirers! With that thought, he pulled himself a little more upright and stood against the front of the counter. "Just a couple of questions, if you would be so kind?"

"You not a copper." It was more a statement than a question.

"No. No, nothing like that," he said quickly.

The old man's eyes took in the size of Arnold, towering behind his brother-in-law. Bertie saw the direction of his gaze and smiled.

"Nothing to be afraid of."

"It's about that missing woman, i'n it?"

"Actually, yes. Yes, it is. I'd – we'd like some details. The newspaper report was very sketchy."

"I told the police all I know. Don't know nothin' more."

"If you'd just be kind enough to repeat what you said," said Bertie. He saw the defiance in the old man's eyes and, slipping a shilling out of his pocket, placed it on the edge of the counter. The old man eyed it suspiciously but said nothing. Bertie sighed and brought out another shilling.

"I didn't even know she were in the shop," said the pawnbroker, swiftly scooping the coins into his palm and dropping them, with a clink, into some receptacle behind the counter. "It seems she was in the queue, waiting."

"There was a queue?"

He sniffed and tossed his head as though it was a stupid question. "'Twas the end o' the week, weren't it? They always comes in toward the end of the week, hocking anything and everything, to redeem it a couple of days later when the old man gets paid."

"Of course." Bertie nodded as though that was common knowledge, though actually new to him. "And she was in the line waiting to be served?"

"What I just said, ain't it?"

"They say that she disappeared." Bertie pressed on. "Her husband was waiting outside. He saw her come in but she never went out again. And she wasn't here when everyone else had gone."

The pawnbroker sniffed. "That's what they say."

"Back door?"

Bertie jumped. He'd almost forgotten that Arnold was standing behind him.

"Ain't no back door," said the pawnbroker. "As I told the police twenty times! Now, you got any more questions for me to waste my time on? I got work to do."

Bertie stood a moment in thought. "How many people were in line here?" he asked.

"Dunno. P'raps a dozen. I don't keep count. Too busy doing the money."

"And you didn't notice this woman at all?" persisted Bertie.

"I don't even know what she looked like. Not even now!"

Bertie could see that he'd get no more information out of the man. He raised his bowler hat to him, more out of habit than feeling any respect. "My thanks." He pulled a piece of paper from his waistcoat pocket and scribbled his name and address on it. "If you think of anything else, please let me know," he said. "G'day to you. Come Arnold."

Outside in the street, as they pressed in against the wall to let a heavily laden brewer's dray roll past, Arnold looked intensely into his brother-in-law's eyes. "So what did we learn?"

Bertie fingered his mustache and squinted his eyes, to let Arnold know he was processing what they had gleaned. Then he led the way back along the street, in the tracks of the dray, trying not to breathe-in the stench of the street.

"First of all, we know that she was not alone in there," he said. "Secondly, we know that there were enough women . . . I should have asked if they were all women or if there were any men. Anyway, there were enough people there that the pawnbroker didn't notice her in particular."

"So are we any farther along than before?"

Bertie looked up at his partner. "Do you know, you sometimes have the knack of asking the obvious, Arnold?"

Arnold beamed, and then looked serious. "Is that good?" he asked.

"I'm not sure."

Bertie sat at the kitchen table, pen wet with ink, staring at the blank page in front of him. Nellie had purchased the large ledger book for him and he now had to write a report of his enquiries on the right hand page, with an account of his expenses on the left. The first expense was, of course, the ledger itself – 1s/3d – and the second the two shillings he had paid the pawnbroker.

Nellie sent Isobel out on an errand and then sat down beside Bertie. Arnold was doing some work at Covent Garden and wasn't expected before supper.

"So what is the result of the first day of enquiry?" Nellie asked.

Bertie cleared his throat. "The missing young lady is Mrs. Emily Squire, married to one Thomas Squire," he said. "They reside in Bread Street, off Fenchurch Street. On the morning in question Mrs. Squire entered the pawnbrokers on Sunbury Street, while her husband waited outside."

"He didn't go in with her?"

Bertie shook his head. "There was no point. There was a queue of women, all waiting to hock one thing or another. I think Mr. Squire only waited to make sure Mrs. Squire didn't run off and spend any of the money she received."

"But she never came out again," said Nellie.

"Right." Bertie sat quietly for a moment, stroking his mustache. Nellie waited. "It's strange. There was no rear entrance; no back door she could have left by. And the pawnbroker didn't even recall seeing her. It seems she went in all right – there seems to be no question about that – but just never came out again."

"So what do you think happened?"

Bertie shrugged. "Obviously she *did* come out. She had to have done. But she did it in such a way that no one saw her."

"And how could that be?"

He continued stroking his mustache. "We have to do a little more digging, I think, my dear," he said. He looked at her and his eyes gleamed. "This is most intriguing!"

Nellie smiled. "Intriguing, yes. But the question is, will it pay for itself?"

His face clouded. "What do you mean?"

"Even if you solve the mystery – how she got out of the shop – who is going to pay you for doing that . . . for the three shillings and thrupence you've spent so far?"

Bertie spoke his thoughts aloud. "She has disappeared. I will not only find how she got out of the pawnbrokers but I will also find her; find where she is now. I would think the husband would pay me something for that?"

Nellie laughed a mirthless laugh. "I don't think we can count on that, Bertram. No, I think we need something else; some other challenge for you, that will pay you money enough to cover whatever you might spend on this case."

Bertie looked worried.

"I – I don't know . . ."

Nellie got up and moved over to the stove to start preparing their supper. "I think I might have something for you."

"Oh?"

"You know my good friend Hattie?"

"Mrs. Parker?"

"Yes. Hattie Parker. I was talking to her about the Penny Court Enquirers and she asked me a question."

"What was that?"

Nellie stoked up the stove and put water on to boil. "She said that she's worried about her husband."

"Mr. Parker? Herbert?"

Nellie nodded. "It seems that Mr. Parker has been coming home very late recently and even stayed out all night last Tuesday."

"He did?" Bertie had trouble imagining Herbert Parker philandering but waited to see what Nellie had to say.

"Hattie said she'd be happy to pay whatever it cost to find out just what her husband is doing." She paused. "Hattie has always been very careful with money, and Mr. Parker earns a good wage at the bank. She can afford to pay and to pay well."

"So you want me to check on Parker? Follow him, perhaps?"

"I would imagine it's not a big job. And if it would help bring in enough to justify what you need to do to solve the Emily Squire case . . ." She left the rest unsaid.

Bertie smiled at her. "Nell, my love. You are even smarter than your brother!"

Chapter Three

"First things first, Arnold," said Bertie, as the two men walked along Cheapside towards the financial district. Traffic was heavy, which was not unusual, but with the horses' hooves pounding the roadway, the rattle of the iron-bound wheels on most of the vehicles, and the general shouting of cab drivers and lorrymen, it was not easy to make oneself heard.

Herbert Parker worked as a clerk at a small bank on Leadenhall Street. Bertie planned to get there at six o'clock, as Herbert would be leaving, and to follow him wherever he might go.

"We keep out of sight of Mr. Parker but keep him *in* sight, if you follow me."

Arnold did not respond. Bertie presumed it was because he was still trying to understand exactly what it was that Bertie had just said. Bertie sighed. "We just follow him but make sure he doesn't see us," he said.

"Ah!" Understanding dawned on Arnold's face.

Herbert Parker was prompt in leaving his place of employment. From across the street, The Penny Court Enquirers spotted their man and set off in pursuit. Herbert Parker looked neither to right nor to left and finally dashed across the road, avoiding hansom cabs, carts, and even a horse-drawn omnibus. Turning south from Leadenhall Street, he set a brisk pace down the India Road and on into Lime Street. At the end of Lime Street he turned into a pub called *The Turk's Head*. Bertie and Arnold, a hundred feet or so behind him, came to a halt.

"What do you think, Bertie?"

"Probably gone in for a bite to eat. A good sign that he's not planning on going home, I would say."

Arnold nodded sagely then, after a moment, said "Shall we do the same, d'you think? Get a bite to eat, I mean?"

Bertie's mind had a sudden vision of pounds, shillings and pence mounting up at a frightening rate in his ledger book, under the heading "Expenses". He shook his head as though to clear it. "I think we had best hold on for a while, Arnold. We don't know for sure that he's gone in there to eat. He may just be asking directions. He could be out again in two minutes. Besides, we can have a late meal when we get home."

"Perhaps we could just pick up a pie?" Arnold sounded hopeful. Bertie didn't encourage him.

But Herbert Parker was not out of *The Turk's Head* at all quickly. It became obvious that he must be partaking of a substantial meal, in all probability washed down with good porter, thought Bertie. The two Enquirers stood shifting their weight from one foot to the other for a very long time.

"Ah!" Bertie let out a long sigh of relief as they saw their prey emerge from the hostelry and continue on, at a less hectic pace. He crossed Fenchurch Street and entered Philpot Lane.

"He's making for the river," muttered Bertie.

"Why would he do that?"

By now it was getting quite dark and the lamplighters were making their rounds. A gas light burned at the corner of Botolph Lane and Eastcheap, enough to allow Bertie a glimpse of his quarry now hurrying past Pudding Lane and then down Fish Street Hill.

"He can move fast for a city clerk," muttered Arnold. "Sitting at a desk all day doesn't seem to have done him any harm."

Bertie grunted in agreement.

Fifteen minutes later Bertie pulled Arnold back into the shadows as, ahead of them, Herbert stopped outside a darkened doorway in a row house above Old Swan Stairs. They watched him look carefully up and down the narrow alleyway before knocking on the low, blackened door. It seemed a long time before a candle flame was visible through the small pane of glass in the door. Herbert reached out and tapped again on the door, this time in a series of short and lengthy raps. The door was opened a crack and Herbert disappeared inside.

The two pursuers stood for a long time waiting to see if Herbert Parker would come back out again. He did not.

"What d'you think, Bertie?"

"One thing I think is that our friend Herbert is not doing any philandering. Nellie's old friend Hattie doesn't have to worry about any rivals. No, my bet is that Mr. H. Parker has been bitten by the opium bug. I'm betting that the hovel we see before us is one of the many opium dens scattered about our fair city."

"Opium? You think so?"

"I do indeed." Bertie's bowler hat nodded back and forth. "And there's only one way to make certain."

"Wh-what's that?" asked Arnold. From the quaver in his voice, Bertie felt that his brother-in-law knew the answer.

"We have to go in there," he said quietly. Arnold said nothing. Bertie sighed. "I suppose only one of us needs to actually go inside . . . You can wait out here, Arnold."

"Thanks, Bertie." Arnold's voice was quiet. Then he spoke louder. "How are you going to do it? Isn't that a sort of secret knock that he gave?"

"Very good, Arnold. Yes. I'm sure it was. Let me think on that."

They stood for a while. Two men, in evening dress, came unsteadily down the alleyway and made for the darkened doorway. They spoke together in hushed voices and then knocked on the door. The same procedure was gone through as with

Herbert Parker. The men were admitted and the door closed. Bertie began to get an idea.

Within a few more minutes a group of five men, similarly dressed for a night out on the town, moved unsteadily along to the door and rapped loudly on it. They were obviously the worse for drink and made no attempt to keep quiet. After a moment, and the required secret signal, the door was opened. As they started to go in Bertie squeezed Arnold's arm.

"Stay here," he said. "If Herbert comes out without me, follow him." Then he was gone. Arnold saw him slip quickly but quietly across the street and follow the group into the building as though he was one of them. The door closed and Arnold was left alone.

It was a short, emaciated, Chinese woman who closed the door behind Bertie when he followed the other men into the facility. She was dressed in a worn, silk gown that, when Bertie saw it in brighter light, was dirty and unkempt. They all stopped and let her take the lead. She said not a word but pulled aside a bead curtain separating the entrance area from a larger, slightly better illuminated, room.

"You will remove shoes," she said. They all did as she told them. "Now please to not speak. Silent! No talk."

They followed her along a short passage, around a corner, and into a large, ill-lit room with a low ceiling. Crudely constructed beds – little more than edged wooden pallets holding soiled cushions – filled the area. More than half of them were occupied by men from all walks of life, it seemed to Bertie. Dense clouds of sweet-smelling smoke billowed over everything. Two young Chinese boys, in shabby canvas trousers and soiled blue jackets, squeezed between and over bodies, to fill pipes and to light them with glowing charcoals. Many of the men lay with eyes closed while others had glassy, fixed stares that seemed to see nothing yet everything at the same time. The smell of sweat, tinged with urine, mingled with the sweet smell of the opium. Bertie wrinkled his nose in distaste. The evening-dressed men lost no time in tumbling down onto empty beds and groping about for pipes.

Bertie quickly spotted Herbert Parker, already unaware of his circumstances as he lay with a half smile on his lips and his eyes screwed up as though to shut out life itself.

Bertie was almost afraid to breathe in case the thick, cloying smoke claimed him and dragged him down into the hell that he knew existed in such dens. He felt his throat constricting from the cloying, all-pervading smoke and wondered how and why anyone could be seduced into accepting its dubious release. For release is what the addicts claimed to receive; release from stress, from worry, from all the miseries of life. Opium, they sang, was the great deliverer. The uncritical, non-discriminating, pleasure satiation that was no more nor less than a heaven on earth. That is, until they came back down to earth.

As Bertie shrank down on a bed close to Herbert, the better to watch him, he was suddenly made aware of that crash landing that awaited the unwary. A young man alongside Herbert suddenly cried out in agony and starting thrashing about, his arms and legs striking unheeding neighbors. The woman owner cried out something in Chinese and the two young boys leapt over recumbent bodies to grab hold of the customer. As he screamed and thrashed – beginning to intrude on the forced meditations of those about him – the boys were hard put to hold him. The woman shouted loudly and a second bead curtain at the far end of the room was thrust aside to admit a bare-chested giant of a man, head bald but for a tightly braided pigtail that bounced about his neck as he strode down the room. He reached to grasp the drug-induced victim and plucked him out of the sea of pallets, propelling him on toward the door through which Bertie and the others had entered.

Bertie jumped up and followed the giant, the woman, and young man out of the establishment. Bertie's soft heart was working overtime.

"Wait!" he cried. "Wait! The boy needs help."

The giant tossed the young man out of the door into the alleyway and then turned and disappeared as quickly as he had come. The Chinese woman made to close the door but Bertie stuck his foot in it and glared at her through the opening.

"This is not the first time, I'm sure, that someone has been so badly affected," he cried.

"Where can I take him? He needs a doctor, and quickly."

She made a short sharp comment in Chinese and tried to force the door closed, but Bertie would not budge. "A doctor!" he cried. "Or do you want me to bring the police here?"

"*You-tai!*" she spat.

"What?"

"*You-tai!* Jew! Take him to Jew place!" She stamped on Bertie's toe and slammed the door as, with a cry, he pulled back his foot.

Arnold came rushing out from where he had been hiding in a dark recess. Bertie quickly explained what was happening. "I think the young man is in real danger," he said. "You stay here, Arnold, and wait for Herbert. When he comes out, follow him and don't lose him. I'm going to find someone to help."

Bertie looked around. Against a wall, not far from the nearest flickering gas lamp, he saw a wheelbarrow filled with dung. Hurrying over to it he tipped it over on its side. The dung fell out and Bertie hurried back with the now empty cart to where Arnold stood with the young Jewish man – quiet now but for a steady moaning. Together they lifted the man into the wheel barrow.

"Remember," said Bertie. "Wait for Herbert. I'm going to see what I can do." And he set off up the street, unsteadily pushing the barrow with its human cargo.

Chapter Four

"What am I doing here?" Bertie asked himself. He sat in the front parlor of the *Beth Holim Temporary Shelter and Care Facility* on Lower Thames Street. Somehow he had pushed the ungainly wheelbarrow, with its human cargo, over two miles to a Jewish hospital-shelter housed in a shabby tenement house. Happily he had encountered a Jewish student near Fresh Wharf, who had not only directed him but had helped him push the patient all the way past the Custom House to the facility.

Bertie hoped that Arnold was still at his post. He determined that when he had got his breath back, and now knowing that the young Jewish boy was in good hands, he would return to Old Swan Stairs and relieve his brother-in-law. He looked at his palms, at the blisters starting to break-out from man-handling the rough old wheelbarrow. Perhaps this Enquirer business hadn't been such a good idea? He tugged at his mustache.

"Mister Hawkins?"

Bertie came to his feet as an attractive middle-aged woman, with her long black hair hanging loose but pulled back in a kerchief, came into the room. She had dark eyes and olive skin. She wore a plain, dark brown, walking skirt of heavy cheviot and a soiled white lawn-waist.

"*Sholem aleichem*," she said. She carried a dented metal bucket, filled with steaming water, which she put down on the floor. "Your friend is going to be all right."

"He's – he's actually not my friend," stuttered Bertie. "In fact I never saw him before tonight."

Her big brown eyes opened wide and she stared at him.

"I . . . we . . . that is, it was just a case of being in the right place – or the wrong place – at the right time . . . I suppose," he finished lamely.

She looked at him long and hard, but did not smile. He got the feeling that she seldom had anything at which to smile. She picked up the bucket again and turned to go. "You do know that he is – that we are – Jewish?"

"Oh! Oh, yes. I didn't think that . . . I mean . . ." He felt strangely at a loss for words. "Do you not get many non-Jewish persons here then?"

She paused and then once again put down the bucket. "Normally, no. No, we do not. But this seems to be the week. Perhaps the astrologers would say it has to do with the moon, I don't know."

"What do you mean?"

She shrugged. "Oh, it is nothing. There is yourself here and then, just two days ago, a young woman – non-Jewish – was brought in here by two rivermen; the Rosenthal brothers. They had pulled her from the water. They didn't know where else to take her and, of course, we took her in. Poor child. She is in a coma. In a bad way."

"What happened?" Bertie couldn't help asking.

The woman pushed a stray lock of hair back into the headscarf, wiped her hand on her skirt and then extended it to Bertie. He uncertainly shook it. "I am Ruth Weisman, director of this establishment," she continued. "The young lady had been assaulted. Not uncommon of course. Hit over the head with some object. My guess is that she was struck and then robbed – probably while crossing a bridge – and then tossed over the side into the river."

"Good God!"

"By rights she should have died. But it seems there was sufficient air caught up in her clothing to keep her afloat long enough for the tide to drag her along and tangle her in the footing of London Bridge. That's where Israel and Jakob found her."

"You say she is still alive?"

"Yes." Once again she picked up the bucket. "I really must take this along before it gets cold. Here! You may follow me, if you wish, and see her. She is in a coma so will be none the wiser for a visitor."

Bertie was anxious to get back to Arnold but couldn't resist the opportunity to see more of an establishment to which he would never normally have access. You never knew when it might be useful for the enquirer business, he thought. He followed the rapidly departing figure ahead of him, noting the occasional spill of water from the bucket she carried.

Bertie's first thought was that the young woman laid out on the narrow bed was strikingly beautiful. She had fine blonde hair, though the side of her head had been much bloodied where she had been struck by the footpad. Her cheekbones were well defined and her lips fine and delicate. Her eyes were closed but he almost expected her to open them at any moment. He walked on tiptoe to her side.

"She can't hear you," said Ruth Weisman. Bertie nodded and let out his breath, realizing that he had been holding it.

The girl was wearing a broadcloth dress devoid of trimmings. It had once been a soft blue but now was badly torn and stained with tar and grease from the river. The right sleeve had been ripped open to the elbow and her lower arm was badly scraped and angrily red. He saw that someone – presumably at the facility – had placed a dressing on the worst of the wound. The young woman's shoes had been removed and set down at the side of the bed.

Bertie glanced around and saw other figures in similar beds; four figures in total in the small room. The other occupants seemed not to be comatose but were obviously very ill, two of them swathed in bandages. He wrinkled his nose at the strong smell of carbolic acid. No one took any notice of him. Behind him, Bertie heard Miss Weisman move off with her bucket. "I will leave you to let yourself out, if you don't mind," she called.

Bertie nodded mutely and had a last look around the room. Something tugged at the corner of his memory. Something he couldn't quite pin down. He looked back at the silent figure in the stained blue dress.

Mrs. Emily Squire was last seen wearing a high-necked blue dress with a black woolen shawl across her shoulders. Her hat, so far as her husband can recall, was also black and of straw, with a feather "of some type" about its brim. Her boots were good quality pebble leather, fully laced.

So had said the report in the newspaper. Bertie looked down at the side of the bed, at the pebble leather fully laced boots. Was this pathetic figure Mrs. Emily Squire? If so, how had she gone from entering a pawnbroker's shop to being fished out of the River Thames at London Bridge?

He bent down and picked up one of the shoes. It was of good quality – despite the soaking it had suffered in the river – and was only slightly worn down at the heel. He picked up the other one. Something caught his eye.

Putting down the one shoe, Bertie poked his fingers into the other one. A piece of paper was wadded up against the side, close to the top of the boot. He pulled it out and unfolded it. It seemed that the tight lacing of the boot had helped protect it from the worst of the water. On the paper he read a name and address: *Mrs. Grey, 9 Friday Street.*

Chapter Five

"Mr. Bertram Hawkins?"

"Yes," answered Bertie. "Who wants to know?" He stood at the front door of his house, very much aware of the fact that he did not have on a collar and that he was in his stocking feet. He hadn't even shaved and his breakfast was getting cold on the kitchen table. Somehow he seemed to have overslept and to be all behind.

"*I* want to know," responded the tall, gaunt figure imperiously. He wore a Paramatta Inverness coat that was soaked with rain. Water ran off the stranger's equally wet bowler hat and even dripped off his mustache, as the downpour continued in Penny Court. "Might I come in? It's as wet as an otter's pocket out here."

Bertie could see that it was yet another cold, rainy, overcast morning and, not caring for the attitude of the taller man, took his time in stepping back and allowing him to enter. He received no thanks. Bertie, more for his own comfort than that of his visitor, turned and led the way back into the warmth of the dining room. Nellie and Isobel were about the house, making beds and clearing grates, so the room was empty. Bertie ushered the man to a chair and then returned to his kippers and toast. The Inverness coat dripped puddles onto the carpet.

"Would you like a cup of tea?" Bertie's good nature got the better of him. The man grunted his acceptance and placed his soaking wet bowler hat on the floor beside the fireplace. Bertie poured him a cup from the teapot on the table. "Now," he said. "Perhaps you'd be good enough to tell me who you are and what you want with me?"

"Inspector Campbell Moss of Scotland Yard."

Bertie choked on his kipper and had to take long gulps of tea to recover. "Scotland Yard?" he finally asked, much subdued. He found the inspector studying him with dark brown gimlet eyes, peering out from under bushy eyebrows. The policeman had a thin, pinched face with a sharp nose. A straggly grey mustache was the only point of interest on his face. His thin, grey hair – revealed when he removed his hat – was plastered across the top of his head in a vain attempt to hide its thinness. He had the trace of a Scottish accent, which Bertie thought strangely appropriate for a man from Scotland Yard.

"Correct." The inspector pulled a dog-eared, blue-covered, notebook from the depths of his Inverness coat and turned the pages till he found what he was looking for. "It is my understanding that on Wednesday, 14th day of April of this year of Our Lord, at approximately two fifteen p.m. of the clock, you did speak with – 'question' was the word used by the subject – a Mister Levi Lieberwitz at his pawnbroker's establishment on Creed Lane."

"The pawnbroker? Yes, I spoke with him. Why?"

"If you dinna' mind, I will ask the questions."

"But I do mind. Since when has it been a crime to talk to a pawnbroker?"

"Whether or not a crime has been committed is for me to decide, laddie. Now . . ." The inspector turned back to his notebook. "You were asking questions of Mr. Lieberwitz concerning the case of a missing young woman, as I understand it."

"You understand correctly." Bertie settled back to eating his kipper.

"Why?"

Bertie delicately removed a kipper bone from between his teeth and placed it on the edge of his plate, along with several others.

"Why were you asking questions of the pawnbroker?" persisted the policeman.

"Why are you asking questions of *me*?" responded Bertie. "I've done nothing wrong. I saw the story about the young lady's disappearance in *The Morning Post* and decided to look into it a little further."

"This is a police matter."

"Which doesn't mean a great deal," said Bertie. He pushed aside the plate bearing the kipper bones, brushed toast crumbs from his shirt, and poured himself another cup of tea. He did not offer more to his guest.

Inspector Moss, ignoring his own cup of tea and obviously feeling the need to assert himself, rose to his feet and glared down at Bertie. His bowler hat was beginning to steam in front of the fire. "We are in the middle of an investigation to determine what has happened to a young woman who has disappeared."

"And have you found her?" asked Bertie, with quiet pleasure.

"What? Speak up!"

"I asked if you had yet found her?"

There was a long period of silence, broken by the door opening and Nellie bustling in followed by the sniffing Isobel. Nellie stopped short when she saw that Bertie had company. Isobel bumped into her back.

"Ah, Nell," said Bertie. "This is Inspector Moss from the police."

"Scotland Yard," added Moss.

"Quite." Bertie found he was enjoying himself. He moved away from the table and, taking up his collar from where it lay on the mantelpiece, proceeded to attach it to its studs. Nellie took her cue from her husband and turned away to direct the maid down to the kitchen and her duties.

"The Inspector is apparently still looking for that missing woman," said Bertie, tying his tie.

"Did you tell him . . ." Nellie started to say.

"That I went and spoke to the pawnbroker?" said Bertie quickly, giving her a wink. "Oh, the police are smart, my dear. They already knew I had been there. That is why the good inspector has come to pay us a visit." He gave his tie a tug. "That, and to get out of the rain."

The inspector took up his steaming bowler hat and moved towards the door. "I must repeat that this is entirely a police matter, Mr. Hawkins, and you should leave it as such. Do I make myself clear?"

"Oh, absolutely," said Bertie.

"So you didn't tell this policeman about finding the girl in the coma?" asked Arnold. He sat with Bertie and Nellie in the drawing room, where they had retired after eating dinner. Isobel was down in the basement kitchen, cleaning dishes.

"I nearly let out that piece of information," said Nellie. She caught her husband's eye. "Sorry, Bertie."

He smiled at her over the top of the glass of sherry he nursed. "No problem, Nell. I just didn't see making the job of the police any easier, especially since we don't yet know whether or not this young lady *is* the missing one."

"I bet she is," murmured Arnold.

"Well, I want to check on it a bit more. Talk with the husband, if I can. We have a lot of work to do yet, Arnold."

The big man nodded.

"And what about Hattie Parker's husband?" asked Nellie. "Is that all finished?"

Bertie took a sip from his glass and then placed it carefully on the occasional table at his elbow. He took up his favorite curved pipe and started charging it with Gallaher's Rich Dark Honeydew tobacco – the only tobacco he ever smoked. "We managed to get Herbert home that night, and explained to Hattie what he'd been up to. She wasn't pleased with him but I think she was grateful that it wasn't another woman that was keeping him away from home."

"So you've finished with him?"

Bertie sighed. "I think it probably best that I have a long heart-to-heart with Herbert. He was getting hooked on that opium. Nasty stuff. But I think we got to him just in time. Yes, otherwise I think we can close the Parker case." He felt a certain satisfaction saying such things. He struck a lucifer and started puffing clouds of rich aromatic smoke into the room.

"I'll ask Hattie to pay our fee then," said Nellie. "Good. Well done, you two."

"So what's our next move?" asked Arnold, sticking his tongue down into the wine glass to lick the side of it and get the last hint of the sherry.

"Well first, I hope it's a nicer day tomorrow than it was today," said Nellie. "We can't spend two days sitting around just doing paperwork and complaining about the police. What had you in mind, Bertram?"

Bertie contentedly drew on his pipe. "As I said, I'd like to speak to this Mr. Squire, if possible. Or perhaps you could do that, Arnold?"

"Me?"

"You are part of the team, you know."

"Yes. Yes, of course I am." Arnold looked uncomfortable but, catching his sister's eye, straightened up and spoke with a slightly deeper, more business-like voice. "Yes, I can manage that. And what will you be doing, Bertie?"

"This address I found in the girl's shoe. It's Friday Street, which just happens to be one street over from where the Squires live. I'd like to go there and talk with this Mrs. Grey."

Isobel Wilson's working hours were long and hard, as they were for all maids-of-all-work. She was lucky in that she had her own bedroom up in the attic at Penny Court – many girls in her position had to make do with space in a corner of the pantry, off the kitchen – but since this was her first maid's position she didn't appreciate that point. She was up at 6:00am and immediately took care of the big kitchen stove, first cleaning and blackening it, so that it would be ready for Mrs. Hawkins making breakfast. Isobel saw to it that the chamberpots were emptied and that the coal skuttles were filled. She had to see to the fireplaces, make the beds, gather clothing and linens needing to be washed, clean the silverware and cooking pots and pans, scrub the sink and kitchen table, mop the floors and sweep the passage. It seemed there was always something needing to be done, from the washing on washday, to beating carpets, and going to the market for the day's shopping. This last Isobel especially liked, though usually it was in the company of Mrs. Hawkins herself.

Isobel had become aware of the new business that Mr. Hawkins and Mr. Middleton had started and she thought it exciting. She had been taught her letters and could read tolerably well, enjoying the occasional "Penny Dreadful", even though the stories were aimed at young boys rather than girls. The copies Isobel managed to acquire were usually worn and grubby, having passed through many hands but, learning of her interest, Arnold Middleton would once in a while bring her a copy he had found in one of the markets where he worked. Her favorite was *The Adventures of Tommy Turnbull*, an orphan boy who seemed to stumble upon one mystery after another.

The latest episode dealt with a young woman who had disappeared from her home, driving her parents to distraction. Tommy Turnbull was hot on her trail. Isobel thought that the story was much like what she had heard of the lady who disappeared from a pawnshop. She was frustrated in not having the next installment of the penny magazine to find out what happened. She thought that if she had it, she might be able to help Mr. Middleton and Mr. Hawkins with their enquiries.

Chapter Six

Number nine Friday Street was one of a long row of attached houses, all exactly the same. At one point in their existence the front doors and window frames had been painted different colors – probably bright and fresh – but now they had all deteriorated and, with the constant fog, dirt and aging, they were all a dingy grey. It seemed appropriate, Bertie thought, that Mr. and Mrs. Grey should live there.

He rapped hard on the bare door – there was no door knocker – and waited. He heard footsteps inside and then someone peered up at him through the letter slit.

"'oo are you? Watcha want?" It was a female voice.

"Are you Mrs. Grey?"

"'oo wants to know?"

"My name is Hawkins. Bertie Hawkins, Mrs. Grey. I'd just like to ask you a question or two about the young lady who disappeared."

"What? The one from Levi Lieberwitz?"

"That's the one." Bertie was beginning to feel conspicuous, standing on the top step and talking to a letter box.

"I told all I know to the coppers."

"Mrs. Grey, do you think you could at least just open the door so that we can talk?"

She took a moment to think about it before finally, with a lot of mumbling, she let the letter-box cover fall and started undoing bolts on the inside of the door. When she finally opened it, Bertie was slightly taken aback. Mrs. Grey was a very tall, formidable woman, who peered down at him as though he were some specimen. She wore a grubby tea gown that must have been handed down from several previous owners. The fasteners were missing from the front and she clutched it about her. The sleeves were too short for her large form.

"Watcha want?"

"'oo's that?" Another voice – a man's – issued from the depths of the hallway.

Mrs. Grey responded over her shoulder, keeping her eyes fixed on Bertie. "It's some nark asking questions about Lieberwitz again."

Bertie knew that a nark was a person in the pay of the police, who informed on people.

"No! No, I'm not a nark," he protested. "I'm just a – an ordinary person making enquiries."

A short, grubby little man in a collarless shirt and with his braces dangling down over soiled, wrinkled trousers, appeared in a doorway off from the hall where they stood. A half-smoked cigarette was stuck in the corner of his mouth. It was unlit. His thin, greasy hair stood out at all angles as though completely foreign to a brush and comb.

"I was there. Why don't you ask me your questions?" he said, the cigarette wagging up and down in his mouth as he spoke.

"You were there? At the pawnbroker's?"

"What of it?"

"I was the one inside," said Mrs. Grey, as though establishing her importance to the situation.

"And can you tell me exactly what happened?" asked Bertie, looking from one to the other of them; up to the wife and down to the husband.

Mrs. Grey let out a sigh. She looked at her husband. "I'll handle it, Mr. Grey," she said. He sniffed, removed the cigarette and studied it for a moment, replaced it in his mouth, then turned and disappeared back into the room. Mrs. Grey turned back to Bertie, blocking his view of anything behind her.

"Did you speak to Emily Squire while you were at the pawnbrokers?"

Her eyes did not waver as she studied him. Bertie found it rather unsettling.

"She was in the queue right in front of me."

"Was she?"

"Yes. She was there to pawn a gold watch. *Real* gold. A corker. Reckon it must 'ave bin worth all of fifty quid . . . though old Levi wouldn't give you more than a fiver for it, if that."

"She showed you the watch?"

"Oh, yes. Her old man was *making* 'er pawn it. Seems she'd only just got it from her grandpa. 'e'd sent it to 'er, through the post. She didn't want to part with it. But as soon as old Tommy Squire saw it, 'e saw only money. Told her to take it to uncle's."

"I was standing outside with 'im." The voice of Mr. Grey came from the room into which he had retired.

"I'm telling 'im," snapped Mrs. Grey, over her shoulder. Turning back to Bertie she said, "Mr. Grey was standing outside the shop with Tommy Squire. They was both waiting on us."

"May I ask what you were pawning?"

"My old heavy raglan coat. Very warm it were, but I needed the money till '*e*," she tossed her head in the direction of the door behind her, "till 'e gets 'imself another job."

Bertie nodded understandingly.

"Seems I have to hock that old coat every winter; just when I need it most."

"Did Mrs. Squire – the young lady who has gone missing – did she say anything to you? I mean, other than to tell you about her grandfather's watch?"

"Yes. She took me coat."

"I beg your pardon?" Bertie wondered if he'd misheard.

"She took me coat. I know tight old Lieberwitz would only give me 'alf a crown. That's all 'e ever gives me for it. She said as how she'd give me three bob."

"She gave you three shillings for the coat? But why? What did she want with it?"

"Don't ask me! She said she only needed it for a couple of days, so I wrote down me address for 'er, took the money, and got out of there."

"She came out with the money," volunteered the voice of Mr. Grey.

"Did you tell all of this to the police?" asked Bertie.

"Nar! They weren't interested. They just wanted to know where Mrs. Squire 'ad gone. I told 'em I didn't know. She was still there when I left."

Bertie felt a warm glow spread over his body. Suddenly he knew the answer to the mystery of Emily Squire's disappearance.

Bertie sat at a table in a corner of an ABC teashop, a half-drunk cup of tea beside him as he laboriously wrote notes in a notebook Nellie had given him. She had got the idea from watching the Scotland Yard inspector.

"You should write down what you find out at the time you find it," she had said. "That way you won't forget it."

Bertie felt it unnecessary but not worth arguing with his wife. He pulled out his silver pocket watch and checked it against the clock on the wall of the ABC.

"What have we got then?"

He looked up as Arnold came into the shop and moved across to join him at the table. A waitress appeared as if by magic and Arnold asked for a pot of tea and some cakes. She moved away.

"Some interesting bits and pieces." Bertie carefully wound his watch and then returned it to his waistcoat pocket.

"Me too!" Arnold was obviously bursting to tell what he had learned so Bertie let him tell his story first. "I went and spoke to Mr. Squire. Nasty piece of work, if you ask me."

"Oh? In what way?"

Arnold shrugged. "I don't know. Hard to put a finger on it." He looked intensely into Bertie's eyes. "It's just something I *felt*. Sensed, I think you'd say. I'm good at that. I sense things."

Bertie said nothing but drank some tea.

"He was very short with me, as though he didn't want to give me the time of day."

"What did you ask him?"

Arnold sat up straighter as the waitress brought him a pot of tea and a plate of small cakes. When she had gone he continued. "It so happened that when I got there he was putting a sign in his window saying 'Flat to let'. My guess is that he's not waiting to see if the police find his wife, he just wants to rent out her room. He must be presuming that she's dead."

"Well done, Arnold," said Bertie, finishing his tea and then pouring a second cup. "And did you speak to him? What did he have to say?"

Arnold looked less enthusiastic. "I asked him if it was his wife that was written about in the newspapers and he told me to get lost."

"He did?"

Arnold focused his attention on the plate of cakes. "Didn't give me a chance to ask any of the things you wanted me to ask him." He chose a petit-four covered in vanilla icing and took a bite from it before even getting it to his plate.

"Hm." Bertie sighed. Although he didn't say so, he somehow knew that he should have gone to speak to Mr. Squire himself. Perhaps it wasn't too late. "Never mind, Arnold. The information about renting the room might be important."

"You think so?" Arnold brightened up, and finished the petit-four. "How did you do, then?"

Bertie sat back and glanced at the notes he had scribbled into his new notebook. "The residents of 9 Friday Street are a Mr. and Mrs. Grey. I spoke to Mrs. Grey . . . and, indirectly, to Mr. Grey. It seems that she was in the queue at the pawnbrokers at the same time that Emily Squire was there. And, in fact, her husband was waiting outside with Mr. Squire." He looked up from his notes and studied his brother in law. "It would seem not uncommon practice for husbands to send in their wives to do the actual act of pawning, while they wait outside."

Arnold nodded, his mouth full.

"But, here's the interesting part," said Bertie. Arnold stopped chewing. "Mrs. Grey was there to pawn a large, heavy, winter coat but she claims that Emily Squire offered her more than she knew the pawnbroker would give."

"What do you mean?"

"Apparently Mrs. Grey had pawned the coat before and knew that she could only count on half a crown for it. Mrs. Squire gave her three shillings and said she would return the coat within a couple of days. That's why she wrote down Mrs. Grey's address, so that she could return it."

"So the young lady in the coma *is* our missing Mrs. Squire?"

Bertie nodded. "Indeed."

"Then what happened?"

"Mrs. Grey couldn't say. She said that she left the shop right away, with the three bob. She doesn't know what Mrs. Squire did after that."

Arnold focused his attention on the choice of the two cakes left on the plate. Finally selecting one, he glanced up. "So where does that leave us, Bertie?"

Chapter Seven

At five minutes to midnight, the last train from Brighton pulled into Victoria Station and the few passengers disembarked. It was in the early hours of the following morning that one of the cleaning crew happened to look out of a window, down at the tracks, and saw the body. It lay under the rear portion of the train, the head severed. The last carriage, which happened to be the baggage car, was unhitched and pulled back to allow the police access to the victim.

Police Sergeant Samuel Wheatley came to attention as Inspector Moss entered the scene.

"At ease, Sergeant," said Moss, bending over to look at the decapitated figure on the ground. "What can you tell me about the victim?"

"Conveniently, sir, the victim had his passport in his pocket so we were immediately able to identify him as Colonel Sir Dennis Ardsley Bart."

"*Sir* Dennis Ardsley?" Moss whistled through his teeth.

"Sir Dennis Ardlsey Bart," corrected the sergeant.

"*Bart* means 'baronet,' you idiot," snapped Moss. "Now, what can you tell me about Colonel Ardsley?"

"What we've found so far, sir, is that he served in the army in British India, in Madras. When he retired from the army he undertook a number of diplomatic missions for the Foreign Office. Probably on his way home from one of them when this happened, sir."

Moss nodded sagely. "Any sign of foul play . . . what's your name?"

"Wheatley, sir. No, none, sir. My take on it is that he was perhaps anxious to get off the train as it came into Victoria, being so late and all, and he slipped and fell under the wheels."

"More haste less speed, eh, Sergeant?"

"What, sir?"

"Nothing you need Scotland Yard for, by the look of it. I'll leave this in your capable hands then, Wheatman."

"Wheatley. Yes sir."

Inspector Moss hurried away. He had more important things on his mind than accidental deaths. They should not be disturbed by the actions of an impatient retired colonel, even if he was a Baronet.

"You'll be reading anything new we've got on Mrs. Squire in the afternoon edition, Bertie."

Evans "Taffy" Lloyd was one of the lucky ones who had been retained when *The Daily Chronicle* had been taken over by *The Morning*

Post. Older than Bertie by about fifteen years, he was an editor who worked on the most recent crime stories. For years Bertie had worried him for more details than the paper printed about all of the cases.

"I've met this Inspector Moss," said Bertie. He wrinkled his nose. "I was not impressed. No more clever than the majority of the Scotland Yard boys."

Taffy laughed. "Well at least we agree on that," he said. "But he's got this bee in his bonnet that the husband somehow did it, you know?"

"He thinks Mr. Squire made his wife disappear?"

The two men were sharing a drink in *The Printer's Imp*, on the corner of Fleet Street and Shoe Lane; a favorite watering hole for the newspaper men.

"According to the good inspector, the wife either *did* in fact come out of the pawnbroker, or – his favorite theory – she was never even in there in the first place. He says the husband claimed she disappeared and he actually did away with her."

"And why would he do that?"

Taffy took a long drink from his porter, wiped his not inconsiderable mustache, and looked at his friend. "I think you'll find that he hasn't thought that far ahead yet."

They both laughed.

"Well," said Bertie, "I happen to know of someone who was waiting outside with Mr. Squire, so she most certainly did go in."

The Welshman put down his beer and leaned towards Bertie. "You know this?"

"Oh, yes." Bertie took a long drink himself. "But let's not upset Inspector Moss's theory . . . not just yet anyway."

Taffy smiled. He was the one who had originally helped get Bertie a steady job with the newspaper. They always got along well. Bertie looked up to Taffy like a son to a father. Bertie's own father had died when Bertie was ten. He liked to say that the drink killed his father. Whenever asked if his father was an alcoholic, Bertie then responded: "No. He worked for a brewery and drove a dray. One day a hogshead of beer rolled off the wagon and crushed him into the cobblestones. So, the drink killed him!" His mother had died of consumption shortly after that, leaving Bertie an orphan. He had quickly learned to support himself, mainly by selling newspapers.

When working as a pressman, Bertie still managed to spend some time with Taffy, who encouraged him to read as much as possible. He was allowed ready access to the small but adequate reference library of books in the editor's office and often sat in there reading until Taffy chased him out at the end of the day.

Bertie knocked on the door of 35 Bread Street and stood on the top step studying the notice in the window.

Flat to let. No pets, no noise, no salesmen.
3s/6d a week in advance.

He knocked again. The house was an exact duplicate of the home of Mr. and Mrs. Grey, one street over. He studied the piles of ashes and cinders, vegetable peelings, rags, paper, meat bones and broken furniture on the pavement and could see that the dustmen did not get to such streets as this as often as they did to Penny Court. Refuse collection was supposedly free of charge in London but slipping the dustmen a tip was the best way to ensure its regular occurrence.

Bertie knocked on the door a third time. He was about to turn away when the door finally opened.

"Yes?"

Bertie presumed that the man staring at him was Thomas Squire. He had black hair, was clean-shaven but had a distinct five-o'clock shadow. His dark eyelashes seemed unnaturally long for a man. Despite his face being pitted from smallpox, Bertie could see that he would probably cause many a female heart to flutter.

"Good day to you." Bertie smiled his friendliest of smiles. He nodded toward the sign in the window of the front room. "I see that you have facilities available? I would like to have a look at them, if I may?"

"Are you a salesman?"

"No, sir, I am not."

"Or a purveyor of patent medicines?"

"It says nothing about that on your sign," protested Bertie.

"Are you such?"

"No, sir, I am not. Now, may I see this room you screen so solicitously?"

Squire grunted and then opened the door wider to give Bertie entrance. He glanced up and down the road outside, as though to be sure that no one was watching, and then followed Bertie inside and closed the door.

"Up here," he said, and led the way up the staircase.

The room Bertie was shown was small but held an iron bed with brass rails, a five-drawer bureau, a bedroom commode, and an antique-finished ash wardrobe of respectable size. A lady's mahogany-finish dressing table stood beside the wardrobe. There was a tiny fireplace with a wall-mounted gas bracket to one side of it. Bertie noticed that the fireplace had not been cleared of its ashes. He looked about the room and then moved across to the window. It overlooked a small yard that contained an untidy pile of wooden boxes, barrels, and bric-a-brac. There was an overgrown vegetable garden that looked as though it had not been tended for several years.

"Not much of a view," Bertie observed.

"You were planning on spending a lot of time in the room?" asked Mr. Squire sarcastically.

There was an adjoining door to another room, the key obvious in the lock. Bertie surmised that the Squires may not have shared a bedroom; the one in which he stood being Mrs. Squire's – now vacant. He decided to press Mr. Squire a little.

"The wife no longer here, then?" he asked, trying to sound innocent.

"What?" Squire's face grew dark. "What the hell . . . ?"

"Oh, sorry," said Bertie hurriedly. "Didn't mean to intrude. Just natural curiosity, you see." He smiled his friendliest smile. It was thrown back at him.

"If you've seen enough, Mister, you can either fork over three shillings and sixpence or get out of here."

Bertie's eye caught sight of something in the fireplace grate, half buried in the ashes. He eased over toward the window, looked out, then turned back and said "Oh! Are you expecting the police, then?"

"What?" Mr. Squire rushed to the window.

"Just went aound the corner, I think," said Bertie. "Perhaps going to the front door?"

As the landlord opened the window and leaned out, Bertie swiftly bent down and scooped out a small piece of paper from the cold ashes and slipped it into his pocket.

"You'd better make up your mind," said Mr. Squire, coming back in. "I've got to get downstairs."

"Hmm . . . No." Bertie shook his head as though reluctantly arriving at a decision. "No. I'm afraid it's not quite what I'm looking . . ."

"Then let's not waste any more of my time, eh?" snapped the other man, and stomped off out of the room and down the stairs. Bertie followed and was unceremoniously shown the way out. Mr. Squire seemed surprised that in fact there were no police waiting outside.

The death of Colonel Sir Dennis Nigel Ardsley (1814-1886) was reported in *The Times* in a short article on page 7. It recounted his years in India. As a young officer under Sir Alexander Burnes, he had traveled to Afghanistan and was there for the Afghan uprising in 1842. Ardsley and Dr. William Brydon, an army surgeon, were the only two men of the more than 16,000 people retreating from Kabul, who made it back alive. The colonel's later years in Madras, while Lord Ripon was the Viceroy, were relatively quiet. When Colonel Ardsley retired his faithful batman, one Cedric Bromley, moved to civilian life with him as his servant; a not uncommon occurrence. Bromley became an excellent aide in Sir Dennis's various missions undertaken, in post army life, for the Foreign Office. It was Cedric Bromley who identified the body and who carefully went through the colonel's baggage. According to *The Times*, Bromley was "most disconcerted" over the death. It didn't go so far as to report that the valet broke down and cried, but the implication was there. The colonel left one son, Hugh William Dennis Ardsley – now Sir Hugh Ardsley.

The Times did note that the colonel had been a major figure at the Treaty of Berlin of 1885, being one of the authors of its actual wording. This was an accomplishment of which the colonel was apparently most proud, to the point where he adopted the habit of always carrying around with him a copy of the 1,458-page treaty. The treaty regulated European colonization and trade in Africa. The copy was found by Bromley, in with the colonel's other belongings in the baggage car.

"Why are you reading us this obituary?" asked Nellie.

Bertie removed his spectacles and put them down, on top of the newspaper. *The Times*, he found, insisted on using a type font just a size or so smaller than that used by the old *Daily Chronicle* and it made it difficult to read without resorting to his old steel-framed, small-lens spectacles; something to which he rarely had to resort.

"I want you to look at this," said Bertie mysteriously, tugging at his mustache. He produced a tiny piece of paper from his waistcoat pocket and laid it on the table. Nellie and Arnold leaned forward to see what it was.

They all sat around the kitchen table. The two men tended to gravitate to the kitchen if they were there during the day, if only for the proximity to the warmth of the stove and the ever-present pot of tea. Nellie enjoyed the company of the two of them while she did the cooking, though she complained that they were both "under her feet". Isobel would be in and out of the small area, constantly sniffing, as she took care of the making of the beds, the blacking of the grates in the house, the scouring of pots and pans and the preparation of vegetables.

"Pretty," said Arnold. "Oh, by the way . . ." he dug into his pocket, pulled out a crumpled magazine, and tossed it to the maid-of-all-work.

"Here! This is for you, Isobel. I managed to get it down Petticoat Lane."

The girl squealed with glee, shaking her mop of carrot-red hair, when she saw that it was another of *The Adventures of Tommy Turnbull,* and then she looked anxiously at her employer, her freckled brow puckered. Nellie nodded her head in approval. "You spoil the girl," she said.

"Aw, she doesn't get much," said Arnold. "No harm. Just a bit of nothing I picked up for her."

"You're a softy," said his sister. She returned her attention to the piece of paper Bertie had produced. "It's a coat of arms," she said. "Where's it from?"

Bertie couldn't help smiling complacently, like a stage magician astounding his audience with a trick. "Taffy Lloyd tells me, it is the 'armorial bearings', they call them, of the Ardsley family," he said. "And I found it in the fireplace at 35 Bread Street; the home of Thomas and Emily Squire."

"What – what was it doing there?" gasped Nellie. Arnold was still digesting the information.

The piece of paper had been burned around its edges, including the upper edge of the arms. Bertie turned it over. On the back could be read the words "… extremely ill. Please return …"

"Looks like a woman's hand," observed Arnold. Bertie nodded agreement.

"But . . . if this is connected to that dead colonel, what has it to do with the missing Emily Squire and what was it doing in her fireplace grate?" asked Nellie.

"Yes. That's what I was going to say."
Arnold nodded, his face still screwed up in doubt.

"I have a theory," said Bertie, his smile
fixed on his face. "And that is that our Emily Squire
is an ex-servant from the Ardsley household." His
smile faded as he had a further thought. "Of course,
she might have left them under a cloud."

"Why, then, would they be asking her to
come back – if that's what the scrap of message
says?" asked Nellie. She had got up from the table
and began to clean the tableware laid out on the
back sideboard.

"Perhaps she's the prodigal son," said
Arnold with a wide smile. "Oh! I suppose that
would be prodigal daughter . . . wouldn't it?" His
face was now a frown.

Bertie looked at him for a long moment.
"Arnold, my old friend . . . you may just have hit
the proverbial nail on its bent head."

Arnold looked pleased but surprised.

Nellie turned back to them. "You think she
may be a daughter?"

"I'm remembering the solid gold watch that
she was supposedly carrying when at the
pawnbrokers," said Bertie. "Perhaps it was the
mother who wrote the letter – asking her to come
home?"

"It doesn't say 'home'," said Arnold,
studying the scrap of paper.

"No," conceded Bertie. "You're right again,
Arnold. It doesn't. Any more than it says it's from
the mother, but . . . well, you're the one who says he
senses things. What do you think?"

Arnold's face went through a number of changes, from pleased to worried, to puzzled, to thoughtful. He scratched the top of his head and squinted his eyes.

"Well, never mind," said Bertie. "I intend to follow up on this. Do a little more enquiring."

"How are you going to do that?" Arnold asked.

"I'm going to find where this Ardsley family lives and pay them a visit."

Chapter Eight

Nellie had quite happily agreed to it when Bertie suggested that they needed to have some professional business cards to hand out, especially since he would be going to see Sir Hugh and Lady Claire Ardsley. They designed a tasteful one and had it printed:

The Penny Court Enquirers
Bertram G. Hawkins
Arnold Middleton
Discreet enquiries for a reasonable fee
27, Penny Court, Paternoster Row, London, E.C

"I didn't know you had a middle name, Bertie," said Arnold when he saw them. "What does the G stand for?"

Bertie smiled a satisfied smile. "Actually I don't have a middle name," he said. "But I've always liked the look of a name with a middle initial, so I added the G."

Arnold studied the card. "Perhaps I should do something like that?" he murmured.

Bertie had got the address of the Ardsleys from Taffy Lloyd. They lived on Merrick Square, between New Kent Road and Great Dover Street, on the Surrey side of the river. It was an area of respectable upper middle class families, with large homes possessing coach house, stables, and other out-buildings. Bertie took one of the light green omnibuses to the omnibus center at the Elephant and Castle hostelry, paying the 4d fare and riding on the top in one of the pleasant garden seats, since the weather was unusually fine. He made a notation of the fare in his notebook.

A man dressed as a costermonger – wearing the old-fashioned smock and a bright red Kingsman neckerchief – sat in the seat immediately beside Bertie and, shortly after the omnibus had crossed the river, unfolded a greasy newspaper package and took out a pork pie, which he proceeded to eat with grunts of pleasure. Bertie found his mouth watering but was more concerned that his clothes not pick up the pie's aroma.

Leaving the conveyance at the inn, Bertie took a hansom cab to Merrick Square, wanting to arrive in a style befitting the residence. He had intended to have the hansom deposit him on the doorstep, under the imposing *porte-cochere,* but at the last moment lost his nerve and banged on the trapdoor above him. The cab driver opened it and looked down.

"You can drop me here," said Bertie, indicating the pavement just before the Ardsley residence.

Paying off the cab, Bertie walked up the curving driveway to the massive front door and, taking a deep breath, lifted the polished brass knocker and let it fall. The sound seemed to echo off into the far distance. He heard no other sounds from inside but the door suddenly and silently swung open on well-oiled hinges and a beak-nosed, bewhiskered man in startlingly white shirt and black tailed coat stood appraising him.

"The tradesmen's entrance is around the back," he said and made to close the door again.

"One moment, my man," said Bertie, in his most forceful voice. He extracted one of his new business cards from his breast pocket and extended it to the snooty footman. "Please be so good as to convey this to your mistress, with my compliments, and ask that I might have a few moments conversation with her." He fixed the man with steady eyes, as though daring him to refuse. After a moment of standing with eyes locked on each other, the footman gave in and stepped back.

"Please come in and wait a moment, *sir*," he said, as though there might be some doubt as to whether the *sir* was applicable. Bertie ignored that and stepped inside.

"Thank you, *my man,*" he said.

Looking around the high-ceilinged entrance hall, hung with oil portraits of those he presumed to be family members, Bertie wondered if he should have rented a frock coat and top hat for this visit. Suddenly his brown three-piece sacque suit and bowler hat seemed inappropriate. He could hardly blame the footman for trying to push him off around to the tradesmen's entrance.

Bertie was just considering slipping outside again and perhaps returning at a later date more appropriately dressed, when an older lady, wearing a royal blue and gold, embroidered Japanese silk house robe, descended the curving staircase holding his card in one hand and cuddling a Pekinese dog with the other. She had a quizzical look on her face but a not unpleasant countenance.

"And you are Mister Hawkins or Mister Middleton?" she asked, as she reached the bottom of the steps.

"Hawkins, ma'am – I mean, your ladyship," said Bertie, giving a slight bow. *How does one address a lady?* "Lady Ardsley, I take it?"

She gave a quick smile. "You are not a salesman, I hope?"

"No, no, Lady Ardsley."

She beckoned him to follow her, leading the way into what turned out to be the library. "I am not yet used to the title myself, Mister Hawkins," she said. "My father-in-law only just passed and, since he was a baronet, my husband has inherited the title."

"Yes. So I understand," said Bertie.

"Oh?"

"I read of the late colonel in *The Times*," continued Bertie, as though *The Times* was his normal morning newspaper.

"I see. Won't you please sit down?" The footman had followed them into the library and now hovered near the door. She spoke to him without turning. "Hunter, bring us some sherry." To Bertie: "You do drink sherry, Mister Hawkins? It's not too early in the day?" The Pekinese sat quietly on her lap, fixing Bertie with an inquisitive eye.

"Oh! Oh, yes. I mean no. I mean, thank you ma'am." He couldn't help looking hard at the footman to see how he was taking having to serve the man he'd tried to turn away.

To his credit, Hunter did not look Bertie's way but moved smoothly over to a sideboard and poured sherry into two crystal wine glasses. When he placed them on the occasional tables beside their respective chairs, the Pekinese growled at him. Bertie smiled. Lady Ardsley dismissed the footman.

Lady Ardsley took a small sip of the liquid and then set down the glass and looked at Bertie. "Now, Mister Hawkins. Let us get to your business. Your card says that you are an enquiry agent, is that the correct term? And if so, then what is it you are here to enquire about?"

Bertie set down his own glass, though he had taken a more sizeable sip than had his hostess. "This may be entirely incorrect, your ladyship," he said, "in which case I apologize profusely, but I have to ask. Do you have a daughter named Emily?"

Isobel couldn't wait to read the next installment of *Tommy Turnbull*. When Mrs. Hawkins went out to visit her best friend Gladys Sykes and her seven children, instead of blacking grates as Isobel had been instructed to do, she settled down at the kitchen table and smoothed out the crumpled pages of the Penny Dreadful. Its back page was missing but that didn't matter, for Isobel knew that it only ever carried advertisements for things like *The Oberman Exerciser – most popular on the market – to build your muscles and develop your chest,* the boys' favorite book *The Queensbury Rules for the Sport of Boxing; superseding the old London Prize Ring Rules*, and the inevitable advertisement for *Indian clubs, made of choice hardwood*. She turned quickly to Tommy and his adventures.

The enterprising boy had hidden away amongst the luggage of a stage coach and traveled with the runaway young lady as she went to meet her young man. The couple then made their way north to Gretna Green, in Scotland. Tommy was able to alert the Peelers, with their long blue coats and tall black hats, who prevented the young lady from ruining her life by marrying a worthless man who only wanted her money. Thanks to Tommy Turnbull, the missing young lady was returned to her delighted parents.

With great satisfaction, Isobel closed up the magazine and hugged it to her chest. She sniffed and determined to tell Mr. Hawkins where he might look for the lady missing from the pawnbrokers . . . Gretna Green.

"Your daughter Emily eloped with your coachman?" said Bertie.

Lady Ardsley nodded and stroked the dog. "It broke my heart," she said. "My husband could not find it in himself to forgive Emily. He said that he knew that Squire – Thomas Squire, the coachman – was only interested in her for her inheritance, so he cut her off without a penny."

"He disowned her?" Bertie was aghast.

Lady Ardsley nodded mutely and, after a quick sip of her sherry, extracted a lace-trimmed handkerchief from her sleeve and dabbed at her eyes. Bertie felt embarrassed.

"It preyed on him," she went on. "I know it did. He had worshipped his daughter. I am sure that this is what led to his present collapse."

Bertie swallowed more from his glass. This was going from bad to worse. Sir Hugh had collapsed? Well of course, he reminded himself . . . that was what was meant in the letter that said "extremely ill. Come home." He asked her ladyship about that.

"Yes." She nodded. "It's his heart, though his doctor keeps saying that it is nothing to worry about for a man of his age. But I'm not so sure. He keeps talking about Emily." She sighed. "I had no idea where she had gone until I finally got a short note from her. It just said that she was married, though I don't know how or where. However, she intimated that she was not happy. I must presume that Squire – her husband – had discovered that she no longer had any money. I couldn't stand it and wrote to her, imploring her to come home. I felt sure that her father would forgive her. But I have heard no word from her."

"Have you not heard about the young woman who disappeared from the pawnbrokers?" asked Bertie, looking at her intensely.

"Disappeared? Pawnbrokers? What are you talking about? What has this to do with Emily?"

"It was in the majority of the newspapers," said Bertie. "It seems it was a mystery that the police could not solve." He smiled to himself. "But let me point out that the name of the young lady who disappeared is Emily Squire."

Lady Ardsley sat up straight and looked at him, her handkerchief forgotten. The Pekinese jumped down from her lap and stood looking bewildered. "You mean . . . you think . . . that this is *my* Emily; *our* Emily?"

"Indeed I do," said Bertie. He produced the burned scrap of letter from his pocket and passed it across to Lady Ardsley. "This is what I found in the fireplace of her home and what led me to you. I went there to speak with this Thomas Squire."

"And you saw Emily?"

"No. Leastwise, not there; not at the house." He quickly told Lady Ardsley the story of the disappearance from the pawnbrokers, with Thomas Squire left waiting outside.

Lady Ardsley scooped up the Pekinese and again cradled it in her arms. "Forgive me, Mr. Hawkins, but I am confused. What has happened to my daughter?"

"Where the police were unable to solve the mystery, my lady, I believe that I have done so," Bertie said. He smiled and allowed himself the final drops in the sherry glass. Then he told her about his

interview with Mrs. Grey and what he had learned
of Emily's acquiring the top coat. "It is my belief,"
he said, "that Emily, having acquired the coat while
inside the pawnbrokers, then put it on and left the
pawnbroker's, going the opposite way from where
her husband stood. He, of course, didn't even look
at her in that big coat since he had only seen her in
her blue dress with the black shawl thrown over her
shoulders. He most certainly believed that it was
simply one of the other women from the queue
inside the shop who was leaving. So when all of the
others *had* left, he thought that Emily had
'disappeared' and so informed the police."

"But you say that you *have* seen Emily?"

"Yes, my lady. I have." Bertie wished that
there was more sherry. "Quite by chance I came
across her in a care facility on Lower Thames
Street, not far from the Customs House."

Lady Ardsley's hand went to her mouth. "A
care facility? Would you care to elucidate on that,
Mr. Hawkins? Is Emily all right?"

Bertie ran a finger around his collar. "I - I'm
sorry to say that she is not in the best of health, my
lady. Oh, she is alive," he hastened to add, "but is
presently in a comatose state."

Lady Ardsley came to her feet, the Pekinese
sliding off her lap onto the floor, where again it
stood looking bewildered. It was obviously not used
to being left to think for itself, thought Bertie.

"Do not alarm yourself," he said quickly.
"She is in very good hands."

"Can you tell me what happened?" she reseated herself and the Pekinese, uninvited, jumped up back onto her lap.

"I have not yet been able to confirm all of this," said Bertie, "but my theory is that your daughter spent her last few coins in acquiring the overcoat she needed to escape the pawnshop and the control of her husband. She had the gold watch, of course, but it seems she was not willing to part with that."

"A gold watch? Oh! It was her grandfather's – he must have sent it to her – and it was of great sentimental value to her."

"Of course. So my suggestion is that, without money, she set out to walk home to you here. However, on the way, whilst crossing a bridge over the river, she was set upon by a footpad who struck her and then took both the topcoat and the watch. This villain then – perhaps thinking that he had killed her – pushed her over the side of the bridge into the river. It was only by chance . . ."

"And the grace of God," murmured Lady Ardsley.

"Of course," muttered Bertie. "Only by chance that she was found by two boatmen and taken to this establishment."

"I must go to her!" Lady Ardsley started to her feet but the dog was ready and sprang down of its own accord.

Chapter Nine

By the time Bertie approached home the sun had long since disappeared and fog had started to come up from the river, as it did every day at this time of the year. With a long sigh, Bertie turned into Penny Court. He came to a stop as a not-unknown figure stepped towards him, out of the fog.

"Inspector Moss! What a coincidence."

"Coincidence? I think not, Mr. Hawkins. Oh dear me no, laddie." The policeman's bright beady eyes gleamed at Bertie through the gathering mists. "I made enquiries at your residence and, not being able to extract the information as to your whereabouts from your wife, I stationed myself here where I knew you would have to pass on your way home."

"Have you been waiting long?" asked Bertie solicitously, silently thanking Nellie for not saying where he had gone.

"Much too long! Now then! I have information that you have been interrogating Mr. Squire and certain of his neighbors."

"Interrogating?" asked Bertie innocently.

"Aye! And I choose my words carefully, laddie. I'd advise you to do the same."

Bertie shifted his weight from one foot to the other and back again. It had been a long day and he wanted nothing more than to get home to Nellie. He looked about him, squinting through the fog, then back at the policeman. "I think it's getting thicker, Inspector, don't you? Tell you what . . . why don't we just trot on along to number twenty-seven and see if there might not be a nice hot pot of tea waiting, or even a cup of cocoa?"

There was a very brief moment's hesitation on Inspector Moss's part before he nodded curtly and turned to walk with Bertie, along Penny Court.

Ten minutes later Bertie and the Inspector sat on either side of the kitchen table, each with a steaming cup of cocoa alongside a plate of gingernut biscuits. Nellie and Isobel busied themselves preparing dinner. Bertie looked, with satisfaction, about the old kitchen and allowed himself a deep sigh of satisfaction. Inspector Moss's eyebrows knitted across the top of his sharp nose and he carefully stirred three spoonfuls of sugar into his cup.

"All right," he said, less sharply than he had been speaking out in the evening fog. "Now let's get to it, Mr. Hawkins."

"Why don't you call me Bertie? Everyone does."

"I am not 'everyone'," replied the inspector sharply. "Now, as I said earlier, I have it on good authority that you have been questioning the people who are involved in my investigation into Emily Squire's disappearance."

"Oh, are you still working on that?" Bertie spoke as though surprised.

"What do you mean? Aye, of course I'm still working on that. As it happens, I am about to take in our Mr. Squire for further questioning. He has a lot of explaining to do, it seems to me."

"What, even though we know where Mrs. Squire is and what had happened to her?" Bertie put a single spoonful of sugar into his own cup and stirred the cocoa.

"What are you talking about?" The inspector had stopped with his cup halfway up to his mouth, a biscuit held in his left hand.

"Oh, of course." Bertie chuckled as though at some private joke. "You Scotland Yard gentlemen work as your own pace, do you not?" He took a sip of his drink and then put down the cup and looked at the policeman. "While we private enquirers go out and solve the mysteries."

"You – you've solved it?" The biscuit and the cup both slowly descended back to the table.

Bertie glance at Nellie, who was looking at him. They smiled at one another. Bertie turned back to Inspector Moss. "It really wasn't too difficult," he said. "Not once I'd spoken to Mrs. Grey."

"Who?" His hand, still clutching the biscuit, came up to cup his ear.

"Mrs. Grey."

"Mrs. Grey?"

"Mr. Squire's neighbor. She had been inside the pawnshop with Emily but you didn't question her very thoroughly."

"What do you mean?"

The policeman seemed to have lost a lot of his fight, thought Bertie. He drank a little more cocoa and then went on to tell the inspector how he had solved the mystery of Emily's disappearance and also of locating her at the Beth Holim Temporary Shelter and Care Facility. He did not mention his visit to, and conversation with, Emily's mother.

Inspector Moss nibbled on his ginger biscuit and sipped at his cocoa as he listened. Bertie was uncertain as to what sort of a response he would get to what the policeman could only see as interference. But he was pleasantly surprised.

"It seems that I have misjudged you, Mr. Hawkins. Aye. Misjudged . . . and that's nay a thing I do very often, I might tell you."

"Inspector . . ." began Bertie.

Moss held up his hand. "Nay, laddie, I like to think that I am a fair man." He spent a moment nibbling the biscuit again and gathering his thoughts. "You've spoken to Emily Squire, then?"

"Well, yes. Yes, I have now, inspector."

Nellie looked up, surprised, and Bertie addressed her. "I spent some time with Lady Ardsley – which I'll tell you all about later, my dear – and then she wanted to see her daughter. Only natural, I would think. So we went, together, to the Care Facility. When we got there, we found that Emily had finally come back to consciousness."

"Oh, that's wonderful." Nellie beamed, as did Isobel, listening with open mouth. Then, suddenly, Isobel burst out.

"Oh! Mr. 'awkins! I have to tell you! Tommy Turnbull . . ."

"Isobel!" Nellie was aghast that Isobel – maid-of-all-work – should burst in on a conversation, especially one between Bertie and a police inspector from Scotland Yard.

Bertie held up his hand. "That's all right, Nellie. It looks as though the girl has something important to say – though you should not interrupt others, Isobel. Now, what is it?"

"It's about the missing lady, Mr. 'awkins. The one what disappeared."

"Emily Squire? Yes? What about her?"

The three of them – Bertie, Nellie, and Inspector Moss – hung on her words.

"She went to Scotland, Mr. 'awkins. To Grenter Green." She sniffed loudly.

"*Gretna* Green," said Inspector Moss, correcting her. "Aye, that's just over the border into Scotland. Under Scottish law young lads of only 14 years and lasses of 12 may get married without their parents' consent, which they canna' do in England."

"Aha!" cried Bertie. "So Emily and her coachman could have gone there to get married. Lady Ardsley was wondering where it happened."

"They'd have been married at the old blacksmith's anvil by the 'anvil priest' himself." The inspector sat back in his chair, smiling, as though it brought back old memories.

"Does that solve the mystery, then, Mr. 'awkins?" asked Isobel anxiously.

Bertie smiled and nodded. "It certainly completes the picture for us, Isobel. Thank you very much."

The maid's freckled face was all smiles, and she went off to clean out chamberpots with a soft song on her lips. For days afterwards Arnold claimed that she didn't sniff as much as she used to do but neither Bertie nor Nellie were aware of that.

"So Squire married her for her money and then found she no longer had any," mused the inspector. "She got jumped and foxed by a rampsman, who thought he'd killed her and so tossed her into the Thames."

"What a blessing those two boatmen found her," said Nellie.

"Jews, weren't they?" asked the inspector.

Bertie nodded. "Yes. Who took her to a Jewish facility and probably saved her life."

"What did Lady Ardsley think of it all?" asked Nellie.

"Well, she's taken Emily home with her. Now she's got two invalids to take care of: her daughter and her husband."

"Wait a minute! Wait a minute!" The inspector had a deep frown on his face and looked, greatly puzzled, from Bertie to Nellie and back to Bertie. "Lady Ardsley? *Ardsley?* Where have I heard that name before?"

"Ah, yes." Bertie nodded his head understandingly. "I was wondering when Scotland Yard would unravel that part of the puzzle."

"Wait just a minute! Wasn't that old soldier who fell off the train and got himself killed, wasn't he Sir Something Ardsley?"

"Indeed he was," said Bertie. "He was Emily's grandfather . . . and original owner of the gold watch that the footpad stole from Emily Squire."

"Where was I, then?" Arnold sounded indignant.

"You were working in Covent Garden, of course," said Nellie.

She, Bertie and Arnold were at dinner in the Hawkins dining room. Inspector Moss had taken his leave, reluctantly it seemed to Bertie, declining an invitation to join them at the meal. Arnold had arrived at Penny Court not five minutes after the policeman left. Over dinner, Bertie and Nellie had brought him up to date on what had happened.

"I miss all the interesting stuff," grumbled the big man.

"You may not have to for long, Arnold," said Bertie, winking at Nellie.

"That's right," she said, smiling at her brother. "You may have to give up working at Covent Garden, or any of the markets, so that you can devote all of your time, with Bertie, to the Penny Court Enquirers."

The knife and fork clattered from Arnold's hands onto his plate. He looked, dazed, from one to the other of them. "What do you mean? How can that be?"

"When I helped Lady Ardsley place Emily in her carriage, to take her home from the Jewish facility," said Bertie, "her ladyship said that she believed that Sir Hugh would want to get in touch with me as soon as he was able, to 'express his appreciation', she put it."

"And you know that can mean only one thing," Nellie chimed in, all smiles.

"Money!" Arnold picked up his knife and fork again, a smile on his face.

"We do not yet know for certain," cautioned Nellie. "We must not count our chickens."

"But I'd bet on it," said Bertie. He continued eating, and then returned to his narrative. "Well, as I told Inspector Moss, it was another of those 'it's a small world' occasions when we realized that the late lamented Colonel Sir Dennis Ardsley was actually Emily Squire's grandfather. It seems he had posted the gold watch to her just the day before he got killed falling from the train."

Arnold looked at his brother-in-law. "I thought the police inspector was the enemy?"

Bertie laughed, though a little uneasily Nellie thought. "No, no, Arnold. He was never the enemy. Oh, he is a policeman I grant you. And from Scotland Yard no less. The very people I despaired of and wanted to show up."

"You didn't really want to show them up, did you?" asked Nellie.

"Well, no I suppose not. It was really for my own satisfaction. I just wanted to be able to prove to myself that I could do better than they were doing."

Bertie dug into his roast beef and Yorkshire pudding. "Pass the gravy, Arnold, would you?"

"Yes, but that would take more than just one case, wouldn't it?" He passed the gravy boat to Bertie.

Bertie grunted. "You are right, as always, my friend." Arnold smiled. "And I think we will have plenty more opportunities."

"So the colonel – the grandfather – was returning from somewhere abroad?" asked Nellie, as they finished their main course and watched Isobel gather up their plates before serving dessert.

"Yes," said Bertie, and then stopped with his hand halfway to his water glass. "Oh, my God!"

"Bertie!"

"Sorry, my dear. But . . . Arnold, where was the colonel's body found?"

"At Victoria Station. He had fallen out of the train before it came to a stop . . . they said."

"They said! Yes!" Bertie came to his feet, throwing down his dinner napkin. "I've got to go after Inspector Moss. My God! I think the colonel may have been murdered!"

Chapter Ten

Bertie was agitated enough that he hailed a hansom cab and asked the driver to take him to Scotland Yard with all possible speed. He knew he'd have to justify the expense to Nellie but that was to be worried about later. He gazed out over the leather apron trying to see through the fog, as the cab moved down Ludgate Hill and into Fleet Street. The fog had become thick but the traffic was light.

The hansom had a near miss with another cab coming in the opposite direction, leading the cabman to let loose a string of curses that Bertie hadn't heard since his days on the street corner selling newspapers. Down Charing Cross and into Whitehall, Bertie found himself sitting on the edge of his seat, straining his eyes. He chastised himself and sat back, trying to relax. He couldn't make the vehicle go any faster just by willing it to do so. Bertie hoped that the inspector had returned to Scotland Yard after leaving Penny Court, and not gone home himself. If he wasn't in his office, Bertie didn't know what he would do.

As the hansom came to a stop at the gates to Scotland Yard, Bertie flung aside the cover and jumped to the ground. The cabman leaned down for his fare, cursing the terrible driving conditions to indicate that a tip would be appreciated. Bertie gave him three shillings – more than necessary, even with a tip – and hurried through the murk towards the blue light burning at the entrance door.

"Inspector Moss?" The police sergeant at the enquiry desk, who seemed reluctant to stop perusing his copy of *The Police Gazette*, repeated the inspector's name as though he had never heard it before. He looked Bertie up and down before, apparently, deciding that he was a respectable person. "Oh, yes. Yes, I believe the inspector may still be 'ere. I'll 'ave to go and see. What did you want with 'im?"

Bertie passed one of his cards across the well-worn counter.

"Give him this and say that I'd like to speak to him . . . urgently."

The sergeant moved away, studying the card and shaking his head. He went down a short passageway and tapped on a door. There was a muffled response and the policeman went in, closing the door behind him. Bertie looked around the cramped outer office. On the wall behind the sergeant's counter two portraits looked down on him – one the inevitable picture of Queen Victoria and the other the newly appointed Police Commissioner, Major-General Sir Charles Warren. The commissioner's new picture frame gleamed brightly beside the dusty, somewhat dingy, old frame around Her Majesty.

Bertie strained his ears. He was a little surprised – annoyed, even – to hear laughter come from inside the office the sergeant had entered. Surely they did not find his business card amusing?

The sergeant emerged from the room, a smile on his face, and beckoned Bertie forward.

"In 'ere," he said.

Bertie entered the room, the sergeant closing the door on his heels.

"Well now. Mr. Hawkins . . . once again."

The inspector's office was small and cramped. A double gasolier hung from the ceiling, though only one mantle was alight, giving little illumination into the farther reaches of the room. These seemed to be piled with books, magazines, box files, and numerous papers and reports tied into clumps with faded green string. The desk over which the gas fixture was suspended was an ancient wooden one, deeply scarred and burned from carelessly placed cigarettes and cigars. There was a large stain at one corner where an inkwell, at some time in the furniture's history, had been overturned. Black and red inkwells stood in a dual holder with a single pen nearby. Piles of papers covered much of the desk, though the section in front of the seated policeman had been cleared to accommodate a crumpled newspaper opened to reveal a portion of fish and chips. A cracked mug of strong looking tea sat beside it. Inspector Moss held a potato chip in his fingers as he looked at Bertie.

"You'd have done better staying with us for dinner." Bertie nodded at the greasy paper on the desk. "We had roast beef and Yorkshire pudding."

"Peas?" asked the inspector.

"Brussel sprouts," said Bertie.

Inspector Moss sighed and then popped the chip into his mouth. He slid the paper to one side. "Why are you chasing after me?" he asked.

Bertie looked around. There was one chair on his side of the desk but it was bearing up under a pile of police reports. He took them and set them on the floor, then pulled the chair closer to the desk and sat down. "I had an idea about the death of Colonel Ardsley," he said.

"Did you now?" A hand reached across and dipped, once again, into the pile of chips. "And what might that have been?"

"Do you have sketches of the body, as you found it?" Bertie asked. He knew, from his days at *The Daily Chronicle*, that when a body was found a police artist would sketch the details of its discovery: position, condition, relative placement of other items.

"Those are not for public scrutiny."

"I'm not exactly 'public'," said Bertie, looking the inspector in the eye. "I really do think I might have stumbled on to something."

Two more chips and then the inspector pulled open a drawer in the desk and pulled out a folder. He moved the fish and chips slightly farther away and, placing the folder in front of him, opened it. He dug through and produced some well-thumbed sketches which he turned so that Bertie could see them.

"Not pretty," he said. "But then, a decapitation never is."

"I used to work for a newspaper," said Bertie. "I've seen worse." He leaned forward and studied the sketches. "The body is lying on its back," he observed. "With the neck – or what remains of it – conveniently across the rail."

"Conveniently?"

"Were there any marks on the head?" asked Bertie. "I see it was right where you'd expect it to be, after being severed."

Inspector Moss nodded. "There was a gash and bruise across the left forehead."

"Across the forehead?"

The policeman pushed the greasy supper away from him, as though he suddenly had more important things to do. "Wait a minute," he murmured. He took the sketch from Bertie and studied it.

"If the gash on the forehead came from the fall to the rails," said Bertie, quietly, "then the body would surely have been face down, not face up, would it not? Is it possible the blow to the head came *before* he fell from the train?"

Inspector Moss waved a dismissive hand. "Wait a minute. Wait a minute," was all he said, as he looked closely at the sketches.

"And the body looks to me," Bertie pointed to the pencil drawing, "to be very neatly laid out perpendicular to the track, so that the neck could be over the rail."

Inspector Moss drew in his breath through his teeth, making a hissing sound.

"You think he was hit on the head and then laid there, for the train to go over him?"

"The train is always shuffled about a bit, once the passengers have disembarked," said Bertie.

"They have to oil and clean things, I suppose. The murderer . . ."

"Murderer?"

"Oh yes. I think it was murder. I'll explain more in a moment."

"There's more?" The inspector screwed up the remains of the fish and chips, dropped them into a waste basket at the side of the desk, and then leaned forward attentively with his hand cupped behind his ear.

"The murderer would have known, or guessed, that the train would move, so he placed the head where it would be sliced off and look like an accident," said Bertie. He was excited. He found that as he put his thoughts into words, he saw the events more clearly; the crime seemed to come alive.

"All right. All right." The inspector got to his feet and, scratching the bald spot on the top of his head, walked back and forth in the small space behind the desk. "Let us say – just for the moment, now – let's say that it was as you describe. The big question, then, is who would want to kill Colonel Ardsley and why?"

"That's actually two questions," said Bertie, frowning. "But yes," he went on as the inspector opened his mouth to respond. "Yes, who and why? You are right . . . of course, inspector."

Inspector Moss nodded, and continued pacing and scratching. Finally he stopped and looked hard at Bertie. "All right, Mr. Penny Court Enquirer! Who and why? You have obviously worked this out."

Bertie did not smile but continued to frown as he thought it through. "I still have a lot of gaps, but I do have a lot of suspicions," he said. He had come to his feet on his side of the desk. "The thing that started me thinking on all of this was, why was the colonel coming into Victoria station?"

"We know that! He was returning from somewhere abroad. He did 'things' for the Foreign Office, though don't ask me what. We checked with the Office and they agreed he had been out of the country."

"Exactly," said Bertie, nodding. "He was returning from abroad. So I say again, what was he doing arriving at *Victoria* Station? The Cross Channel Ferry arrives at Dover. He should have been arriving at Charing Cross Station, on the Dover line, not at Victoria on the Brighton line!"

There was a long silence.

They both sat down again and the inspector went back to the open file in front of him. He turned several of the loose pages.

"The colonel's luggage was all there, in the baggage car, as you'd expect," he said, looking through the papers. "His batman . . . valet . . . whatever he calls himself now – Bromley; Cedric Bromley – he went through everything. Real cut-up he was. Been with the colonel for years, it seems; here and in India or somewhere. My Sergeant Wheatley went through everything with him."

"Why wasn't Bromley traveling with the colonel?"

"Said he'd been sent on ahead to do some special errand. Didn't say what it was, exactly."

"Did he look through the luggage?" asked Bertie. "I mean, not just *at* it to see that it was all there?"

"Aye, he went through it all, according to Wheatley. Opened cases and everything. Said he had packed it, in Germany, and so he could tell it was all as it should be."

They both thought about what they had discovered. Finally the inspector, once again, gave in and looked at Bertie. "What do you think, then? Why was he coming from Brighton and not Dover?"

Bertie spoke slowly, forming his words as he formed his thoughts. "He was coming from Germany, you say?" The inspector nodded. "Suppose – just suppose, mind you – that he was being followed . . ."

"Chased!" said the inspector, eagerly.

Bertie nodded. "All right. Suppose he was being chased, and realized it? He might well have left the Channel steamer and jumped on a train along the coast to throw off his pursuer. Finished up at Brighton and then came up to London from there."

"But his pursuer caught up with him and gave him what for!" Inspector Moss's eyes gleamed with excitement.

Bertie smiled. "It's all possible, Inspector, isn't it? What we have to do is to find out if it's what actually happened."

Chapter Eleven

Cedric Bromley was forty-five years old and had spent much of his adult life associated with the late Colonel Sir Dennis Ardsley. Bromley's father was curate of All Saints parish church in Kilham, East Yorkshire. Cedric had attended St. John's College Cambridge but, much to his parents' dismay, he had left there prematurely and joined the British Army. Cedric had taken easily to the discipline of army life. He had seized the opportunity to become batman to the well respected officer and gentleman, on Colonel Ardsley's deployment to Madras in 1861. When the colonel eventually retired, Cedric followed him into civilian life as Sir Dennis's valet, adapting easily to regular travel between England and the Continent. Cedric Bromley frequently undertook what the colonel referred to as "exercises"; carrying private documents to and from individuals on both sides of the English Channel. Whether or not such secret missions were connected to Foreign Office business, it was not Cedric's place to enquire.

Cedric stood in the middle of his small flat looking at a pair of silver-backed hair brushes that his employer had given to him on his birthday the previous year. He thought wistfully of the colonel's many generosities. He would miss him greatly, he knew. A knock at the door interrupted his thoughts. He laid aside the brushes and went to answer the knock.

"I'm thinking," said Bertie, standing by the kitchen stove and stirring the big cook-pot with a large wooden spoon, "I'm thinking that we need to find the gold watch that was stolen from Emily Squire."

Nellie rolled out pastry on the kitchen table while Isobel peeled potatoes. Arnold incongruously balanced on one foot while brushing his shoe with the boot brush.

"Why do you need to do that?" asked the big man, admiring his handiwork.

"Yes, Bertie. That's a good question." Nellie sprinkled flour across the pastry and rolled again.

Bertie peered into the steamy depths of the cook-pot, sniffed the mouth-watering aroma, and then returned to his appointed task. "If you recall, Emily received the watch in the post just the day before her grandfather was killed. I'm wondering if the colonel didn't send it to her because he needed to be rid of it."

"Be rid of it?" Arnold echoed.

"You mean, he didn't want anyone else getting it?" Nellie took the pie dish and lined it with half the pastry.

"Exactly. He needed to hide it and thought that it would be safe if it wasn't on his person. The only one he could think of, to give it to, was his granddaughter."

"But she was going to pawn it," chimed in Isobel. A sharp look from Nellie silenced her.

"No," said Bertie, addressing the young girl. "She was being *made* to pawn it, by Thomas Squire. And we know that he was only interested in what money it was worth. Emily was smart enough to then run away, *with* the watch, and try to get to her parents' house."

"So how are you going to find it?" Arnold stood up and looked down at his feet.

"How are *we* going to find it, you mean," said Bertie. "Well, what do you think the man who stole it would have done with it?"

"Fenced it!" cried Isobel gleefully, having learned the word from her Penny Dreadfuls. Nellie merely sighed.

"No," said Bertie.

"No?" said Arnold.

"When he assaulted Emily he stole not only the gold watch but also the old top coat she had worn to escape the pawnbrokers."

"So?"

"He wouldn't be likely to try and fence an old coat," Bertie continued, sneaking another smell from the cook-pot.

"Another pawnbrokers!" cried Nellie.

"Of course!" Arnold looked pleased with himself, as though he'd come up with the answer.

"Yes," agreed Bertie. "If he wanted a quick return on his ill-gotten gains then he would have made off to the closest pawnbroker and got whatever he could for both the watch and the coat."

"And then probably drank away the proceeds," said Nellie bitterly. "To think that a poor young woman almost lost her life for that."

Bertie laid down the spoon and moved over to the sink to fill the big tea kettle. "We need to find that gold watch," he said. "Not just to return it to Emily, but to examine it."

"Why?" Arnold sat down at the kitchen table and broke off a small piece of the pastry. Nellie slapped his hand.

"To see what was so important about it that the colonel needed to send it to his granddaughter for safe keeping."

"You really think that's what he did?" asked Nellie.

"Yes, I do."

"There is a lot of pawnbrokers in London," said Isobel with a sigh, obviously determined to be part of the discussion.

"Not in one area," said Bertie. He put the kettle on the stove and then sat down at the table alongside his brother-in-law. "Where was Emily attacked? On a bridge over the Thames." He answered his own question.

"We know that," muttered Arnold.

Bertie went on unabashed. "Which bridge, though? Well, if she was going to be walking to her parents' home, which is off the New Kent Road, then she would almost certainly cross by Blackfriars Bridge."

"And how does that help?" asked Arnold.

"I can tell you that," said Nellie. "It means we – you – have to start checking on all the pawnbrokers closest to the end of Blackfriars Bridge. Not the whole of London."

Isobel beamed around at everyone.

Inspector Campbell Moss turned off Whitehall and walked along Downing Street. On his left towered a lofty block of government buildings with the Home and Colonial Offices at the east, Whitehall, end and the Foreign and India Offices at the far end, overlooking St. James' Park. He rounded the large, square, corner tower of the building and crossed to the entrance. People were strolling into and out of the park. The weather had turned warmer and those not gainfully employed were making the most of it. Inspector Moss spared them no thought but focused on his purpose.

In one way he cursed the over-zealous Bertram Hawkins for pointing out that Colonel Ardsley had been murdered, but at the same time he grudgingly gave him credit for noticing any number of things that should have alerted the Scotland Yard men. Not necessarily himself, he thought, since he was not focused on that case . . . though he had not declared it a "case" as such because he had failed to see what Bertram had seen! Very sobering.

He entered the Foreign Office and ascended the wide, curving staircase to the second floor. At a highly polished mahogany enquiry desk he asked the clerk, peering at him over half-glasses, where he might find Mr. Snype. He was directed back down the stairs to the first floor. At another, similar, polished mahogany enquiry desk – could it be the same clerk, he wondered? – the inspector was directed along one of a number of corridors that spread before him, like the passageways that must have lured Theseus into the presence of the Minotaur. After two wrong turns, the inspector finally came to a paneled door bearing the name "Nathaniel Snype". He knocked and went in.

After explaining his business to a bespectacled woman with a tight mouth and close-cropped hair, he was persuaded that in fact he did not need Mr. Snype after all – which was just as well since that gentleman was in conference with "the Minister". He was directed next door, to speak with a Mr. Biggersley who, happily for the inspector, was in attendance. Biggersley was a large man who came out from behind his desk to shake hands with the inspector and to explain – withdrawing his gold watch from his waistcoat pocket and reading the time – that he could give the policeman only a few moments.

"Colonel Sir Dennis Ardsley," he continued. "Ah, yes. Very sad, his passing." Mr. Biggersley's full face was framed by a wealth of whiskers, from which protruded a node-like, ruddy, nose. His virtually colorless grey eyes were perpetually watery, their lids drooping. "We here at the Foreign Office were acquainted with Sir Dennis for many years. Ah, yes. Very sad." He gave a long, obviously heart-felt sigh and the whole of his large frame shuddered. "I, myself, worked with him on occasion over the past decade, including his legendary work on the Treaty of Berlin."

"Did he do a lot of work in Germany?" asked the inspector.

"Germany? Oh, yes. I wouldn't say exclusively. No, certainly not exclusively. There was that episode in Paris . . ."

"Was that recently?" interjected the inspector.

"Recently? Oh, no. No, that was several years ago. Not that it wasn't important, of course. The work of the Foreign Office . . ."

"Aye, aye, aye!" Inspector Moss's time was also valuable. "I understand he had only just returned from Germany when he . . . when he was . . . when . . ."

"Ah, yes." Another large sigh and bodily shudder. Then, after a pause, Mr Biggersley went on. "It is my understanding that he was returning from the Fatherland, as they term it, when he had his so unfortunate accident. However . . ."

The inspector had his notebook out and ready.

"However, I do not believe that he was doing any government work on that particular visit. As I understood it – from Sir Dennis himself, just before he left for the continent – he was participating in some private negotiations with Herr Benz."

"Herr Benz?"

"Yes. Karl Benz, the industrialist and inventor. Surely you must have heard of him, inspector?"

"Oh! Oh, aye. *That* Herr Benz!" Inspector Moss nodded vigorously and made a notation in his little book. "Er, would you happen to know just what those negotiations were, Mr. Biggersley?"

The large man spread his hands expressively and squinted at the inspector through his watery eyes. "As I said, they were private negotiations."

"Of course." The inspector nodded again, understandingly.

"I can tell you, though . . ." Mr. Biggersley turned away from the policeman as though to indicate that, so far as he was concerned, the interview was over. "It had something to do with our own inventor, Mr. Edward Butler. Now, if you will excuse me?"

As the large man moved behind his suitably large desk and took his seat, the inspector threw out a final question. "Of course, sir. Er, Mr. Butler being . . . ?"

"Edward Butler." Mr. Biggersley busied himself shuffling papers and doing his best to ignore his visitor.

"Of course." Inspector Moss made a final notation before leaving Mr. Biggersley to his important Foreign Office work.

Arnold Middleton stood in the center of Blackfriars Bridge and looked first towards the Blackfriars end and then towards the Embankment. The trouble with checking on pawnbrokers at the end of the bridge, as Bertie had suggested, was that there were *two* ends to the bridge – two sets of shops he would have to look into. The bridge's five great wrought-iron spans strode across the busy river like an undulating wall attempting to hold back the waters. Barges, paddle-steamers, and river traffic of all sorts plied up and down, going with and against the tide. Rivermen shouted to one another and were echoed by drivers of carts, carriages and omnibuses up on the bridge itself; the roadway busy at all hours of the day, it seemed. The bridge was a tidal turning point and, when opened by Queen Victoria in 1869, had drawn many compliments with its stone carvings of birds on the piers. Arnold had no thought for these niceties, however, as he stood pondering his first move.

To the north end were the Inns of Court and Temple Church. Less likely to have pawnbrokers scattered about them, he decided, though he might have a look down Apothecary Street. He turned south and walked, with and against the multitude of pedestrians, toward Commercial Road, Stamford Street, Holland Street and Blackfriars Road itself. Pawnbrokers Arnold soon found aplenty and spent the next three hours enquiring of surly, suspicious male and female proprietors as to whether a particular overcoat and gold watch had been pawned within the past few days. He eventually turned for home, tired but happy in the knowledge that he could report back to Bertie the locations of three different hock shops that admitted they *might* have the said items. It would need Bertie himself to wring from them the absolute truth.

Lady Ardsley led the way into the drawing room, where Emily and her father both lay resting on day beds. The curtains were partially drawn to block out any strong sunlight that might happen to intrude. Bertie stepped as quietly as he could, afraid of disturbing anyone or anything.

"We are not asleep." It was Sir Hugh, who lay back wearing an elegant, maroon velvet smoking jacket with quilted shawl collar. His steel grey mustache was waxed and pointed, giving the suggestion of a military air; his softly waving hair parted precisely in the center. His white shirt and stand-up collar made a stunning background for what Bertie assumed was his regimental tie, though which regiment that was Bertie had no clue. Sir Hugh's trousers were sharply pressed, seemingly contradicting his relaxed position on the day bed. "You will, I trust, pardon me if I do not rise, Mr. Hawkins?"

"Oh, yes sir. Sir Hugh, sir. Of course. Please, don't . . . er . . . don't . . ." his voice trailed off.

"I understand I have you to thank for bringing me back together with my parents." It was the young lady who spoke. Emily's head was still heavily bandaged but it did not detract from the elegance of her deep rose-colored, lace-trimmed, French cashmere, tea gown. "That was so very good of you."

Lady Ardsley indicated an armchair. "Won't you please be seated, Mr. Hawkins?"

Bertie waited for her ladyship to seat herself first and then did the same. "I'm just so delighted that I was able to be of service," he said. "It was not really too difficult," he directed his words to Sir Hugh. "Everything just sort of fell into place."

"You are too modest." His lordship reached to a small table beside the chaise-longue and picked up a slip of paper. "It was my unpleasant duty to have to disown my own daughter." His voice caught in his throat and he feigned a cough. "Happily, not for too long."

"It was Thomas," said Emily, in a small voice.

Sir Hugh nodded, tapping the edge of the piece of paper on the surface of the table. "Indeed it was, my dear. A conniving, scheming young man if ever I met one. You were too innocent for his ways, I fear."

"He had us all fooled," said Lady Ardsley.

"Well, enough of that!" Sir Hugh sat up as straight as he was able on the reclining surface. "We have all learned from the experience, I trust."

"May I ask, sir?" Bertie interjected. "What about Emily's . . . er, Miss Ardsley's . . . or Mrs. Squire's . . ."

"Her marital status?" Sir Hugh fixed Bertie with a hard stare, almost as though it was Bertie's fault. "I have spoken with my lawyer. As it happens the union was not consummated. We may apply for annulment. We have, in fact, already started a Deed of Separation."

"Such a relief," murmured Lady Ardsley.

"Indeed," Bertie agreed. He turned to Emily. "Another unhappy subject I must broach, Miss Ardsley. Your grandfather."

"Here!" Sir Hugh brusquely extended in Bertie's direction the piece of paper he had been playing with. "Before we get on to the subject of my father's demise, I would like to give you this, Mr. Hawkins, . . . with the thanks of all of us."

Bertie rose and retrieved the piece of paper, which he found was a check, made out to "The Penny Court Enquirers". The amount made him stagger. He looked hard at it and then up at Sir Hugh.

His lordship waved his hand dismissively and took up a glass from the same small table. Bertie could not tell whether it was medicine or whiskey. He suspected the latter.

"Now!" said Sir Hugh. "It is my understanding that my father's death was not an accident. I must say that I am not surprised. Not like an Ardsley to go falling off a train, especially when it is just arriving at Victoria Station!"

"Quite so, sir," agreed Bertie. "I did go over the facts with an inspector from Scotland Yard and he was kind enough to acquiesce that my findings were correct."

"You straightened out the fella, as I heard it," snorted his lordship. "No place for false modesty, Hawkins. Own up to it, now."

"Yes. Well – thank you, Sir Hugh. Anyway, it appears that the colonel – your father – was in fact murdered . . ."

Lady Ardsley gave a small gasp.

"Sorry to be so blunt, my lady. But yes, he was murdered and the inspector and I are determined to track down his killer."

"Very noble of you, Mr. Hawkins."

"Not at all." He addressed Emily: "Miss Ardsley, I understand that your grandfather forwarded a gold watch to you, just before he died?"

"Yes." She struggled into a more upright position. "That's what led to . . . oh, so many things! As soon as he saw the watch Thomas insisted that I pawn it and give him the money. He was . . . rather 'persuasive', I must say."

"Which led to your escaping from the pawnbrokers?"

"Yes. But only to lose the watch anyway, to the footpad who attacked me."

"We are on to that," said Bertie. "My partner and I feel that we have narrowed the area where the watch may have been disposed of and we think – we hope – that it is only a matter of time before we can restore it to you."

"Oh, that would be so wonderful." Emily's face beamed. She clapped her hands together. "It has great sentimental value to me, you see. My grandfather used to let me play with it, as a child. He would swing it on its chain and I would . . ."

"Yes, well I'm sure Mr. Hawkins doesn't need all those details." Sir Hugh waved his whiskey glass. Bertie was now sure that it *was* whiskey and not medicine, having detected a slight smell of the alcohol. "What more do you need from us, sir? I think both my daughter and myself might benefit from some rest now."

"Of course, Sir Hugh. Of course." Bertie came quickly to his feet. Just then there was a discreet knock at the door and the footman, Hunter, came in.

"Mr. Cedric Bromley has called, my lord."

"Has he, by George? Well, have him hold on a moment, will you. One visitor at a time."

Bertie made his goodbyes and followed Hunter out of the room. In the hallway he passed a tall, brown-haired, clean-shaven man in a black frock coat. His top hat, cane and gloves were evident on the hall table, where Hunter had placed them. He nodded briefly to Bertie as they passed, peering down at him through a gold-rimmed monocle.

So this is the colonel's batman/valet? thought Bertie. Hunter showed out Bertie and closed the front door firmly behind him. Bertie stood for a moment on the top step and considered his next move. *Yes, damnit! I am an enquiry agent*, he thought to himself, as he moved quickly down the steps and then turned and walked briskly around the hedges and planted borders in the direction of the drawing room windows.

The gravel of the pathway crunched under his feet and Bertie moved forward carefully and cautiously. He quickly found the windows he wanted but was disappointed to find that none of them was open. He had hoped – though couldn't remember from his time inside the room – that the French windows might have been ajar to allow some modicum of air to enter the confining room. But it seemed that Sir Hugh preferred to keep the warm air inside and the slightly cooler air outside.

Bertie could just make out the low murmur of voices, if he placed his ear up against one of the window panes. He thought he heard Sir Hugh's firm voice say the word "tragedy" but wouldn't swear to it. Another, higher, voice said something about sorrow. It seemed that Cedric's visit was a simple one of visiting bereaved relatives. Bertie turned aside and made his way back towards the street.

Chapter Twelve

"Do ye not have an office?"

Inspector Moss looked around the drawing room at 27 Penny Court as though suspicious of the heavy furnishings, comfortable chairs, and warm fireplace. Bertie noticed that he didn't hold back from enjoying a slice of Nellie's blackberry and apple pie, on the occasional table beside him.

"To tell you the truth," said Bertie, tamping down the tobacco in his briar pipe, "I do most of my office work, if you want to call it that, down in the kitchen. Besides," he couldn't help adding, "this is a lot more comfortable than your office at Scotland Yard, I would say."

The inspector took another bite of pie to save himself the trouble of having to respond. After a long silence he allowed himself: "I will admit, they dinna' have pie like this at the Yard."

After another quiet moment Bertie commented, "I saw – I don't think you could say I 'met' – that Cedric Bromley. Seemed a nice enough sort of chap, though he didn't strike me as having much substance."

"Substance?"

"He was all dolled up, with his monocle and all. I couldn't see him being anything but a lackey of the colonel's."

"Hmm." Inspector Moss reluctantly pushed away the empty pie plate and settled back to enjoy the warmth of the well-banked fire. "Well, as I told you, from the Foreign Office I learned that the colonel was not on any sort of official business at the time of his death. He'd been to see an old German pal of his, one Karl Benz. Apparently the two of them became good friends when Ardsley was over there for that Berlin thing. Benz is apparently working on some sort of version of the horseless carriage, or at least the engine to drive it."

"Was the colonel involved in that?" asked Bertie, puffing contentedly at his pipe.

"I dinna' think so, though I'm beginning to wonder just what the colonel *was* involved in and what he wasn't."

Bertie took the pipe out of his mouth and examined the Chinese amber mouthpiece. He put it back in his mouth. "So we still don't know who might have been chasing after him, with intent to kill."

"One thing this Biggersley – at the Foreign Office – mentioned was that there was an English inventor named Butler and that the colonel was acting as some sort of go-between for him and the Kraut."

"So the murderer could have been acting from the English end, if the colonel's murder is connected with them?"

"I dinna' think so," said the policeman. "I think, as we said, that the murderer was chasing him from the Continent."

"That would certainly explain why he cut across to the Brighton Line." Bertie nodded.

The door opened and Arnold came in. He waved cheerily to the Inspector, seeming not to be surprised to see him there, and then moved across to tower over Bertie.

"So I hear that I don't have to go out to the markets any more?" He sounded excited and pleased. "Nell said as how we were now solved . . . solvement . . ."

"Solvent," said Bertie. To the inspector he added "Her word, not mine. Yes, Arnold, Sir Hugh Ardsley was pleased enough with what we accomplished in getting his daughter home to him that he 'showed his appreciation', as your sister would say. We have enough in the Penny Court Enquirers' coffers that you can join me in devoting *all* of your time to our crime solving."

"Oh, Lord! There'll be no stopping you now!" Inspector Moss threw up his hands in mock surrender. "I canna' stand people interfering with police work, especially the work of the detective police, and especially not amateurs butting in. I might say that you two have been a real thorn in my side . . . until you proved your worth, at any rate." He scratched the top of his head. "So long as you dinna' go getting under foot, I guess I can turn a blind eye your way. But dinna' go telling anyone I said as much!"

"Perish the thought," said Bertie, with a smile. "Arnold, why don't you sit down and join us?"

"Was that pie?"

Bertie sighed. "All right. Duck down to the kitchen and see if your sister will part with another slice."

"Ahem." The inspector cleared his throat.

"And another one for the inspector, if she would."

Arnold picked up the inspector's empty plate and disappeared out the door.

"I have no jurisdiction in Germany, of course," said the inspector. "So I intend to check on this Mr. Butler that Biggersley mentioned." He pulled out his dog-eared notebook and consulted it. "I understand that he was featured at two different exhibitions in recent times. The Stanley Cycle Show in '84, in the Agricultural Hall, and the '85 Inventions Exhibition last year, in the Albert Hall Galleries in South Kensington. Apparently he has been showing plans for what he calls 'The Butler Petrol Cycle'."

"Would that be a conflict for Herr Benz, do you think?" asked Bertie.

"How would I know? I know nothing about engines or horseless carriages or cycles or whatever!"

Arnold arrived with the slices of pie, including one for Bertie. There was silence for some moments while they each enjoyed the fruits of Nellie's cooking.

"Could you – in your official capacity, of course – speak to the colonel's man, Bromley, and see exactly what he knows about any communications that have gone between Benz and Butler?" asked Bertie.

The inspector nodded. "I certainly could, Bertram." Neither Bertie nor Arnold commented on the fact that the policeman had used a familiar term to Bertie. "And I will make a point of it. I'll also try to make heads or tails of these vehicles that are being introduced by the gentlemen in question."

"Very good . . . Campbell." Bertie followed the inspector's lead, without making a display of it. "We – Arnold and I – are following up on the missing gold watch that was taken from Emily Squire. Emily Ardsley, as she is once again. And I do think it might yet be advantageous to keep an eye on that ex-husband of hers. Thomas Squire does not seem to me to be the sort who will take kindly to losing what he wanted so very badly."

"I'll watch him," volunteered Arnold.

Bertie nodded agreement. "Good, Arnold. Very good."

*INVENTOR MURDERED
SON KIDNAPPED!*

The headline screamed from the newspaper in Bertie's hands. He had stepped out, right after breakfast, to go to the corner shop for tobacco, when he saw the paper and heard the newsboy shouting the headline.

"'orrible murder! 'orrible murder! Small boy taken. Getcha noos 'ere!"

Bertie felt a knot develop in his stomach when he read that the murdered man was Edward Butler. The story was not long; apparently the police had little in the way of evidence, or little that they would divulge to the newspaper reporter. The murdered man's body had been discovered in his study, which had been ransacked. His five year old son, Eric, had been snatched from his bed while sleeping. Butler's wife, Kate, claimed she had slept soundly through it all, having taken laudanum. The newspaper gave an address on Great Sutton Street, in Clerkenwell, and said that Inspector Campbell Moss of Scotland Yard was handling the case. Bertie hailed a hansom right away.

Standing in Butler's study, Inspector Moss was ticking off items in his notebook when Bertie was shown in by a police constable.

"Is this the same inventor we were looking for?" Bertie asked.

The inspector looked up briefly. "Now how did I know that you would show up, Bertram?" He sighed and then returned to his notebook. "Aye, it's the same. I was planning on seeing him this morning, but not this way."

"What have you got?"

His eyes still on his notebook, the inspector said, "The wife, name of Kate Gildersleeves – now there's a mouthful – claims she was sound asleep through it all. Laudanum, she says. Has been having trouble sleeping so she took it last night. Claims she 'doesn't use it a lot'. Now how can a woman simply sleep through her husband being murdered and her son kidnapped?"

"If she had the laudanum then she certainly could," said Bertie. "She could sleep through just about anything, I would think."

"Hmm! Well, we'll see. Now then . . . was the boy kidnapped, or did he perhaps off his old man and run away?"

"He was how old?" asked Bertie.

"Let's see. I've got it here . . . Oh! He was five. Well, we have to examine all possibilities, you know."

"Of course." Bertie smiled. He looked about him. The body had been removed by the coroner. "How was Butler killed?"

"Garroted. Someone must have broken in and, while Butler was sitting at his desk, come up behind him and slipped the rope over his head. Seen it a dozen times."

Bertie gazed around the room. It looked as though everything had been upended. Books and papers lay all over the floor, pictures had been pulled down off the walls, curio cabinets were standing open, even the corners of rugs and carpets had been turned back.

"Looks as though he was looking for something; not just a haphazard robbery."

The inspector nodded. "Just what I was thinking." He scribbled in his book.

"Why are the corners of the rugs turned up? Did the police do that?"

"No; the perpetrator. He was looking to see if there was any hiding place in the floor boards. There isn't."

"To do with this Butler Petrol Cycle, do you think?"

"Undoubtedly. The plans for it, in all probability." The policeman thought for a moment. "Would they be worth much, do you think?"

Bertie nodded his head, as he looked around the room. "To the right person, yes. I'm sure they would. The horseless carriage, and all associated with it, is brand new and open territory. I would imagine that whoever is first at just about any aspect of it will become very influential." He moved over to the desk and studied it. All of the drawers had been pulled out.

"And very rich?"

"If the idea actually takes off, yes," said Bertie. He picked up a small, square, leather box with a flat lid. "Of course, right now we have the Red Flag Act in force. I'd heard from my friends at the old *Daily Chronicle* that this is seriously hindering progress, not just for the motor vehicles themselves but for any manner of things that can and will be developed from it." He looked inside the box to find a half dozen or so calling cards. After a quick glance at the inspector, who was still deep in his notebook, Bertie slipped the visitors' cards into his pocket and returned the box to the desk top.

"Well, all that is beyond me," muttered the inspector, closing his notebook and once again prowling the room. "I've got my hands full just trying to solve a murder. *Two* murders now . . . and a kidnapping!"

Bertie nodded sympathetically. "I presume the murderer took the child to hold for ransom when he couldn't find what he wanted." He thought for a moment. "Well, speaking of the murders, Campbell, since you're tied-up here why don't I go along and have a word with Mr. Cedric Bromley regarding the colonel? Perhaps find out just what sort of correspondence he was carrying back and forth across the Channel for the colonel?"

Chapter Thirteen

Cedric Bromley had rooms in Pimlico, on Charwood Street, off Belgrave Road. It was a modest but well kept house run by a Mrs. Brush. Bromley rented rooms on the second floor. Bertie found Mrs. Brush to be an elderly but spry woman in perpetual mourning, with a sharp face and personality to match. She questioned him closely before deigning to show him up the stairs to her lodger's rooms.

"You look familiar," Bromley greeted him. "Have we met before?" He took in Bertie's sacque suit and bowler hat. "Obviously you are not a member of my club, so it wasn't there." He indicated a straight-backed chair for Bertie, remaining standing himself. He wore a plain silk, ivory colored waistcoat with a dark green cravat tucked into it. He did not bother to put on his jacket for his visitor.

Bertie looked about him and then, when Bromley didn't offer to take his hat, placed his bowler on the floor beside him. "We didn't really meet, as such," he said. "It was more a passing as I came out and you went in. At Sir Hugh Ardsley's, you may recall?"

"Ah! Yes." Without asking if Bertie minded, Bromley removed a cigarette from a silver box on the mantle-piece and lit it with a paper spill, from the fire in the fireplace. He did not offer one to Bertie. "And your reason for coming to my residence?" He tucked his monocle into his eye and looked disdainfully at the card that Bertie had sent up, with Mrs. Brush. "A private enquiry agent is it, Mr. Hawkins?" The monocle dropped from his eye again. He caught it and swung it into his waistcoat pocket.

"It is." Bertie took in the state of the room. Typical bachelor residence, he thought. Also, typically a man with a military background. Books were about the place, but all in neat little stacks. Any clothing in evidence was carefully folded. Bertie did, however, find his attention drawn to a decanter of whisky on a silver server, resting in the center of the walnut sideboard. The decanter, he noted, was almost empty.

"I am – er – assisting Scotland Yard in their enquiries regarding the death of Colonel Ardsley."

Bromley moved over to the sideboard and Bertie felt that the man wanted to pour himself a drink, but refrained.

"The colonel? I have already spoken – at some length, I might add – to both Scotland Yard and to *The Times* newspaper. I do not feel there is anything more I might add . . . even to an enquiry agent." Apparently making up his mind, he poured himself a glass of the liquid. As an afterthought, he waved the decanter in Bertie's direction, with a questioning look on his face. Bertie shook his head.

The decanter, virtually empty, was returned to the sideboard.

"You had been with the colonel for a long time," said Bertie, making it a statement rather than a question.

Bromley moved and stood with his back to his visitor, gazing out of the window. Despite the closed window, Bertie could hear the sounds of traffic outside: the clip-clop of hooves, the muffled shouts and calls, the clatter of hansoms, the rumble of larger vehicles.

"He was like a father to me." The voice was soft and subdued. It was as though Bertie was no longer there and Bromley was merely reminiscing; talking to himself. He held his half-smoked cigarette in one hand and his whiskey glass in the other. "We had been on a long march together, the two of us. India, Madras, Bangalore, Bombay, Surat. Then afterwards, Germany, France, Switzerland. Germany had a special attraction for him, I think. I didn't care much for it myself, but then what did that matter? I got to being sent back and forth, like a shuttlecock. The treaty was the big one for him. He never forgot that. Lived it and relived it." He paused for a long time and Bertie didn't think it right to interrupt him. After what seemed an age, Bromley took another long drink from his glass and turned back to face his visitor. "What are you looking for, Mr. Hawkins? Grief? I can give you grief."

Bertie felt decidedly uncomfortable. "What will you do now?" he asked.

Bromley shrugged. He took a long drag on his cigarette and then tossed it into the fireplace. "He was talking about retiring anyway. Really retiring. Going back to live with his family. He would no longer have needed me."

Bertie thought he sounded bitter. It was time to change the subject. "These assignments between England and Germany. Was it always between the same people, that you were asked to act?"

"No." He drained his glass, looked at the near-empty decanter, and held on to the glass as though for support. "There were a lot of different people at different times. Oh, the last couple or so times, yes. While the colonel remained in Germany, I came across to speak with one individual in particular."

"Mr. Edward Butler?" said Bertie. He noticed that Bromley's eyebrows went up a fraction, though he made no comment. "And the gentleman in Germany was Herr Karl Benz, I believe?"

After the briefest of pauses Bromley said, "There is no secret about that. This was not a Foreign Office affair."

"No, of course not."

"The colonel was acting as liaison between the two parties. They were trying to arrive at a mutually satisfactory agreement on . . . whatever it was."

"You didn't know what they were negotiating?"

"No, I did not."

Bertie didn't believe that but he said nothing.

"There seemed to be a lot of back and forth," continued Bromley. "Offers and counter offers, perhaps?"

"I would imagine so." Bertie nodded. "And I understand that you were away on just such a negotiating quest at the time of the colonel's passing?"

"Correct." Bromley looked long and hard into his empty whiskey glass then put it down on the mantle-piece next to the cigarette box.

"What was so urgent that you had to leave the colonel – go on ahead – to see Mr. Butler?"

"I really don't know. The colonel insisted. Said he wanted me to deliver the latest letter from Benz to Butler at the earliest opportunity. He did not enlarge on that." Bromley took out another cigarette, looked at it and then replaced it in the cigarette box, closing the lid. He turned to face Bertie.

"If there is nothing more, Mr. Hawkins, I will bid you good day. I am already late for an appointment and must be on my own way."

"Certainly, sir." Bertie picked up his hat and came to his feet. He lost no time in leaving Mrs. Brush's establishment. He walked to the corner of the street, turned onto Belgrave Road, and then stopped. He stayed there for some time, looking back around the corner to see if indeed Cedric Bromley did leave for his claimed appointment. He did not. After more than half an hour, Bertie turned and made for home.

Nellie decided to take the Red omnibus to Holborn Viaduct and from there walk to Great Sutton Street. The omnibuses on that route ran every five minutes so she didn't have long to wait. She paid her penny fare and sat back to enjoy the ride. It was a dull, overcast day but not as cold as it had been and the sun did break through the clouds on rare occasions, to add a brightness and promise to life. She always kept Bertie's dire warnings against pickpockets in mind and so she held her reticule close as she sat in the uncomfortable omnibus seat. The unevenness of the road transferred the jolts and bumps throughout the heavy vehicle as the horses plodded up the slight hills and trotted down the inclines. It was a seldom experienced sensation for Nellie and she sat with a slight smile on her face.

Located between Islington and Hatton Garden, Clerkenwell was well known for its watch-makers, goldsmiths, and opticians. The name derived from "Clerk's Well" which had once been situated there. Parish clerks from London used to gather there annually for celebration of miracle plays and similar. But Nellie thought there'd be no celebrating this day, or any time soon until the Butlers' child was found and restored to his mother.

She had determined that she needed to take a hand in the actions of the Penny Court Enquirers by going to talk to Kate Butler. It called for a woman's touch, to give the poor woman what comfort she was able and, at the same time, to make the enquiries that she knew Bertie needed to make.

The house at Great Sutton Street was small but neat, with fresh paint on the front door and on the window shutters. In sharp contrast was the black wreath that hung on the door. The brass door knocker had obviously not been polished that day but showed signs of having been well and regularly burnished. Nellie raised it and let it drop with a bang. She stood there for some considerable time before she heard someone respond. The door was opened by an auburn-haired woman in her late twenties. Her eyes were red-rimmed and heavily shadowed underneath. She wore first mourning; her bombazine dress covered with black crepe and a widow's cap on her otherwise striking hair. She looked at Nellie with a blank expression.

"Yes? What is it?"

Nellie suddenly felt out of her depth. What was she doing imposing herself on this woman's grief? She probably just wanted to be left alone. But no! Nellie pulled herself up straighter and, with what she hoped was a friendly smile, looked the woman in the eyes.

"Mrs. Butler? I am so sorry to intrude at this time but I thought you might appreciate a sympathetic ear. My name is Nell Hawkins. May I come in?"

With the slightest of hesitation, Kate Butler stepped aside and allowed Nellie to enter. She then led the way through to the drawing room where she excused herself for a few moments to make a pot of tea. Soon the two women were sitting opposite each other, with tea and digestive biscuits.

"I have no maid," Kate said, by way of explanation. "Edward . . . Mr. Butler . . . was very involved in his work and at times it could be very expensive."

Nellie waved her hand. "I know just what you mean, my dear. I have only the one maid-of-all-work . . . and sometimes I wish I didn't have her!" She smiled, but the other woman did not respond. Nellie looked around at the bands of black crepe along the mantelpiece over the fireplace, and around the picture frames. The mirrors in the room were all covered. The curtains of the room were drawn, so that the gasolier was burning.

"Your husband was here when the police were here, you say?" said Kate, offering milk and sugar to her guest.

Nellie accepted both and stirred them into her tea. "Yes. He has been working with Inspector Moss . . ."

"He is a policeman, your husband? Oh, I beg your pardon. I did not mean to interrupt. Please forgive me."

"That's quite all right," said Nellie, with a smile. "No, he is not a policeman himself. He is a private enquiry agent. We – he has had occasion to be of assistance to the inspector in the past and, as part of an investigation, the two of them were interested in speaking with your husband . . . your late husband, I suppose I must say. Oh, I am so sorry!"

She reached out and touched Kate's arm as the woman looked away for a moment, obviously upset. "No. Please. Go on," Kate said. "What would they want with Edward? He was not a part of any police investigation that I was aware."

"They were investigating the death of a Colonel Ardsley," explained Nellie. "It seems that this colonel was coordinating some kind of a deal between your husband and a German named Benz."

"Ah! Herr Benz. Yes." Kate nodded, as she cupped her teacup in both hands. "There was something. I don't know the details but as I understand it Herr Benz had been making offers to buy Edward's invention – the one for a carburetor, I think it was called. The German was most anxious to obtain it but Edward just couldn't decide whether or not he wanted to part with it. I believe Herr Benz made several offers. A man kept calling here and speaking with Edward." She paused and Nellie didn't interrupt her. Kate drank some of her tea and then set down the cup very deliberately. "I wish he'd sold it! I wish Edward had sold his carburetor. Whether to Karl Benz or whomever, I don't care! I just wish he'd got rid of it!"

Nellie was surprised at the outburst. "You felt strongly about it, I see," she said quietly.

"Edward had burned himself out on this thing. He had been the 'belle of the ball' at the Stanley Cycle Show a couple of years ago, and then again at the Inventions Exhibition last year. It seems that he had solved a problem others couldn't. Something to do with spraying some liquid into the engine. Benz was at the Stanley Show and had a representative at the other one. He kept on and on at Edward to sell his idea."

"And Edward wasn't keen on that, I take it?" said Nellie.

"It was the Red Flag Act that was killing him," said Kate. She poured herself another cup of tea. Nellie declined one. "Over twenty years there has been this hold on development. A top speed of two miles an hour in built-up areas and four miles an hour in rural areas. And you have to have a man with a red flag walking in front of your vehicle plus two other men present! It's barbaric! I heard Edward bemoaning it for so long. Every year they said they'd repeal the Act or they'd increase the speed, or something. But they never did!"

"I had not realized the restrictions," said Nellie. "It would be enough to stifle anyone."

"Benz said that it would be different on the Continent. He said that he would be able to make use of Edward's carburetor in his own engine and then the whole automobile movement would benefit. He offered Edward a lot of money."

"And Edward didn't take it?"

"I think he was about to. I believe Herr Benz was making one final offer. Quite large. And I think Edward was ready to accept it."

Nellie thought for a moment. "This invention of Edward's? It would, then, be something that other people would also want? Would, perhaps, even be willing to try to steal?"

"Oh, yes!" Kate laughed mirthlessly. "We had a break-in two or three weeks ago. Nothing was taken. I suspected they were looking for my husband's work though he didn't think so. And now one of them has tried and killed Edward in the process. Not to mention kidnapping my son! I'm sure I will soon be getting a ransom note asking for Edward's plans in exchange for my son's safe return!"

"Did you tell the police of this previous attempt?"

She shook her head. "Edward said best not to publicize what he had." She paused before continuing, bitterly, "I must just await this ransom note, that is sure to follow."

"And you'd be willing to do that, I'm sure; to give up the plans to get your son back?"

"Of course." Kate suddenly broke into tears. The teacup fell from her hands and broke as it hit the saucer. Nellie rose and moved to her, putting her arms around the woman. Kate leaned against her and sobbed.

"What is it?" asked Nellie.

"I don't know where the plans are! How would I know where Edward hid them? How can I get back Eric if I can't give them what they want?" Kate's whole body shook as she cried.

Nellie held her close.

Chapter Fourteen

Bertie laid out the seven cards in front of Taffy Lloyd. They were the visitors' cards he had taken from the box on Edward Butler's desk. He read aloud the names: "Cedric Bromley, Harold J. Lawson, Frederick William Lanchester, Bromley again, Frank B. Shuttleworth, Wilhelm von Bernstorff, Maurice Whiteway."

"Do any of them mean anything to you?" asked Taffy.

Bertie nodded his head. "Cedric Bromley, of course. I've told you about him. He was just a transporter and deliverer of messages, it seems. Lawson sounds kind of familiar, though I can't quite place him. The others . . . no. No, the other names don't mean anything to me, which is why I came to you, Taffy."

The Welshman picked up two of the cards and read the names and addresses carefully before putting them down again. "Harry John Lawson is an interesting gentleman, if I might call him that. Some have labeled him a fraudster."

Bertie tugged at his mustache. "A fraudster?"

Taffy nodded. "Nothing he's been brought to task for . . . not yet, at any rate. He dabbles in a number of enterprises, including this budding automotive thing. He was a bicycle designer and then turned to horseless carriages. I think he has a small factory, or warehouses or something, down near the London Docks. He designed several different bicycles in the '70s and made a bit of a name for himself with some sort of chain drive to the rear wheel. However, he seems to have enriched himself mainly from garnering important patents and shell companies."

"Shell companies?"

The two men were in Taffy Lloyd's office at *The Morning Post*.

"A shell company is one that is used to transact business without itself actually having any assets of any significance," he explained. "Shell companies are not in themselves illegal, though many of them come very close to the line. They are sometimes used to disguise true profits in order to avoid payment of taxes."

"So why would he have been visiting Edward Butler, I wonder?"

Taffy shrugged. "Perhaps he saw some sort of opportunity in Butler's patents on this engine thing that everyone seems so interested in."

Bertie nodded slowly. "You may be right. Hmm! How about this German gentleman, Wilhelm von Bernstorff? Have you heard of him?"

"No. But you say this Karl Benz – who I *had* heard of, by the way – was negotiating with

Butler, so perhaps von Bernstorff was part of that deal?"

"From all I've found out so far, that deal was strictly negotiated through the colonel, so I doubt this gentleman," he tapped the card, "was part of it. But, of course, there may well be more than one German interested in what Butler had." Bertie looked along the line of cards again. "What about Lanchester? Do you know him, Taffy?"

"F. W. Lanchester. Yes, as it happens I do." Taffy swung around in his chair and pulled a well-worn reference book from the shelf behind him. He opened it and flicked through the pages till he found what he was looking for. "Here! This is a book of biographies of notable and up-and-coming people in London in recent years. Here's our Mr. Lanchester. Quite a brilliant young man, it seems." He read: "*Frederick William Lanchester, born in Lewisham on October 23, 1868, is in the process of turning a hobby into a profession. Fresh from his studies at the Hartley Institution in Southampton, Mr. Lanchester took out his own patent on an isometrograph. He has recently taken a job with the Forward Gas Engine Company and is said to be working on an invention to control engine speeds and is patenting a pendulum accelerometer together with another patent for a self-starting device for gas engines.*"

"He sounds quite the brain," Bertie commented.

"Word is that he's a young man to watch. Interesting that he's been in touch with Edward Butler."

"What about the others?"

Taffy shook his head. "The names don't mean anything to me right away, but let's have a look through this volume. It has brought me several surprises in the past."

Half an hour later the two men had learned a lot. Taffy drew up a list of the men whose cards they had, together what they had discovered about them.

Cedric Bromley – aide to Colonel Ardsley.
Messenger between Butler and Benz.
Harold J. Lawson – Entrepreneur. Opportunist.
Recently interested in automobiles.
Frederick William Lanchester – Inventor with
interests in engines and their development.
Frank B. Shuttleworth – Manufacturer located in
Erith, Kent.
Wilhelm von Bernstorff – Unknown German, might
or might not be associated with Karl Benz.
Maurice Whiteway – Supplier of sheet metal and
metal castings.

"A general cross-section of the sort of people you'd expect someone like Butler to associate with," Bertie commented.

"All right," said Taffy, sitting back, lacing his fingers behind his head, and gazing at the ceiling. "Let's look at this from the newspaper reporter's point of view, boy. Regardless of who these people are, what could they possibly want with Edward Butler?"

Bertie started counting off on his fingers. "Number one, Butler seems to have come up with an invention that is wanted – no, *needed* – by this new automobile industry. Number two, he didn't seem to have advanced very far on his own but was reluctant to let anyone else have it."

"He was dickering with Benz, don't forget," said Taffy.

"Dickering, yes. So Benz might have got frustrated."

"Enough to murder Butler to get what he wanted?"

Bertie shrugged. "It's possible. We've got to look at all possibilities."

"Any and all of them might have got the same treatment from Butler."

"That's true," agreed Bertie. "So any and all of them might have been frustrated to the point where they decided to act for themselves."

"Again, to the point of killing the man?" Taffy raised his eyebrows.

"It is possible. We don't know what sort of temper any of them has," said Bertie. "They say the Germans have bad tempers," he added darkly.

Taffy laughed and brought his hands back down to the desk. "No, I don't think we can go on generalizations, Bertie. We've got to have specifics. Real clues, boy."

Bertie got to his feet. "Well, I'd better let you get on with your real work, Taffy. I very much appreciate the time you've spent. Would you keep an ear and an eye open, in case anything else should pop up, or you have any ideas?"

"Of course, Bertie This makes a nice change from the local government elections we're covering just now!" The two men shook hands.

Inspector Moss had taken to regularly calling in at 27 Penny Court. Ostensibly it was to review the progress on the Ardsley and Butler murders, but Nellie swore it was because he had become addicted to her cooking. Bertie suspected there might be a grain of truth to that.

"Something smells good," said the inspector, as he sat down at the kitchen table.

Nellie winked at Bertie and then turned to the policeman. "As it happens, Campbell, I'm just about to take a steak and kidney pie out of the oven. But I'm sure you've already eaten. We seem to be a little late today."

"Nay! Nay, I havena' eaten," said the inspector quickly. "Matter of fact, I'm kind of behind myself. With all of these investigations, I'd quite forgotten about food."

Bertie smiled. "Can we talk you into joining us for dinner then?" he asked.

The inspector had the grace to allow a second or two to pass before he answered. "Well now, I'm sure I should be getting along but . . ."

"You've only just got here," said Arnold. As usual he had his nose in the newspaper but added to the conversation.

At that moment Isobel came into the kitchen and stopped when she saw Inspector Moss had joined the kitchen group. "Oh!" was all she said. Then she went to the sideboard, took out another set of cutlery, and went back up to the dining room to lay the extra place.

When everyone was sitting back from the table, having had their fill of steak and kidney pie, mashed potatoes, peas, carrots, and an apple pie dessert, Bertie poured himself a coffee and then passed the pot to Arnold.

"Any developments at the Butler household?" he asked the inspector, while watching his brother-in-law fill his cup so full that he had to spoon out a few mouthfuls before he could lift the cup and not spill it.

"Not a great deal." Inspector Moss sighed. He took the coffee pot from Arnold and filled his own cup. "There were some letters we found that established a tentative contact from another German – fellow by the name of Daimler – who was working on a similar attachment for the engine to the one Butler had perfected." He reached into his pocket and withdrew his ever-present blue-covered notebook. "Daimler is working with another Kraut name of Maybach. But it appears that Butler had scooped them all. His design is something they'd all like to get their hands on. It's an engine powered by mineral hydro . . . hydrocarbons, whatever they are. It's a two cylinder engine and it works – now this, apparently, is the revolutionary part – by spraying Benzoline," he pronounced the word very carefully, "a petroleum product, carbureted by air." He looked around at the others to see their response.

Bertie sipped his coffee and nodded sagely, as though he understood everything the inspector had said. "The only problem is," he said, "that no one seems to know where this miraculous design is. The plans have apparently disappeared."

"Hmm." Inspector Moss nodded his head as he took a mouthful of apple pie. He chewed for a while before continuing. "That's obviously what the intruder was looking for. He killed Butler to get the plans, but then couldna' find them."

"Or, he killed him *because* he couldn't find them," put in Arnold.

"True."

"Or . . ." Arnold's face was screwed up as he started filling in blanks. "He *did* find the plans, which is why we can't find them. He stole them after all." He sat back with a satisfied smile on his face. It faded when Nellie said:

"Then why did he kidnap the son? Anyway, even Kate doesn't know where the plans are." Nellie went on to tell the inspector what she had already told Bertie, of her visit to the widow and what little she was able to learn.

Bertie reached into his own pocket and produced the list that he and Taffy had compiled. He passed it to the inspector. "See if you know any of these names, Campbell. They are all people who, apparently, visited Butler in recent days. I suspect that one of them could just possibly be the murderer, though, of course, the murderer may not have come with calling card."

Moss studied the list while finishing his pie and washing it down with coffee. "Where did you get this?" he finally asked.

Bertie waved a non-committal hand. "I was able to put it together from . . . from names that were associated with Butler." He didn't elaborate. "Most of them seem to be tied-in to the automobile."

"Well, we certainly know of your Mr. Lawson. Though he's been fairly quiet of late. Either he's turned over a new leaf – *not* very likely to my mind – or he's plotting some new infamy. You say he saw Butler recently?"

"So I believe," said Bertie. "He'd been there and left his calling card."

The inspector continued looking at the list. "Lanchester I believe is up north at the moment. I think I read somewhere that he was doing some work in Birmingham. Bromley, of course, we know. Now Shuttleworth and Whiteway, I have no idea, but it should be easy to check on them. The Kraut I dinna' know what to say."

Bertie turned his attention to Arnold. "Weren't you going to follow up on Squire, Arnold? What he might be up to? Did you get anywhere?"

Arnold looked up with eyes wild. He reminded Bertie of a rabbit who was looking down the wrong end of a double-barreled shotgun. "What? Oh, yes. Yes, I did manage to do some checking, as a matter of fact."

They all looked surprised. Even more so when Arnold continued. "I found that his usual watering hole is the Mucky Duck on Lombard Street"

"Mucky Duck?" Nellie looked bewildered.

The Inspector smiled. "It's a pub named the Black Swan," he explained. "But the locals all refer to it as the Mucky Duck."

"Go on, Arnold," urged Bertie.

"Well, I found that Squire goes in there a lot. And he always seems to have plenty of money to spend these days. It wasn't always the case, it seems. Buys a lot of rounds."

"Really? That's unusual for a man who is out of work," said the inspector.

Arnold looked pleased with himself. "No longer out of work," he said. "It would appear that he now does odd jobs for Mr. Lawson."

"There it is, on the corner," said Arnold, nodding towards the Black Swan Inn. It was an old public house, even for that part of the town, but seemed to be well maintained. It had started raining so Bertie was glad to lead the way inside. They found themselves a table not far from the bar but against the wall. He sent Arnold up to the counter to get them each a pint of porter. Settled with their drinks, the two of them looked about but could see no sign of Squire.

"He usually comes in around this time," said Arnold. "Though not always, I suppose."

They had finished their drinks and Bertie was giving due consideration as to whether or not they should have another round when Arnold nudged him. "There he is. Just came in."

Bertie recognized him right away as the man who had shown him the room for rent. He was wearing a dull-finished, rubber-sheeting coat, glistening with rain. Squire's bowler hat, which looked as though it had seen better days, was dripping water onto the sawdust of the floor. He stood just inside the door looking all around the public bar, checking every single person there. Bertie looked down and lifted his empty tankard in front of his face.

"Don't look at him, Arnold," he muttered. "Just relax and . . . I think perhaps you'd better go and get us another round of drinks."

Arnold needed no urging. By the time he returned with their refilled tankards, Squire had made his way up to the counter and was exchanging banter with two men who had been there before Bertie and Arnold came in. Bertie tried to overhear what was being said but the general chatter from the now-crowded bar made it difficult.

"Arnold. As casually as you can, wander up to the counter and see if you can lean on it with your drink, close to Squire. Then keep your ears open to hear what he's talking about."

Arnold did as he was told. Bertie was pleased to see that he could be quiet and inconspicuous when he wanted to be. Soon he was leaning on the counter right next to Squire but with his back to the man.

"Perfect!" Bertie smiled to himself.

He noticed that Squire paid for drinks for himself and for the two men he was talking to. The men looked like dock workers. Eventually they downed their drinks and made their farewells, turning to leave. Arnold must have heard them and glanced towards his brother-in-law. Bertie held up his hand, palm towards Arnold, to indicate that the big man should stay put, and then he got up himself and moved through the crowded room to the door. The two men lingered in the doorway, when they saw the rain coming down, but finally started a fast walk up the road. Bertie stood close to them for the few moments they were there, as if making up his own mind. He let them go and turned back into the bar.

The rain was coming down heavily and neither Bertie nor Arnold had been prepared for it, so Bertie hailed a hansom and they made their way home in style.

"The two men mentioned the East India Docks just before they left," said Bertie as the cab trotted along. "I thought they looked like dock workers. What were you able to pick up?"

"Squire was talking to them about work to be done at a place called Lawson Industries," said Arnold. "He said they were going to be needed by the end of the month, though he didn't say what for."

"Lawson Industries must be the company that Harry Lawson runs," said Bertie. "I was wondering where it was. It looks as though it may be down near the East India Docks, then. Makes sense, I suppose. There are all sorts of warehouses in that area." He grunted. "Hmph! In fact that will be the problem – finding his one in the middle of all the others."

"Sounds like a job for the bloodhound of the Penny Court Enquirers," said Arnold, with a laugh. Then added, "That's me!"

"Yes." Bertie nodded. "I guessed that's who you meant. That's pretty good, Arnold. The bloodhound of the Penny Court Enquirers. Very good."

Arnold beamed the rest of the way home.

Chapter Fifteen

Inspector Campbell Moss kept repeating the name to himself. Wilhelm von Bernstorff. Wilhelm von Bernstorff. Wilhelm von Bernstorff. Why did Germans have such difficult names? Willy Barndoor, or William Barnstead, or something else would make so much more sense! But no! It was . . . he had to look down at his notebook to recapture it . . . Wilhelm von Bernstorff. All right; so be it!

He had experienced one of what he modestly termed his "moments of genius". Who would be most likely to know about this von Bernstorff? Who could tell him what he needed to know? Why, the German Embassy, of course! Inspector Moss marched along to the embassy, at 9 Carlton House Terrace, prepared to knock some sense into a few Kraut heads.

Through questioning others at Scotland Yard, the inspector had assumed that the people working at the embassy would have a good grasp of the English language, since they were working and living in England. He found that in fact their ability to speak the Queen's English was little better than his ability to speak German. There also seemed to be a lot of clicking of heels and stamping of feet.

"*Nein,* we do not 'ave a von Bernstorff 'ere at the embassy."

"I know that!" snapped the inspector. Then he thought a moment. "Well, actually no, I didn'a know that. I just assumed. Hmm. . . All right then, do you know who this von Bernstorff is? *Who is this von Bernstorff?"* For some reason he thought that by raising his voice the German gentleman he spoke to might more easily understand what he was saying.

In fact the embassy official stood quite still and stared hard at Inspector Moss. He wore an immaculate black cut-away frock coat, grey pin-stripe trousers with a sharp crease, a silver waistcoat topped by a deep maroon tie and a gold watch chain that was strung across his ample stomach. Moss noted that the man had a nasty scar across one cheek. His hair was close cropped, though he sported fine mutton-chop sideboards. His large mustache was waxed on the ends with the points sticking upward.

"There is no need to raise your voice, Herr policeman." He spoke precisely. "*Folgen Sie mir ganz nahe."* He beckoned the inspector to follow him as he crossed the vast expanse of Turkey carpet to a large, gilt desk manned by a second gentleman in equally elegant sartorial finery. He addressed the seated man in a long flow of German in the midst of which the inspector picked up the words "Scotland Yard." He then turned to the inspector, gave a half bow with a click of his heels, and walked away.

"The colonel asks me to help you, Herr Moss."

"Inspector. Inspector Moss." He pulled himself up to stand a little straighter. It was comforting to be able to look down on the German . . . until that gentleman rose to his feet and showed himself to be almost six feet tall.

"*Sehr verbunden.* Pardon me, Inspector. I am Secretary to the Head of the Cultural Section at the embassy. Lieutenant Georg Reitsch." He clicked his heels. "Now, I understand that you are trying to find a Herr Wilhelm von Bernstorff?"

Inspector Moss breathed a sigh of relief. "Aye. Aye, that's it exactly. You know him?"

"As it happens, I do know *of* him. I happened to be at my desk here when he briefly visited the embassy a number of days ago. What is it you wish to know, Inspector?"

"Whatever you can tell me. It may help with an investigation I am conducting."

The Lieutenant thoughtfully stroked his chin. "He signed the day book but that will tell us nothing more than the hour at which he visited. But let me see – I have a good memory." His brow furrowed. "As I recall he said he was here very briefly on business. I believe he mentioned he was associated with the Deutz-AG-Gasmotorenfabrik in Cologne. He may have been their technical director but, I regret, I am not certain of that."

"And why was he in London?"

"As an *Eröffnung* – an 'overture' – I remember he used that word, to a British inventor. I regret I do not have that name. He intended to do little more than leave his card and express his company's interests, I believe. Is this of any help, Herr Inspector?"

Moss was making notes in his little blue book. He finished and looked up at the tall German. "Aye. Aye, Lieutenant. Thank you very much. That does move us on a little."

There was a click of heels.

Arnold had done his work well, thought Bertie, locating Lawson's warehouse near Limehouse Reach. It lay between Emmett Street and Garford Street, close to West India Dock Station on the river side of the great West India Dock warehouses. Bertie stood in the gathering twilight watching the fog slowly build as it came off the river. He had sent Arnold on another errand and now considered his plans to check out Lawson Industries by himself. He might possibly be acting hastily, not having thought through everything to its conclusion, he considered. He chewed on his mustache. He was anxious to see where Harry Lawson stood in the overall scheme of things, yet had no real idea of how to go about it.

He thought back to the days when he would pore through *The Daily Chronicle's* reports of police investigations and raids. In some ways he felt extremely confident – there was still the need to prove himself better than the police – yet at the same time he knew he had no practical experience.

It was all a case of going by information obtained, due consideration, instinct, and plain old luck.

The lamplighter came past where Bertie was standing. He was bundled up against the chill wind that blew off the river and mumbled to himself as he peddled his old bicycle along the pot-holed street. There was a gas lamp at the junction of Emmet and Garford streets but then none for a long stretch of either roadway. The entrance to Lawson Industries was a good hundred yards down Emmett Street. Bertie slowly made his way along the rubbish-strewn throughway, the light from the lamppost growing dimmer and dimmer as it dropped away behind him.

He should have come out during the day and had a good look at the set-up, Bertie thought. *Act in haste; repent at leisure.* But then he knew, in his heart, that he was hoping he might have to break into the place, or do something equally drastic, and he wouldn't want to be seen doing that. He thrilled at the thought. *What would Nellie say?* He put that thought out of his head. He was a Penny Court Enquirer and he did what he had to do!

The big, black and rusted, wrought-iron gates into the Lawson compound were locked; a heavy chain and padlock binding the two gates together. Bertie peered through. In the fast fading light he could see a large warehouse, typical of those all around the dock area. It was wooden sided with a corrugated cast-iron roof and small, featureless windows evenly spaced in two rows along its length. Faded, once-white letters spelled out the words *LAWSON INDUSTRIES* across the center section. There were loading platforms at intervals interspersed with piles of wooden boxes, crates, scrap metal and other debris.

Suddenly he pressed his face harder against the bars of the gate. A light had come on in one of the second floor windows at the far end of the building. Through the growing fog and the grime on the window, plus the distance from where he stood, Bertie couldn't make out anything or anyone on the inside. But he knew he had to get closer and discover who was there at that late hour. He looked around, helplessly. He needed to get beyond the big gates. Frustrated, he shook them. With a clang, the chain tying together the two sides slipped a little. It had not been drawn taught when the lock was put on and now the slack hung down. Bertie pushed and moved one side of the gates a few inches before that slack was taken up. He considered the space now apparent at the bottom of the gates.

Bertie had always kept himself in shape – despite Nellie's wonderful cooking – and now was glad of it. Dropping to his knees, he found that he could stick his head between the two wrought-iron barriers and, with much wriggling, might be able to get all the way through. In the end he removed his overcoat and jacket, pushed them through ahead of him, and then squeezed between the gates. He stood up, victorious, on the inside and quickly dressed himself again. He found that he had torn a large ragged hole in the left knee of his trousers. Nellie would be very annoyed about that! Bertie sighed, mentally shrugged, and moved forward.

It was quite dark now and the fog had increased to where Bertie had difficulty seeing much of anything. The lighted window was no more than a vague glow up ahead of him. He moved towards it, holding his hands out in front of him in case he encountered any obstacle. He reached the side of the building and advanced along it with one hand touching the boards. Eventually, after negotiating a loading dock and then several piles of scrap, he found himself underneath the lighted window. It was on the floor above where he stood so he could not see into it. He would have given anything for a ladder.

He moved back to the piles of debris and considered some of the packing crates and wooden boxes. Perhaps he could pile up some of them enough to see into the window? But it was high up and would take a lot of boxes. The packing crates, although empty, were too big and heavy to move, otherwise they would have helped tremendously. In the end Bertie gave up on the idea. He moved on, a short way past the lit window, to the end of the warehouse. He found his hand resting on the water-spout. It came down into a large and nearly-full rain-water barrel. Bertie had an idea.

Moving a wooden box beside the barrel, Bertie was able to clamber up onto it. From there he reached up and grasped the down-spout. He tugged to test its rigidity. It seemed firmly attached. With a deep breath and a silent prayer, Bertie pressed his feet against the side of the building and pulled himself up on the down-pipe. Slowly, inch by inch, he moved up the side of the building. It took more strength than he had reckoned but he kept at it, stopping frequently to catch his breath. Eventually he was almost level with the bottom of the lighted window. What he needed to do was lean across from the pipe, so that he could see inside the room.

Arnold had been sitting with his sister and brother-in-law before Bertie hurried away on what he termed "urgent business". Nellie had said that Hattie Parker was once again concerned about her husband Herbert. Herbert had shaken the opium attraction but it seemed that something else had now caught his attention and Hattie was very worried, according to Nellie. Bertie had suggested that Arnold once again follow the man to see where that attraction lay.

It was already dark and beginning to drizzle as Arnold followed along City Road at a discreet distance behind his quarry. They had taken the underground railway from Bank Station up to Old Street. This had been a completely new experience for Arnold and it was only thoughts of upholding the honor of the Penny Court Enquirers that had helped him overcome his naturally claustrophobic tendencies on finding himself enclosed in a moving vehicle beneath the streets of London. He had sweated profusely and kept his eyes tightly closed, opening them only to watch Herbert Parker when the train arrived at Moorgate station, to make sure he was not disembarking there. Thankfully it had not been a long journey to Old Street; hardly worth the twopence, he thought. The carriages were lit with gas and the stations had large, curved glass roofs lighted from above. Old Street Station was much smaller than Bank had been.

From City Road Herbert turned off onto Featherstone Street, behind the old Bunhill Fields Burial Ground. From there he led into Bunhill Row. The houses all looked the same and it seemed to take Herbert a few minutes to decide which was the one he wanted. Eventually he made up his mind and ascended the front steps to tap on the door. He was admitted right away and Arnold was left wondering what he should do next.

"At the opium den Bertie said 'We have to go in there!'" he muttered to himself, running through his mind the scene at the row house above Old Swan Stairs. "I suppose, then, that's what I should do. . . Go in." But he hung back. Two men – laborers by the look of them – approached from the other direction and tapped on the door. They were admitted right away.

"Doesn't look as though there's a secret knock or anything," Arnold murmured. He looked around, up and down the street, just in case his brother-in-law should suddenly – miraculously – appear. But the street remained empty. Making up his mind, Arnold moved up the front steps and knocked.

A scruffy man smelling strongly of sweat opened the door. He wore a greasy hookdown cap pulled low over his brow. His seaman's jacket was missing a button and was worn over a heavy, dark sweater with frayed sleeves. His trousers were wide-wale corduroys worn thin at the knees. They were stuffed into Wellington boots.

"Better 'urry if you don' wanna miss the first 'un," he said. "That'll be an alderman."

"A what?" Arnold's mouth gaped.

"An alderman, mate. 'alf a bull." He raised his eyes to heaven in desperation. "Lord 'elp us. A bleedin' 'alf-crown, yer gulpin!"

"Oh! Oh, yes. Of course. Sorry," said Arnold, digging in his pocket for the coin.

He was directed ahead along the passageway and told to go down the stairs at the end. Before he got there he could hear the sound of a small crowd; talking and cursing, coughing and spitting, an occasional shout and a laugh or two. He descended the stairs cautiously.

At the bottom it opened out into what had been the basement of the house but had been enlarged by knocking down some of the walls between the cellars. Arnold hoped that the house was still supported and wouldn't come crashing down on top of them. As he pushed and got pushed through the men assembled there, he was able to look over their heads and down into a dirt-floored pit in the middle of the area. It was about six feet in diameter with a fence of wire mesh all around. A single-element gasolier hung down, leaving most of the basement in shadow but Arnold could make out two men holding a sturdy bull terrier against a gate into the enclosure and, opposite, a large cage holding a seething pile of large rats. Arnold's hand went to his mouth. He almost vomited. This was a rat-pit. As with dog fights and cock-baiting, the so-called 'sport' had been outlawed long ago but he knew there were still gathering places in private homes scattered about the poorer parts of London. Obviously this was one of them.

Arnold looked at the rats. They seemed huge. He knew that they would be let loose in the "circus" and then the dog would be released. Bets would be made on how many rats the dog would kill before it, too, succumbed. A recent article Arnold had read in the newspaper stated that a publican had been arrested who claimed to have bought 25,000 rats a year, every year, from rat-catchers in the East End, at threepence a rat. It was rumored that even some of the nobility – gentlemen *and* ladies – would attend some of the displays. And it was not the only illegal blood sport that could be found.

Arnold soon spotted Herbert in the crowd. He was haggling with a man about his bet. Arnold saw the glint of silver as money changed hands. He started working his way around the circle of blood-thirsty onlookers to have a word with Nellie's friend's husband. A strong word.

Suddenly, without warning, Bertie's legs lost their grip on the pipe and his body swung sideways, suspended by one hand still on the down-pipe and the other gripping the edge of the window sill. He hung there, gasping, and trying to assess his situation. He tried to get a grip with his toes on the weathered siding of the building but it had worn smooth with time. If only he could get a small purchase, he thought, he might be able to at least peer in at the window before what he knew would be the inevitable tumble to the ground.

But it was not to be. As he tried to get a better hold with his left hand, the ancient frame of the window sill split and came away, his hand with it. He swung like a pendulum, back over the pipe and then, his hold broken, began his descent to the ground. It was broken at the bottom by the rainwater barrel: he landed, very briefly, on a piece of thin wood which rested across the top of the barrel. This almost immediately gave way and one of his legs descended into the ice cold water while the other traveled down the outside of the barrel. He was stopped abruptly when his groin landed hard on the rim. Bertie let out a yell then tottered over the edge, hit the wooden box, and fell sideways to the ground. He lay there, his hands between his legs, trying to catch his breath and fighting more pain than he had ever known.

It seemed only a short time before Bertie heard the door to the nearest loading platform slide open with a squeal. Turning his head, from his position on the ground, he saw a figure emerge holding aloft a lantern. Beside the figure, in ominous silhouette, stood what seemed to be a giant of a dog.

"Great Dane or Wolfhound?" The question ran automatically through Bertie's ever inquisitive mind before he acknowledged his predicament. He scrambled to his feet and ran with a limping gait around the corner of the building away from the scene of his crime. He heard the man yell and the dog respond with a deep, throaty growl. Bertie could sense rather than see the massive animal launch itself from the top of the loading dock and hurtle after him.

For a moment Bertie thought of trying to hide in one of the many piles of debris that were scattered around the warehouse, but he knew the dog would sniff him out almost instantly. The fog covered the area and he ran on blindly, quite unable to pay heed to where he was going. He could hear strong paws beating the ground behind him. Suddenly, his foot caught in a tangle of wire and he fell to the ground, wrenching his knee in the process.

"This is it! I'm a gonner!" he thought. Nellie's beautiful face flashed before him. He rolled onto his back and brought his hands up to cover his throat, certain that that was where the animal would strike. He closed his eyes and prayed.

Slurp!

A very large, very wet, rough tongue wiped over his face, not once but three times. Hot breath, smelling strangely sweet, was breathed in his face. He opened his eyes to see a string of drool – albeit from an obviously adoring dog – descend and adorn his shirt front.

"I always said I was a natural with animals," he thought to himself.

Chapter Sixteen

"I had to throw away those trousers of yours, Bertram."

Bertie did not respond.

"Apart from the great big hole you managed to tear in the knee," continued Nellie, "the left leg was filthy. It wasn't just rain water in that barrel you put your leg into, it smells as though there was also turpentine or creosote or something in there."

Bertie sighed. "I didn't 'put my leg into' the barrel," he said, quietly. "As I told you, I fell from a great height and my leg happened to go in there."

Arnold looked up from the newspaper he was reading. With his brother-in-law, he was sitting at the kitchen table while Nellie cooked up fried eggs, fried tomatoes, Irish pork sausages, and kidneys. Isobel was sitting before the open front of the stove, balancing a toasting fork in each hand. She kept looking from Nellie to Bertie and back again, sniffing, and had already burned three pieces of bread when they wavered up against the red hot coals of the stove.

"I didn't eat before I came around here," said the big man.

His sister nodded. "I guessed as much, Arnold. Don't worry, I'm making enough breakfast for you." She gave a quick glance at her husband. "Or perhaps I should just give you Bertram's. To help pay for a new pair of trousers."

"Oh, that's not fair, Mrs. 'awk. . ." Isobel dropped a toasting fork and clapped a hand over her mouth. Then she removed it and said, "Sorry, Mrs. 'awkins." She became absorbed in the business of making more toast.

Nellie sighed, then looked at her husband and smiled. "I'm sorry, Bertie. I know it wasn't your fault. And you've been injured too."

Bertie eased his position on the wooden kitchen chair. "It did hurt," he admitted.

"Nasty place," commented Arnold, his nose still in the newspaper.

Over breakfast Bertie once again told them the story of his adventures at the East India Dock. Isobel was allowed to sit at the far end of the table, mouth agape, red head nodding at intervals as she absorbed the details. However, Nellie extracted from her a promise to say not a word to anyone.

"So what did you end up learning, Bertie?" asked Nellie. "Other than that there was someone working late in that particular warehouse."

"I learned who it was." Bertie buttered himself a piece of toast – after scraping some of the charcoal from it – knowing that he had now piqued their curiosity. "And it was not altogether a surprise."

Isobel opened her mouth to say something but Nellie banged down her knife and the maid closed her mouth again.

"So who was it, Bertie?" Arnold could hold his curiosity no longer.

"Our friend Thomas Squire."

"How can you be so sure?" asked Nellie.

"When he held up his lantern and set the dog on me, the light fell full on his face. Happily he thought the dog then took care of 'the intruder' and didn't come after me himself. I was able to crawl away and out the way I had come in – through the slack-chained main gates."

They continued eating in silence for a while.

"But we knew he was now working for Lawson, didn't we?" asked Nellie.

Bertie nodded. "We did. We knew – or thought we knew – that he was doing odd jobs for the man. But odd jobs would not include being at a warehouse late at night, by himself."

"Do we know he was by himself?" asked Nellie.

Bertie had saved the largest piece of kidney for last and was about to pop it into his mouth and savor it. He stopped with his fork halfway to his mouth. Then he lowered it again.

"You know, Nell, my love, you are right. We don't know whether or not he was there alone. I assumed he was, since he was the only one who came looking for me, but perhaps not. Perhaps even Lawson himself was up in that lighted room."

"Doing what?" asked Arnold, pushing aside his plate, freshly wiped clean with the crust from the toast.

"That, my friend, is what I would like to know."

They ate in silence for a while.

"By the way, Arnold," said Bertie. "You did an excellent job with our client Herbert Parker. I swear, that man can get into more kinds of trouble than you can imagine!"

Arnold beamed at the compliment. "I did give him a good talking to, just as you would have done, Bertie," he said.

"And Hattie was once again very gratefully," said Nellie. "Seemed almost happy to pay our fee."

Inspector Moss sat at his desk and studied the list of people who were known to have visited Edward Butler during his final days, according to the cards found by Bertram Hawkins. Of course, as Bertram had himself pointed out when he finally told the inspector how he came by the list of names, this was not an exclusive count; it only reflected those who had visited and left a calling card.

He put a check mark alongside Cedric Bromley's name, since they knew all they needed to know about that gentleman. He also marked off the German, Wilhelm von Bernstorff. Apparently he was merely establishing himself as a contact person between Butler and this unpronounceable German firm. Another check mark for Maurice Whiteway. It seemed the Whiteway people (founder Maurice had died more than twenty years ago) were well known in the industrial world as suppliers of sheet metal and manufacturers of custom metal castings. Presumably these were things Butler was interested in from the point of view of putting his Petrol Cycle into production. The inspector also ticked off Frederick William Lanchester. He had an alibi since he was doing business in the north of England over an extended period.

Frank B. Shuttleworth merited a question mark. The Shuttleworth Company was located in Erith, Kent, on the River Thames a few miles above Gravesend. It seemed to be a well established company and to have a good reputation as a small yet reliable custom manufacturer. What had not been established, however, was the exact whereabouts of Mr. Frank Shuttleworth himself over the past week, nor what his exact relationship might have been with the deceased. Despite a telegram to the local Erith police station, no word had yet come back giving particulars enough to satisfy Inspector Campbell Moss.

This only left Harold J. Lawson, a man not unknown to both Scotland Yard and the inspector himself.

"Harold John Lawson," mused the inspector, studying the list. "Thirty-four years of age. Overly – aye, I think I can say overly – ambitious. The son of a brass-turner. A man who lives above his station, if you were to ask me."

Nobody did ask the inspector, of course, and he sat staring at his list of names for a very long time. Eventually, with a sigh, he got to his feet and went in search of a cup of tea.

It was some hours later that the inspector presented himself at the address on Harry Lawson's card. It turned out to be the Athenæum Club on the south side of Pall Mall. Inspector Moss knew that the Athenæum was an expensive gentleman's club, one of a number in that vicinity. In Neoclassic style, a statue of Pallas Athene stood above the porch looking out over Waterloo Place. A little self-consciously, the inspector ascended the half dozen steps between the paired columns of the portico, and approached the main entrance doors. As he raised his hand towards them, one swung open and he found himself face to face with a liveried figure. The man wore a resplendent uniform with gold epaulettes, velvet knee britches and a powdered white wig. His red face and bulbous nose spoke of regular acquaintance with the bottle. Although slightly shorter than the inspector, this individual managed to look down his nose at the policeman.

"No tradesmen, my man. Be off with you."

He would have closed the door on the inspector but Moss was too quick for him. He stuck his foot in front of the door.

"'ere! I said be off with you! You want me to call the police?"

Inspector Moss restrained himself from smiling and, producing his card, waved it under the fellow's nose.

"I *am* the police, Rumpelstiltskin! I'll thank you to watch yourself."

All pressure on the door ceased. The inspector pushed gently on it and the commissionaire allowed him to enter.

"Now then. Let's have no more malarkey, shall we?" He produced his blue covered notebook and stood looking about him with pencil poised. The functionary gulped and looked all around to see who might be observing the encounter.

Inspector Moss took in the massive pillars, tiled mosaic floor, vaulted ceiling and assorted statuary. His eye was drawn to the clock hanging above the stairs. He saw that it had two figure sevens and no numeral eights.

"Well here's a rum do," he muttered to himself, and made a note in his book.

Smartly dressed gentlemen, in twos and threes, plus individuals, strolled about the area. Some ascended and descended the wide, ornate staircase which branched off to both left and right as it rose to the upper floor. Large white globes hung from the ceiling, emitting bright light. The inspector recalled that just a few weeks earlier the newspapers had made a headline story of the installation of electricity in the Athenæum; the first public building to be so fitted. Apparently it had its own generator.

He turned to the figure beside him. "I'm looking for Mr. Harold Lawson. You know him?"

The short, uniformed man seemed to be regaining his composure. "It is my job to know all of the members," he said, haughtily.

"Is it now? Well then, Mr. Fancybloke, is our Mr. Lawson in residence at the moment?"

"I will need to ascertain that." With as much dignity as he could muster, the portly uniformed figure walked, with rapid mincing steps, over to an alcove and consulted a large, leather-bound book. He turned back a page and ran his white-gloved finger down it.

"Ah!" He looked up at the inspector. "As it happens, constable, Mr. Lawson is in attendance."

"Well then hop to it and tell him that Inspector – *Inspector* – Moss would like a few words with him."

It was ten minutes before Lawson could be located and persuaded to come to the main hall. The inspector introduced himself and then Lawson led him into a small room off the main lobby, obviously kept for such exchanges between members and their business visitors.

Although small, the room was tastefully and expensively furnished. Deep green flock wallpaper covered the walls, with polished walnut wainscoting on the lower extremities. Lawson sat down in a red leather armchair on one side of a fine marble fireplace. He made no move to invite the inspector to take the matching chair on the other side but Inspector Moss sat down in it anyway. A large, gilt-framed portrait of Her Majesty hung over the fireplace and the inspector got the uncomfortable feeling that her eyes were looking right at him. He tried to position himself so that they did not intrude too much.

"Now what is this all about, inspector?"

"Just routine enquiries, sir, if you don't mind."

"Will this take long? I have important business to attend to. We cannot all dither around pretending to do our so-called 'duty', like you policemen claim to do, you know."

"Just some routine enquiries," repeated the inspector, gritting his teeth. "Now sir, I understand that you were acquainted with the late Mr. Edward Butler." He watched Lawson's face carefully for any reaction.

There was none perceptible. Lawson was stocky and fair haired. What hair there was on the top of his head was rapidly thinning and was brushed across his pate to try to hide the condition. His side whiskers were neatly trimmed and elegantly terminated in a slanting cut at the extremities. His fine mustache, although blonde, was waxed and twisted into spikes at its ends, in the manner of the German Kaiser's. The inspector found himself self-consciously touching his own straggly mustache.

"Butler?" Lawson rested his elbows on the arms of the chair and steepled his fingers, looking up at the lofty and elegant ceiling. "Butler? No, the name doesn't ring a bell."

"Really?" sniffed the inspector. "Then how do you account for the fact that you recently left your calling card at his residence?"

Lawson's head came down and around to study the policeman. Then he leisurely dipped his hand into his coat pocket and extracted a cigar case. Still with his eyes fixed on Moss, he brought out a cigar and returned the case to his pocket. He ran the cigar under his nose and then put it to his mouth. "Do you happen to have a lucifer, my good man?"

"Answer my question, Mr. Lawson."

Grumbling, Lawson patted his pockets and then extracted a silver pocket match safe. He struck a light and puffed clouds of blue smoke into the room. Eventually, taking the cigar from his mouth to examine the lit end and then replacing the smoke, he gave a small and, to Moss, unauthentic laugh.

"Oh, Butler! Of course. When you are as busy as I tend to be, inspector, you lose track of where you are and when. Yes, Butler. I believe I did have occasion to pay a call upon him last week."

"May I ask why?"

"Business."

"What business?"

The cigar was waved in the air as Lawson blew more smoke. He ended pointing the cigar at the inspector. "One does not ask a gentleman the nature of his business," he said.

"He does if it happens to tie-in with murder," snapped the inspector.

Lawson seemed surprised. "Murder?"

"You must have read or heard of the murder of your 'acquaintance' Mr. Edward Butler, and the kidnapping of his son. It was in all the newspapers. Or were you too busy to come across that piece of information, sir?"

Lawson seemed suddenly to take the interview more seriously. He sat forward in his chair and tapped the ash from his cigar into an ashtray on the occasional table at his side. He did not, however, look the inspector in the eyes, Moss noticed.

"No, of course I read about it. Very . . . unfortunate. Sad, I suppose. But why are you here asking me questions about it, I would like to know?"

"Just establishing where various people were around the time of the murder. All part of my job, sir."

"Yes, of course." Lawson seemed more subdued.

"Now, if you would be so good, Mr. Lawson, perhaps you would give me some sort of idea as to your business with Mr. Butler."

"I – er – I had an interest in an invention of Butler's. It was nothing of any great importance; I am certain it would never have amounted to anything, but I am an investor and wondered whether or not this might be something I should be interested in. Does that satisfy you, inspector?"

"Did you see the plans for this invention, sir?"

"Plans? No, I did not. Why do you ask?"

"I'll ask the questions, sir. Would you invest in something without seeing plans or an example of the finished product?"

"No. No, of course I would not. Now see here, inspector, my visit to Mr. Butler was simply a preliminary courtesy call, if you like. It was to talk with him and see if there was any likelihood that I might want to deal further with the man."

"Aye, sir. I see." The inspector made several notes in his book.

"Now really," said Lawson, getting to his feet. "I must insist that . . ."

"Aye, sir. No problem." Moss closed his notebook and tucked it back into his pocket. "We mustna' impose any more on the heartbeat of the empire. I take it you have nay plans for leaving the city any time in the near future, Mr. Lawson? Just in case we should need to ask anything more?"

Five minutes later Inspector Moss was outside on the street, breathing a little less strenuously and with the hint of a smile on his lips.

Chapter Seventeen

"That's the last of the pawnbrokers," said Bertie. He and Arnold had spent the afternoon walking up and down Blackfriars Road and neighboring streets, visiting the pawnbrokers that Arnold had suggested to be the most likely recipients of the gold watch and overcoat. None of them had shown any sign of familiarity with either item.

It had not been easy getting the information. At one of the shops the owner, a painfully skinny woman of indeterminate age, with cheeks painted a bright red in contrast to her unhealthy-looking pasty complexion, had cried gleefully that she had the watch but that it would cost one hundred pounds to retrieve it.

"One hundred pounds?" Bertie almost laughed out loud. "Let me see it."

"Let me see your money first," she demanded. Her breath reeked of garlic and Bertie tried not to stand directly in front of her.

"I don't think so. I first need to see if it is indeed the watch I am looking for. Where did you say you got it?"

"From a gent 'oo comes in 'ere from time to time."

"Exactly when was it that he brought in the watch?"

"Oh, I dunno. It's not easy to keep track o' time, you know."

Bertie looked around at the multitude of mantle clocks and wall clocks and smiled. "No," he said. "I imagine it's not. But tell me, was it a week ago? A month ago? Three months ago?"

She squinted her eyes and looked sideways at him. "When did you say you thought it was brought in?" she countered.

He sighed. "Just show me the watch in question," he said. "If it's not the one I'm looking for then we can both be on our way."

She mumbled to herself and eventually brought out a tray of pocket watches, some gold, some silver, some nickel. Some were gentlemen's watches; some ladies.

Arnold loomed behind Bertie, peering over his shoulder at the display of watches. The woman reached out and pulled back the tray closer to her flat bosom.

"This was a solid gold watch, as I've said," stated Bertie.

"Them's all solid gold," she said, despite the fact that most were silver or nickel. Looking closely, Bertie saw that the gold-looking ones were all gold-plate and not solid.

"You cannot pinpoint the one that your friend brought in?" he asked, knowing the answer.

She sniffed, wiped her nose on her sleeve, picked up first one watch and then another. Finally she said "Tell you what, mister. You choose any one o' these and you can 'ave it for twenty thick 'uns. I won't even ask for a ticket."

Bertie sighed. "Thank you. No. We must look elsewhere. Come, Arnold."

As they left the shop she shouted after them "A 'alf sovereign! That's me best offer. You won't find a better 'un anywhere, believe me!"

"They were the most likely of all the 'brokers around here," said Arnold. "I tried them all, Bertie. Honestly I did."

"Oh, I believe you, Arnold. I'm afraid this is going to be much more difficult than I imagined, tracing the stolen watch." They started walking back towards the city, over Blackfriars Bridge. "I still think that the footpad who attacked Emily would have made off to one of the closest pawnbrokers. He would be interested in fast money, I'm sure of it."

"There's the other end of the bridge," suggested Arnold. "I didn't look there because I thought it's all the Inns of Court and such. Not much in the way of hock shops."

"You may well be right," agreed Bertie, "but we'll have a look around just in case."

In the area around Apothecaries' Hall they found a small back street named Playhouse Yard, a reminiscence of the old theatre where Shakespeare himself once appeared, on the site of where the Hall now stood. At the far end of Playhouse Yard was what they were looking for: a pawnbroker.

From the outside it looked as though the shop was closed but when Bertie peered through the bottle-glass windows he could discern a gas light burning within. With Arnold on his heels, he pushed open the door, which squeaked almost as loudly as the bell attached to it, announcing customers. Through the gloom within they saw two duplicate figures look up.

"Twins," murmured Bertie. He approached the counter.

The men each had shaggy, unkempt hair that hung down over their worn and frayed coat collars. Both frock coats were a dirty grey and beneath them were worn, equally grimy, waistcoats of indeterminate color. They sported black ties and the stiff collars on their shirts were unclean. Both men had identical horseshoe-shaped silver pins in their ties.

"And what do you want?" asked one of the figures.

"What you want?" echoed the other.

The one who had spoken first – Bertie took him to be the older, if only by a matter of minutes – had a cast in one eye, making it difficult to tell in which direction he was looking. The other man's eyes seemed ordinary, if bloodshot.

"I am here with a query," said Bertie.

"A what?"

"A what?"

"A query. A question for you." Bertie looked around the shop. It seemed to be all old clothes with no sign of any jewelry, though there were many dark corners. He decided he would ask about the overcoat first. "About ten days ago a man came in here to pawn a gold watch and an overcoat. The coat was a heavy raglan, dark blue in color. A woman's coat. He also had a man's solid gold pocket watch. Do you recall this?"

The two men looked at each other.

"You lookin' to redeem?"

"Redeem?" came the echo.

Bertie shook his head. "First of all I'm just looking to locate the items. Do you have the coat?"

The first man scratched his unshaven chin. "I might 'ave and then again I might not. What's it to you, if you not lookin' to redeem it?"

"Not lookin' to redeem it?"

Arnold leaned forward and put his large hand on the counter. "Show us the coat," he said quietly.

Both men backed up a pace. Then the first turned to the second. "I think it's in rack seven, brother. Go and 'ave a look."

"I'll go and 'ave a look," said the second man and scampered off into the gloom. He quickly returned with a worn, soiled, dark blue coat that seemed to fit the description Bertie had got from Mrs. Grey.

"This the one?"

"This it?"

Bertie studied the coat, taking his time. "It may well be. Did the man who pawned this also give you a gold watch?"

The number one man pulled the coat back towards himself. "That would be a pricy piece, I wouldn't wonder. I couldn't go giving that to just anyone, now could I?"

"Let's first establish that you have the one I'm looking for," said Bertie patiently. "Then we can proceed from there."

The pawnbroker gave a slight nod and his brother scampered away, going through a door at the back of the shop into some rear room. He was gone for a while before returning carrying a large wooden box. The first man pulled a key out of his waistcoat pocket and unlocked the box, throwing back the lid. The top level was filled with jewelry; mainly rings bearing what looked like diamonds, emeralds and rubies. He slid out a lower drawer and placed it down on the counter, closing the box. The drawer held a number of gold watches. Bertie leaned forward to get a better look.

"Which one was brought in by that man?" he asked.

"Don't yer know?"

"Not know?"

"Just point it out," said Bertie.

The pawnbroker lifted out a large, older timepiece that even to Bertie's untrained eye appeared to be of good quality gold. There was a ticket attached to it by a thin piece of string.

"We advanced thirty-five guineas on this fine specimen," said the man, reading the scrawny writing on the label.

"May I see?"

Reluctantly the watch was passed over. Bertie studied it and flipped open the front case. Inside were engraved the initials D.N.A. – Dennis Nigel Ardsley. He noticed that the watch was not working.

"You say you don't 'ave no ticket for it?'"

"No ticket?"

Bertie closed up the watch with a snap. The man held out his hand for it but Bertie kept a hold of it. "Yes, this is the one," he said.

"Without a ticket, I couldn't let that go for less than fifty guineas," said the man.

"Fifty. Yes," added his brother.

"Oh, I think you can," said Bertie. "You see, this is stolen property."

"Stolen? We don't deal in no stolen stuff." He looked suitably shocked.

"No stolen stuff," emphasized his partner.

"But you can see as 'ow we can't let it go without covering our expenses." He reached out and grabbed the watch out of Bertie's hands. Arnold stepped forward but the two of them backed up as far as they could go, out of reach of the big man's hands.

To prevent them from simply disappearing into the back room and not returning, Bertie took firm hold of the wooden box of valuables. Both men let out a cry.

"Now," said Bertie. "Let me explain your position. You can either let me take, without a ticket, both of these objects – and I will pay you the thirty-five guineas you advanced on the watch; nothing on Mrs. Grey's coat – or I can return with an inspector from Scotland Yard and he will confiscate both items and you won't see a penny. Now, which would you prefer?"

The main man came forward and slapped the watch down on the counter, grabbing back the box as soon as Bertie let go of it.

As they left the shop and retraced their steps back along Playhouse Yard, Arnold asked "Why did you pay him the money, Bertie? We could have done what you said and Inspector Moss could have got them for us."

"If the items had still been here when he came," said Bertie. "No, it was only fair to give him what he advanced for it. I have no doubt that Sir Hugh will reimburse me for it. The main thing is, we've got the gold watch."

"And the coat."

"Well, I'll let you return that to Mrs. Grey, Arnold. We don't need it and we don't want her catching her death of cold now, do we?"

Back at 27 Penny Court Bertie sat down with the colonel's gold watch in front of him. He and Arnold had told Nellie and Isobel the story of their search and discovery and then had repeated the story when Inspector Moss came visiting. Bertie picked up the watch and admired it.

"One day," he said, "I will have such a beautiful timepiece of my own . . . instead of my old silver one." He looked down at the watch chain spread across his waistcoat.

"Well, I wouldn't count on it, Bertram. Though it does no harm to dream, I suspect." Nellie took off her apron. "I would suggest we all adjourn to the dining room and have our meal before we go any farther." She nodded to Isobel, who started putting dishes on to trays.

Two hour later they sat around the empty fireplace with a glass of sherry apiece. Isobel had been allowed to sit at the back, after washing the dishes, though without the wine. The days were slowly growing warmer and this was the first evening they had been able to sit without a fire burning. Bertie missed it, feeling that – despite its gift of warmth – it added a deeper, more satisfying dimension to the family gathering.

He breathed a sigh of satisfaction and extracted the colonel's gold watch from his coat pocket. He held it up by its thick chain and watched the reflection of the gas light bounce off it.

"I once again take off my hat to you, Mr. Hawkins," said the inspector. "Always one step ahead of the Yard, it would seem. I need to knock some heads together."

Bertie smiled happily and winked at his wife, who sipped her sherry with great pleasure.

"Bertie is smart," said Arnold, in honest appreciation.

"Thank you, Arnold," responded Bertie. "But it was simply applying enquiry." He couldn't help a dig at the inspector, "Something you could so easily do, Campbell, if you'd a mind to."

"If I'd the time for it, you mean," the inspector replied. "We are not all gentlemen of leisure, able to roam the countryside at will, you know."

Bertie laughed. "If only that were true." He opened the front of the watch.

"It doesn't work, does it?" said Arnold.

Bertie shook his head. "No. I tried winding it but that didn't help."

"Doesn't the back open as well?" asked Nellie. "Perhaps the big wheel in there just needs a push, or poke, or something. My father once had that trouble with his watch."

Bertie smiled condescendingly. "You don't go 'pushing and poking' the innards of expensive watches, Nell. No offense but I guarantee your father's watch was not of this caliber."

"Still, you might take a look," she suggested.

He took another sip of his wine, set down the glass, and examined the back of the watch.

"Hand me that bottle opener, Arnold," he said, pointing to the one on the sideboard. "I think it has a small blade on it. This back is tight and I can't get a fingernail in there to open it."

His brother-in-law did as he was bid. Bertie extracted the blade on the side of the opener, attached like a penknife blade alongside the corkscrew. He carefully worked it at the back of the watch.

"Ah!"

The watch back opened.

"Oh! What's this?" he said.

They all leaned forward to see what had got his attention. Isobel, unable to restrain herself, jumped up and came to stand beside Bertie's chair.

Bertie took a small, folded piece of paper out from the back of the watch.

"A piece of paper stuck in there," he said. "The bent corner of it was restricting the movement, that's why it wasn't running."

Inspector Moss also left his seat to get a better view of what Bertie was doing. "What *is* that paper, Bertram? Unfold it."

Arnold and Nellie put down their wine glasses and joined the group about Bertie. He laid aside the watch and unfolded the thin piece of paper. It was quite small and was covered with a fine handwriting. There was what looked like a signature at the bottom.

"What does it say?"

"What is it?"

"Read it out loud, Bertie."

Everyone spoke at once and Bertie held up his hand for silence. He turned the paper one way and then another. "I don't know," he said. "I can't read it. It's in some sort of funny writing."

Kate Gildersleeves Butler hurried to the front door when she heard the flap of the letterbox fall. It was the afternoon post. On the door mat was a small pile of a half dozen letters which she picked up and looked through. Two were bills, three were letters in black bordered envelopes – obviously of condolence – and one was unadorned, in a handwriting she did not recognize. It appeared, to her untrained eyes, to be masculine with a firmness of form. The envelope was thick, of excellent quality and light cream in color. It had been posted in the East Central district but no return address was obvious on the envelope. Kate carried it up to the first floor drawing room and sat down at her desk. Taking a letter opener, she slit the envelope and withdrew the single sheet of paper inside. It read:

If you would like your son to be returned, please be so good as to place the plans for your husband's float-fed carburetor in a plain envelope and await further instructions.

It was unsigned.

Chapter Eighteen

"You just keep adding to my work, Bertram."

The inspector didn't seem too upset about it, thought Bertie. He followed the policeman into his office and took the chair that was offered.

"You see," said Moss. "I had a suicide that became a murder, then that grew to two murders and a kidnapping. And now you've added a mystery note in a strange language!"

"But they are all connected, Campbell. You must see that."

"Aye. Aye, I do, laddie. Though of course we dinna' really know about this note yet. Wait a minute. Let me get someone in here who I think may be able to help."

He disappeared and Bertie relaxed and looked around the office. Other than the inevitable portrait of the queen, there was a print of the proposed Tower Bridge, clipped from *The Illustrated London News* and suitably framed, one of the front of Scotland Yard and, on a corner of the cluttered desk, a small framed daguerreotype of an elderly couple standing in front of a semi-detached house. Bertie guessed that they might be the inspector's parents. The battered desk was still strewn with the detritus of police business, though he was happy to see that the package of fish and chips was not in evidence.

"Here we are." Inspector Moss bustled back into the office closely followed by a short man in an overly large frock coat and striped trousers. His cravat was askew and his half-pince-nez was likewise at an angle on his nose. His hair was sparse and wild, as though he constantly ran his fingers through it with no regard for its appearance. He had a small, pencil-thin mustache and a tiny rosebud mouth. He kept pursing his lips, as though trawling for a kiss.

"Bertram, this is Dr. Newton. He is something of an expert on foreign languages and may be able to help us solve our problem."

"N-no promises, mind," said the newcomer, in a high tremulous voice. "I can make no promises."

"Of course you can't," smoothed the inspector, propelling Dr. Newton forward. He waved a hand for Bertie to vacate his chair and, when he did, spun the doctor around and sat him down in it. He placed the unfolded piece of paper in front of the doctor who adjusted his pince-nez and inspected it.

"Hmm. This is the Old German Script. Very interesting. Many of the older generation in Germany still use the script. It is not exactly unusual, though may appear so to Her Britannic Majesty's subjects." He held it closer to his eyes. "Signature looks to read 'Karl Benz' I would hazard." He looked up at the inspector. "Isn't he a notable in the advancing field of automobiles?"

Inspector Moss nodded. "That is my understanding."

Dr. Newton returned to his examination, talking while studying the paper. "This is a young man's world, Moss. No longer for the likes of you and me."

"I dinna' think they can count us out yet, doctor," replied the inspector, slightly uneasily it seemed to Bertie's ears.

"Hmm. Let us hope not. I think I saw in *The Times* that Benz just recently patented his – what did he call it? – his *Motorwagen*, but was still having trouble with the engine . . . Does this note have something to do with that?" He seemed suddenly more interested, Bertie thought.

"Can you tell us what it says, doctor?" Bertie asked.

"What? Oh, yes. Yes. It is addressed to one Edward Butler and says, in essence, that the gold presented, in 20 mark coins, is an earnest of his – Benz's – desire to purchase Butler's unique float-fed carburetor design."

"Gold?" interjected the inspector. "What gold?" He looked at Bertie, his eyebrows raised. "There was no gold attached to this was there, Bertram?"

Bertie shook his head. "Just the fact that it was hidden inside a gold watch," he said. "But I don't think that is the gold referred to. Exactly what does it say about it, Doctor?"

"As I said, it states that 'the gold presented' – yes, that's the word – the gold *presented*, 'in the form of 20 mark coins, is an earnest for the design.'"

"Presented where? By whom?"

"I cannot say. I can only tell you what is written here. That is the kernel of it," said the doctor, laying aside the small, thin sheet of paper and removing his spectacles to clean them on a handkerchief he produced from his pocket.

"Colonel!" Bertie and the inspector spoke together.

"The colonel," continued Inspector Moss. "Of course! If I were a betting man I would lay odds that he fits in here somewhere." He suddenly looked uncertain. "But there was no gold found on him or in his luggage when we checked through."

"If there is nothing else, gentlemen . . . ?" The doctor got to his feet.

"No. No, thank you very much doctor. That is all."

Dr. Newton nodded his head and left the office. The inspector and Bertie looked at each other.

"Two questions," said Bertie.

"Questions! You've always got questions, Bertram," said the inspector. "What we need are answers."

"I have questions because I am an enquirer," Bertie pointed out, quietly. "It is by asking questions that we finally arrive at the looked-for answers."

Inspector Moss sighed and slumped down into his desk chair. He waved a hand at Bertie. "I know. I know. And you have proven yourself good at this approach to things, Bertram, I'll give you that. All right. What are your two questions?"

Bertie took the chair vacated by Dr. Newton and pulled it up to the desk so that he could look the inspector in the face. "Number one: why was the colonel on that late train coming from Brighton. And number two: since it *was* a late arrival – was it because he had made a stop along the way?"

The inspector stroked his chin and then tugged at his straggly mustache. "Good ones, Bertram, if I do say so myself. Good ones."

"You are going to return that watch to Miss Ardsley, Bertie, aren't you?" Nellie was busy ironing; blonde ringlets untidily sticking out of her cap.

Isobel was running about moving and folding linen. Bertie stood in the doorway of the basement laundry room watching the activity. He always tried to stay out of the way on washday but couldn't resist looking in on Nellie.

Washday usually started the evening before, with clothes soaked overnight in large vats of water. This morning extra water had been boiled in huge amounts on the kitchen stove and then carried, by both Isobel and Nellie, to the tubs in the basement. The wash was taken out of the soak water, wrung out, and placed in the fresh hot water, there to be scrubbed on the corrugated scrubbing boards. After the soaping, bleaching, whitening, and more – all a mystery to Bertie – there was time on the washing dolly. And then, after much rinsing in numerous baths of rinse water, the wash – by way of the hand wringer – found its way out to hang on the line to dry. When the weather was bad the wash was hoisted almost to the ceiling on the huge drying racks. Finally, as now, the individual pieces were moved to the ironing board where Nellie attacked them with the big, heavy, black irons that were heated on the range.

It was a lot of work and Bertie knew that his presence was not required; in fact his absence was appreciated. But he had wanted to bring Nellie up-to-date on what the mysterious note was that they had found in the back of the watch.

"I was planning on making another trip over to the Ardsleys, to return the watch and to tell them what we found," he said. "I thought Sir Hugh might have some ideas regarding this gold that is mentioned."

"Is Campbell going with you?" Nellie spat, unladylike, on the bottom of the iron to test its hotness. She seemed satisfied and applied it to a tablecloth.

"I would like him to," said Bertie. "It would make the visit that much more 'official' I suppose. But he claims he has too much to do." He looked away and watched Isobel, staggering under a pile of linen, make her way out of the laundry room and head for the stairs. "He's just tilting at windmills, I think, but he seems well satisfied." He sighed. "I suppose it will be up to me again – up to The Penny Court Enquirers – to sort out the case."

"You go and do what you have to do, Bertie." Nellie's concentration was not on the conversation. She had too much work to do herself. Bertie nodded and eased out of the steam and heat.

Emily Ardsley held the gold watch in both hands, and then pressed it to her bosom. "I cannot thank you enough, Mr. Hawkins. I truly thought that I would never see this again. It was, as you know, my grandfather's and was his last gift to me. It is very special." Her voice caught and she turned her head away.

"My thanks must join my daughter's," said Sir Hugh, standing behind Emily's chair. "The intrinsic value of the item is immaterial; it is the sentimental value that we are dealing with here. You were first instrumental in returning my daughter to her family and now, against all odds it would seem, you have tracked down and retrieved that which was stolen. We are greatly indebted to you and, believe me, I shall see to it that you are amply rewarded."

Bertie didn't want to make the actual cost of retrieving the watch an issue, since he knew that whatever size check Sir Hugh now saw fit to write, it would adequately cover his expenses.

"I did bring with me the handwritten note which we found in the back of the watch," he said. He produced the paper and passing it across to Sir

Hugh, who clamped a monocle into his eye and examined the document.

Lady Claire, sitting with her Pekinese on her lap, held onto the dog, rose, and went to join her husband. She flicked open a lorgnette, that hung from a silken cord around her neck, and peered over his shoulder at the tiny writing.

"It makes no sense!" she said, dropping the spectacles and looking accusingly at Bertie.

Sir Hugh held up his hand. "One moment, my dear. Yes, indeed it does make sense, in a way. And yet – as I'm sure you are aware, Mr. Hawkins – it brings us another mystery, does it not?" He looked hard at Bertie, who was perched on the edge of the elegant couch.

"A mystery I was wondering whether your lordship would be able to help solve," he said. A large stuffed peacock was standing close beside the couch; close enough to keep intruding on Bertie's vision. "I take it your lordship is able to read German then?" He was surprised, though he didn't know why he should be.

"My German is rusty – we used to holiday in and around the Alps in my youth – but it is sufficient to take in what it says here."

"Are you familiar with Mr. Benz, my lord?"

Sir Hugh nodded, coming around to stand in front of the fireplace, facing Bertie. Lady Ardsley had returned to her seat and was feeding tidbits to her dog, making kissing noises that Bertie found irritating. "I have been keeping up with the development of the automobile. I believe it to be an inevitable step forward in transportation. One needs to keep a finger on such pioneering work."

Bertie nodded sagely, as though he had given the matter a lot of thought. "Does this mention of gold mean anything to you, my lord? Had your father, the colonel, made any mention of it, I was wondering?"

Sir Hugh shook his head. "No, he had not. I would imagine that it is something that he was in the process of negotiating. Some sort of agreement, it seems, between Benz and this fellow Butler."

"Yes, that was my understanding."

"Have you spoken to Benz?"

"Spoken to him?" Bertie was caught by surprise. "Why no, Sir Hugh. There is no way that I am able to."

His host stood nodding thoughtfully for a moment, tapping his monocle on the back of his hand. Apparently making up his mind, he glanced at his wife and then his eyes focused on his guest. Bertie wished the peacock was not so obvious. It unsettled him. But he tried to look suitable serious as he returned Sir Hugh's gaze.

"I propose that we – you and I, Mr. Hawkins – go and speak with our friend Herr Benz. Would you be amenable to that?"

"What, to G-Germany?"

"Berlin, I believe. Yes. Would that be a problem?"

"I see." Inspector Moss's eyebrows knit together and he pursed his lips.

Bertie wasn't sure just how much the inspector did see but he had felt it only courteous to go to his office and tell him of the plans to visit Germany.

"I think it will be most valuable," Bertie said. "To get Karl Benz's end of the story; to find out exactly what was going on between him and Butler, and what sort of negotiating the colonel was doing."

"Not to mention the question of the gold." The inspector nodded, his eyebrows still drawn tightly together. He looked up at Bertie. "How is Nell taking this, if I might ask? Is she in favor of you gallivanting off to the Continent?"

Bertie smiled and leaned back . . . as much as he was able on the hard wooden chair. "I don't think I'll be doing much gallivanting with Sir Hugh in attendance," he said. "No. Nell is fine with it." The smile slipped a little. "Though she did start giving me a list of things to do and things not to do. Plus a shopping list, of course. Still, it's not like I'm going to Paris."

"Well," the inspector seemed to resign himself to the situation. "I will press on with finding out about the colonel's movements leading up to his murder, and your questions about the time of the train's arrival. I think I'll go and have another talk with his man, what's his name? . . . Bromley." He had a sudden thought and shuffled some of the papers on his desk, finally producing a sheet of fine linen notepaper. "Oh, there is one development, I suppose I can let you in on. Butler's widow came to Scotland Yard to show me this. She received it in the mail yesterday." He handed the paper to Bertie.

"The expected ransom note, eh? What does she say about it? Has she found the plans?"

The inspector shook his head. "No. That's why she came here. She says she doesn't know where the plans are. She was most distraught, as you can imagine. How can she get her son back if she doesn't have what the kidnapper wants?"

Bertie examined the note. "I would guess it to be a man's writing?" He glanced up and saw the inspector nod his head in agreement. "Did she have the envelope? Did you see where it was posted?"

"London East Central, is all we know. That's a big area."

"It includes Lawson's warehouse, and Thomas Squire's residence . . ."

"Lawson's club," added the inspector, "Plus my house, your house, and St. Paul's Cathedral! No, just the postmark doesna' help. I think we've got to wait till he sends his 'further instructions' and then see where they lead."

Bertie got to his feet. "I agree, Campbell. Poor woman. She must be torn apart. Well, I must get on. Got to get packed. I've never been abroad before!"

Moss smiled. "Nor me. I envy you, Bertram, being taken off to the Continent by a baronet. I bet you get the royal treatment."

He sounds envious, thought Bertie. "The main thing is to get the information we need, Campbell. Happily Sir Hugh can speak the lingo and will have any needed connections." He moved to the door. "I'll keep you posted."

"I would appreciate that."

Chapter Nineteen

Approaching Dover, the train ran through the chalk cliffs by way of numerous cuttings and tunnels. After passing through the 766-yard long Martello Tunnel, the track continued through another long cutting and then entered the mile-long Abbot's Cliff Tunnel. The train ran along a terrace supported by a sea wall, and then passed under Shakespeare Cliff by another tunnel three-quarters of a mile in length. The journey ended on Admiralty Pier itself; an impressive 780 yards long.

There was a terminal which gave some small protection to passengers embarking and disembarking the cross-channel paddle-wheelers and steamers. Built partly on piles and partly on the stone quay, the terminal had been constructed for the Paris World Fair traffic in 1867. Prior to that, when a ship missed the tide the passengers had to be transported between the shore and the ship by long boats and had to climb ladders up onto the quay. All this Bertie learned from Sir Hugh as they rode – in First Class, Bertie was delighted to find – on the railway down from London. Bertie was impressed by the famous pier at Dover. It was built of solid stone; huge blocks each weighing several tons.

There were scores and scores of them, piled one on top of another.

The shortest distance across the English Channel was between Dover and Calais – a scant twenty-one miles. On a fine day it was possible to stand on the top of the famous White Cliffs and actually see France. But the day of Bertie's crossing was overcast and the water rough . . . and they were not just going to Calais but taking the longer seventy mile journey all the way to Ostende, in Belgium!

"I've never yet been across when it hasn't been choppy," said Sir Hugh, stroking his fine grey mustache and looking, through lowered eyebrows and polished monocle, at the preparations for departure.

"Is – er – is that bad?" asked Bertie, nervous about leaving dry land. He had once been out in a small rowboat on the Serpentine and had not been impressed.

"What? Oh, no. Not at all." Sir Hugh gave a short laugh, not unlike a snort to Bertie's ears. "No. You'll quickly get used to it. In fact you shouldn't notice anything at all, since we're crossing on the *Calais-Dover*."

"That's good?"

"Very good," said his lordship. "It's a big ship – too big for this puny crossing, if you ask me – and it was designed especially to mollycoddle the public."

Bertie stared across at the strange looking vessel. It reminded him of two ships sitting side by side, with superstructure crossing from one to the other, joining them. The posters pasted on the sides of the terminal dubbed it a "catamaran" and said that it was designed to eliminate roll and pitch . . . the promoters of sea-sickness, apparently. The claim was that it could make the crossing from Dover to Calais in no more than an hour and a half. That still seemed like an eternity to Bertie, and the crossing to Ostende was going to be a little over four hours.

"Damn thing's being withdrawn from service at the end of this year," said Sir Hugh. "I'm not surprised, but I thought it might be amusing for us to make the crossing on it while it's here. It was bought by the London, Chatham and Dover Railway Company. Don't know why they bought it if they don't intend to keep running it." He grunted in disapproval.

Mail bags were tossed on board, together with an assortment of steamer trunks, stateroom trunks, bags, portmanteaux, suitcases, a big American Saratoga trunk, and numerous valises. Their own trunks and valises were taken up and Sir Hugh turned and strode confidently up the gangway. Bertie followed, almost wishing he had never decided to become an enquiry agent.

Bertie gave a wistful last look around at the bustle of the quay before turning his attention to the steamer. Its four tall white funnels, with tops outlined in black, belched smoke as the powerful engines got up steam. The last bell was rung and the ship eased away from the dock. It was 360 feet long and 98 feet wide and dwarfed the paddle-steamers and sailing craft in the harbor.

After they landed on the other side, it was going to take four days of tedious railway traveling to reach Berlin, along some main lines but many smaller connecting routes. From Ostende they would go to Brussels and then loop around by way of Liege and Aix-la-Chapelle to get to Dusseldorf. From there it was fairly straightforward by way of Hanover to Berlin itself. Bertie felt tired before the journey started, as he and Sir Hugh sat in the salon of the ship contemplating that part of the journey and studying a railway map of the Continent.

The first class cabin was furnished with hair-cloth, since even the nobility were not immune to *mal-de-mer*. Stewards, in smart but well-worn uniforms, moved quietly about offering thin sandwiches and Bass ale, as the only available refreshments on the trip. The prices were given in both pounds and French francs. Sir Hugh commented that one always had to carefully count one's change if accepting the foreign money, since the stewards seemed unable to correctly assess the exchange rate. Bertie was glad that he was traveling with a seasoned traveler.

Inspector Moss looked around the second floor room to which Mrs. Brush had taken him. She had tried to pry out of him what his business was with the "nice Mr. Bromley," but Moss had been tight-lipped. Mumbling to herself, she had led the way up the thinly-carpeted stairs and rapped on the door.

"Yes? What is it, Mrs. Brush? You know I don't like to be disturbed."

"Begging your pardon, sir, but this 'ere gentleman insists on seeing you. Says it's important business, but won't say as what it is."

She looked accusingly at the inspector.

"Cedric Bromley?" Moss addressed the face that peered out at him, ignoring the landlady. She gave a shrug and, still mumbling to herself, retraced her steps down the stairs leaving the two of them alone.

"Who the devil are you?" asked Bromley. "And what do you want with me?"

Inspector Moss had a quick look around the small landing. There were three other doors that led off of it.

"This is police business, sir. I'm sure you dinna' want to discuss it out here, 'in public' as it were. Perhaps I should come in?"

After just a brief pause, Bromley opened the door and allowed the inspector to enter his room, closing the door behind him.

"Now what the deuce do you want? And make it snappy, will you? Some of us have agendas to keep to."

"We do indeed, sir," answered Moss, looking around. He recognized the room as Bertie had described it to him. Bromley himself looked pretty much as the inspector expected, apparently prepared to go out on some errand or else recently returned from one. He wore his frock coat, beneath which was a dark grey waistcoat surmounted by a deep maroon cravat held in place with a gold-headed pin. His cuff links matched the pin in metal and decoration as did the watch chain and fob across his waist. His boots were stained and dirty from the street, attesting to the fact that he had in fact recently come in.

"As I said, Mr. Bromley, I am here on police busi . . ."

"Now look here! If this is more questions about my late employer, Colonel Ardsley, then I have nothing further to add. I have been over this before – it might even have been with yourself, though you policemen all look alike to me – and at that time we covered all avenues of your enquiry. Or so it was stated."

"Just one or two loose ends, as it were, Mr. Bromley." Inspector Moss looked expectantly toward one of the few chairs in the room; a wooden, straight-backed one. Bromley brusquely waved him to it.

"Sit down if you must. Though understand that my time is limited. This matter can only drag on for so long, you know."

The inspector set his bowler hat down on the floor beside him and pulled out his notebook. With pencil poised, he had another look around the room. Bromley fidgeted before moving to stand, with elbow resting on the mantle, in front of the fireplace. The fire was unlit.

"Now, sir. As we have it, both you and the colonel were returning from a visit to Germany . . ."

"We had been there on business, yes. *Private* business."

"Of course. And as I understand it, you both arrived back from the Continent together yet you yourself then hurried on ahead, as it were, to catch a train to the city? Is that a fair review, would you say Mr. Bromley?"

"Yes. Yes. You've had all that before." Bromley moved across to a sideboard and unnecessarily moved an empty whiskey decanter from one side to the other.

"Aye! Now what I was wondering was why, exactly, you had to go on so quickly? Did you and the colonel not usually travel together at all times?"

Bromley turned to face the inspector. "Again, we have been over that, sergeant . . ."

"Inspector, sir. Inspector Moss."

Bromley waved a hand dismissively. "There was a message that the colonel wanted me to deliver at the very first opportunity."

"Might I ask, was this to Mr. Edward Butler?"

"As it happens, yes it was."

"You have heard, I presume, of his recent death?"

Bromley's voice was faint. "Yes. Yes, I have." He paused. "Too many deaths."

It seemed to affect him a lot. Inspector Moss thought that he looked as he might if he had lost his cat. But he suddenly rounded on the inspector.

"You police do not seem to be doing a very upstanding job," he said bitterly.

The inspector ignored the barb. "So you were urged to leave the colonel and get on to see Mr. Butler?"

"He bade me hurry on and catch the train shortly leaving Dover station. He assured me that he would oversee the luggage and follow on."

"But even so, sir, did that not seem unusual?"

"Unusual? Not at all." Bromley made a show of pulling out his watch and consulting it. He replaced it in his waistcoat pocket.

"Why, Mr. Bromley, did the colonel then travel from Dover, where you both disembarked, along the coast to Brighton, rather than follow your route directly up to London?" The inspector spoke forcefully and locked eyes with the other man.

Bromley shrugged and gave an insincere smile. "As it happens there is no mystery there, inspector. The colonel said that an old army acquaintance resided in Brighton and he decided that he would avail himself of the opportunity to pay a visit."

"You have the name of this acquaintance?"

"Not off the top of my head, no." Bromley sounded annoyed. "But I am sure I can provide it, if it is actually necessary. Really, inspector, what exactly is the problem?"

"The problem, Mr. Bromley, is that there is evidence to suggest that Colonel Ardsley didna' die from an accident but was murdered. You will appreciate, then, that I need to cover his movements as precisely as possible." He watched the other man carefully, but Bromley turned away and stood looking out of the window.

"Of course, inspector. Of course. Murdered? My apologies if I have been brusque." His tone was more subdued than it had been. "I have an appointment I have to get to and am simply feeling pressed for time."

"Going out again?" replied Moss, and had the pleasure of seeing Bromley start. "I thought you had only just come in?"

"Did – did Mrs. Brush tell you that?" He gave a short, nervous laugh. "Yes. Yes, I did go out on a short errand but I do have to go out again, as it happens. Will this take much longer, inspector?"

"Just a couple more questions, sir. Have you any idea why the colonel subsequently arrived back in London at such a late hour?"

"It doesn't take too much reflection to determine that, inspector. As I've said, he went to visit an old army acquaintance. Obviously they talked until the late evening and he had to catch the last train."

Inspector Moss nodded while scribbling in his notebook. "Hmm. Aye, sir, it does seem that way."

"And now, inspector . . ."

"Of course." Moss picked up his hat and got to his feet. "I do appreciate your taking the time to answer what must seem like inconsequential questions, Mr. Bromley. I willna' take up any more of your time." He moved to the door. "Oh, just one more question though. Were you or the colonel aware of anyone pursuing you back from Germany?"

"Pursuing us?"

"Aye, sir. Any person or persons, known or unknown, who you suspect may have been trailing you, if I can put it that way?"

Bromley shook his head. "No. I have no idea what you are talking about."

Inspector Moss opened the door. "You will let me know the name of that old army acquaintance of the colonel's, in Brighton, will ye not? Here, I'll leave you my card."

Chapter Twenty

Bertie was exhausted and hoped never again to have to see the inside of a railway carriage. He had learned that the second class carriages of the German railway were equal to the British first class carriages in comfort, but other than that he found nothing to commend them. The trains were slow – which contributed to their excellent safety record, he had been told – and the employees were exceedingly polite though very few spoke English. He had never been so glad to arrive at the end of a journey as when the train pulled into Schlesischer Bahnhof and he and Sir Hugh descended, stiff and hungry, onto the platform.

It had been a long run from Hanover, the express stopping only briefly at both Braunschweig and Magdeburg. It had not even stopped at Potsdam, which Bertie had been assured by Sir Hugh was a charming island in the Havel, situated where it expanded into a series of lakes and wooded hills.

"Ah, well," Bertie thought, "I must remember that I am not here on holiday; I am here on business."

A policeman at the exit from the station handed Sir Hugh a metal ticket which bore the number of a cab, Sir Hugh having specified a luggage cab, or *Gepäck-Droschke*. This had only two seats, to accommodate all of their luggage.

"We are at the Reichshof Hotel," Sir Hugh told Bertie. "It's on Wilhelm-Strasse near the Linden."

"Really?" said Bertie, not entirely sure what his host was talking about. "Is that good?"

Sir Hugh looked at him, somewhat surprised. "Why, yes. It may not be the very best hotel in Berlin but I think you'll find it is one of the better and more quietly situated ones. It is much patronized by diplomatists – one of the reasons I chose it – and is on a par with our top London hotels, I think you'll find."

"Oh! Oh, yes, of course, my lord. I didn't mean . . . that is, I mean . . ." He felt miserable and stared out of the window at the passing scenery.

Bertie admitted to himself that he was no judge of hotels but he was very much impressed by the uniforms of the staff at the Reichshof and by the military precision with which they all seemed to carry out their duties. He found himself standing just inside the second bedroom of a suite of rooms that Sir Hugh had taken, tempted to salute as the three porters who had brought up their luggage bowed their way out.

"The valets will unpack for us before we go to dinner," said Sir Hugh. "They have an excellent dining facility here, though I'd recommend foregoing the sauerkraut if I were you. Now, I suggest we meet down in the dining room in one hour. That should give you ample time to dress for dinner."

Happily Emily had warned Bertie that her father always insisted on dressing for dinner. Nellie had run around to see her friend Hattie Parker and had borrowed Herbert Parker's dress suit. Herbert was a Freemason and needed one for his activities there. It was actually a little small on Herbert and so fitted Bertie very well. Bertie hastened to get it as soon as the valet had unpacked. His worn leather travelling bag and suitcase, both also borrowed from Herbert Parker, seemed almost inadequate compared to Sir Hugh Ardsley's stateroom trunk, three valises and top-hat box.

At eight o'clock sharp Bertie entered the luxurious dining room. Giving Sir Hugh's name, he was ushered to a table close to the string quartet that sat, surrounded by small potted palm trees and aspidistras, in a corner where they would not obstruct the floor traffic. Bertie checked his watch to make sure he was on time and then sat back and looked around.

The dining room was elegantly furnished with a multitude of gilt-framed oil paintings about the walls and large crystal chandeliers suspended from the ceiling giving a subdued, almost romantic, light. Waiters scurried to and fro bearing plates and platters, bottles of wine and magnums of champagne.

The quartet was composed of two violins, a viola, and a cello. The violins were caressed by elderly ladies who Bertie guessed to be school teachers during the day. The cello was played by a plain looking young woman who pursed her lips with every note she played, looking to Bertie for all the world as though she were attempting to whistle. The only male of the quartet attacked the viola with panache, throwing back his overly long hair as he wielded the bow like a swordsman, even for the quieter pieces, and obviously intimidating his companions.

A waiter hovered close by and Bertie was unsure what to do. Sir Hugh was late; a trait of which Bertie would never have suspected him. He consulted his watch again. He'd been at the table for fifteen minutes.

After close to an hour alone at the table Bertie decided to order. The waiter – a man with a protruding lower lip and a surly attitude – seemed to speak little English. He repeated everything Bertie said, as though questioning Bertie's choice of dish, choice of words, and right to be there.

"Ich werde ein kleines Stück Rindfleisch nehmen," said Bertie, phrase book in hand.

"Ein kleines Stück Rindfleisch?" said the waiter, his eyebrows raised.

Bertie double-checked the book. *"Ja,"* he said. *"Ja."*

The waiter shrugged and then hurried away, mumbling to himself. Bertie poured himself a glass of wine and drank half of it at one swallow.

"You will pardon me if I intrude," said a female English voice.

Bertie looked up and saw that a lady sitting alone at the neighboring table was addressing him. She had arrived there only a short while before.

"Oh! Oh, no . . . please." He attempted to stand but she waved him down.

"Please don't stand on ceremony. It was very forward of me to address you without introduction, but I couldn't help noticing that you seemed to be having some difficulty with the waiter."

"That is putting it mildly," agreed Bertie.

"This your first time in Germany?"

"Is it that obvious?" Bertie looked about him. There was no sign of Sir Hugh. He turned back to the woman. "Would you care to join me, Miss . . . ? Oh, unless you are yourself waiting for someone?"

"Thank you. I would like that." She waved to another waiter who hurried over and drew back her chair. Bertie rose as she came over to his table and they both seated themselves.

"Bertram Hawkins," said Bertie, introducing himself and extending his hand.

"So very nice to meet you, Mister Hawkins. A fellow Londoner, I presume? I am Mrs. Madeline Fletcher."

She was a blonde-haired woman of indeterminate age, Bertie decided, though he guessed her to be in her late thirties. She wore a gown of light blue with darker blue border stripes that edged the neckline, waist and forearm-length sleeves. Deep maroon was on the bodice reveres and the pleated flounce on the hem. A fine diamond necklace glistened about her neck; matching earrings peeked out from beneath her upswept hair.

"German waiters are not the most agreeable in the world, I'm sure you will agree, Mr. Hawkins."

"This particular one certainly seems to have a chip on his shoulder." Bertie waved for the wine waiter to pour more wine for both of them. "You are staying at this hotel, Mrs. Fletcher?"

"I always stay here," she said, "and I refuse to be intimidated by the staff." She smiled, her eyes studying Bertie. "And what brings you here, if I may ask, Mr. Hawkins? It is a long way from Trafalgar Square."

"Indeed it is." He nodded ruefully. "I'm here on business, though my associate seems, somehow, to have forsaken me." Again he looked hopefully around the dining room, wishing that Sir Hugh would materialize. He turned back to her. "Your husband is with you, I presume?"

Mrs. Fletcher laughed, a musical laugh that Bertie found he enjoyed. "Oh, I'm not married," she said.

"But – but you said . . ."

She waved a dismissive hand. "A lady cannot run about foreign cities unattended, Mr. Hawkins, as I'm sure you are aware. It is convenient for me to present myself as a married woman; it saves a lot of explanations in many situations."

"Oh. I see." But he really didn't.

Much later Bertie and Madeline had finished an enjoyable meal and were sipping cordials. His new blonde companion had proven to be very capable with the German language and more than a match for the surly waiter. Bertie felt very relaxed and had even, momentarily, forgotten all about the missing Sir Hugh Ardsley. The attractive lady had regaled him with stories of her travels about the Continent. An aunt had died and left her an inheritance, she volunteered, and she was making good her dreams from earlier days of travel and exploration.

Bertie, encouraged by the wine plus two or more flutes of champagne – all charged to Sir Hugh's suite – had told a little of his own situation. Madeline was enthralled to find that he was an enquiry agent, especially so since he had hinted at investigating more than one murder.

"So tell me more of what brings you to Berlin, Bertie," she said.

He studied the long stem of his glass, the tall, narrow bowl with its thin sides and finely etched bottom. He was suddenly afraid that perhaps the wine had led him to speak of things he should have kept to himself and wondered what Sir Hugh would think of his unaccustomed loquaciousness.

"Oh, it's simply to make contact with a gentleman who might have some information we need," he said. "Herr Benz is an inventor. . . I doubt you've heard of him but he has been exchanging ideas with an Englishman who is recently deceased."

"Benz, did you say, Bertie? I think I *may* have heard of him, in fact. I have taken a lot of tours around Berlin. Is he, by any chance, the Mr. Benz who is involved with some kind of horseless carriage?"

Bertie looked up. "Why, yes! Yes, that's him exactly. You know of him?"

She frowned. "Let me think." She giggled and drained her own glass. The wine waiter hurried over but Bertie waved him away. He retreated grudgingly. "Benz," Madeline repeated. "Yes. I'm very good with names. Benz and Cie originally of Mannheim, if I'm not mistaken. Mr. Benz himself came to Berlin just last year, though his company remains headquartered in Mannheim."

"How do you know all this?" asked Bertie. "Not that I'm not grateful, but it doesn't seem, what shall I say . . ."

"The sort of thing a lady would be interested in?" Madeline laughed. "My father was coachman to a local squire in Devon," she explained. "He taught me to take an interest in 'transportation', as he put it. Said it was something that would forever be changing and advancing. He was very astute, my father." She looked around for the wine waiter but he had turned his back on their table after Bertie's rejection of him. She shrugged and put down her glass. "I have been out and about Berlin with several tourist groups arranged by the hotel. I recall we did stop to admire Mr. Benz's contraption less than a week ago. A big sort of bodiless seat set up on large spindly wheels. Very strange."

"And do you recall just where, in Berlin, this was?"

"Oh, yes. Mr. Benz complained a lot about the cost of suitable premises in this city. He said his office here was to promote the machine, but the assembly would continue in Mannheim."

"And the location of his office?" persisted Bertie.

"Sorry, Bertie. Yes, it is across the river on Kessel-Strasse, close to the Friedrich-Wilhelm-Stadt Theater."

Bertie lay in bed unable to sleep . . . something he attributed to the unaccustomed amount of wine he had imbibed. He had enjoyed the company of Mrs. Fletcher – Madeline – but was more concerned about what had happened to Sir Hugh. There had been no sign of him in his room and attempted queries at the front office of the hotel had produced nothing but shrugs from the staff. A thousand thoughts and probabilities ran through his head. Among them was a disturbing one. Supposing Sir Hugh had murdered his own father? Bertie searched for a motive. Supposing the son was desperate to inherit the title? Perhaps there was no sign of the father passing on for many years yet, and – for whatever reason – the son wanted to become the new baronet. It was possible, he had to admit.

So why, then, had he disappeared? Bertie mentally scratched his head. Perhaps he had brought Bertie all the way to Berlin just to abandon him; to leave him here with no apparent means of getting home, because Bertie had got too close to discovering who murdered Colonel Sir Dennis Ardsley! He shook his head. No, that was ridiculous. Far easier, if he had committed one murder, to commit a second and kill Bertie without having to leave England.

He climbed out of bed and wandered over to the window. It was a warm night and he had the window partially open. The Wilhelm-Strasse was still very much alive, despite the lateness of the hour. Long after midnight yet still the sound of horses' hooves, the rattle of carriages and cabs, the metal-rimmed wheels, the occasional shout or laughter came floating up to where Bertie stood. Was Sir Hugh out there somewhere? If so, where and why? Bertie sighed. It was far too late for serious thinking.

Madeline – Mrs. Fletcher – had proposed that they meet for lunch but Bertie had said no. He needed to get on with things, with or without Sir Hugh. He had got Madeline to write down the address of the Benz company office and, as soon as possible after breakfast, he intended to pay it a visit and see if Herr Benz was home. He turned back to the bed and, with another deep sigh, climbed up into it.

Chapter Twenty-One

After several repeats of "*Ich will frühstücken,*" to an apparently hard-of-hearing waiter, Bertie had a satisfying breakfast in the suite and then wandered down to the foyer, wondering what to do with himself. The first person he met was Mrs. Madeline Fletcher, resplendent in a tailor-made violet suit trimmed with black silk, the jacket with tiny gilt buttons. She sported a large, pale-yellow, straw hat trimmed with two shades of violet taffeta silk, with folds of black velvet under the brim and a large peacock feather bobbing to one side. She carried a folded parasol to match her outfit. "Bertie! How wonderful! Where are you off to?"

Bertie would have preferred to have been left to his own devices but at the same time felt some relief on encountering someone who was fluent in the language and also knew the city.

"I – I am not quite sure," he said. "My companion, Sir Hugh, has still not re-joined me so I am somewhat at a loss. I thought that perhaps I would see something of the city while I waited."

"Wonderful!" She clapped her gloved hands together enthusiastically. "Then I insist you let me be your guide. No! No protests," she cried as he opened his mouth to speak. "We will take in just a few of the nearby delights and then return for lunch. Perhaps your elusive friend will have materialized by then."

Bertie had no argument and he and Mrs. Fletcher climbed into an open Brett carriage summoned by the concierge. The sun was shining and the day promised to be warm. Bertie rode with his back to the driver in the vis-à-vis vehicle and Madeline, opening her parasol, settled herself where she could point out the places of interest. She directed the carriage driver to first take them to Unter den Linden; the handsomest and busiest part of Berlin.

Bertie was impressed by the Brandenburg Gate, at the west end of the Linden. It had been erected a hundred years before in imitation of the Propylæa at Athens. Madeline pointed out the five different passages separated by massive Doric columns. Most impressive, to Bertie, was the copper sculpture of *Quadriga of Victory* that surmounted everything.

At the corner of Pariser-Platz Madeline pointed to the Palace of Count Redern and a little farther along to the office of the Minister of Religion and Education, with an impressive frieze by Eberlein. She wanted them to go on to the Aquarium and spend some time there, but Bertie was watching the passing hours and insisted they return to the hotel for lunch, which they did at a leisurely pace.

Lunch was passed with Madeline regaling Bertie about the wonders of the Aquarium, enthusing about the grotto-like corridor that extended for 300 yards on two floors. She told him of the Reptile House, the Bird House, the Geological Grotto, and promised to take him there and introduce him to Dr. Hermes, the director and a personal friend of hers.

Bertie was not sorry when his delightful companion suddenly recalled that she had an appointment with a dressmaker that afternoon and would have to put off further sight-seeing till the following day, if Sir Hugh had still not shown up.

Bertie and Madeline bade farewell in the foyer and Bertie determined that he would go on to locate Karl Benz's office, with or without Sir Hugh. At the hotel desk he stopped to get directions and to have the concierge get him a cab. As he stood uncertainly trying to get the concierge's attention, he was hailed by a man hurrying into the hotel.

"Hawkins! There you are. Good!" It was Sir Hugh Ardsley. "Glad I caught you. Where are you off to?"

"I was about to proceed with my investigation and visit Karl Benz," said Bertie, amazed at the sudden reappearance. "I had been wondering where you . . ."

"Excellent! I see you've wasted no time. Well done. Come, let's go up to the suite so that I can change, and I can fill you in on what has been going on. You must have been wondering."

Sir Hugh marched briskly across to the lift at the back of the foyer, leaving Bertie to scurry after him. Nothing was said by either man as the metal cage creaked its way up to the second floor and disgorged its passengers. *Well, I guess he didn't murder his father and leave me to flounder in Berlin*, Bertie thought as he followed along to the suite.

Bertie sat looking at the pictures in a German magazine, and trying to guess at the meaning of the captions, while Sir Hugh bathed and changed. Eventually the man emerged, looking his usual dapper self, in black frock coat and carrying gloves, cane and top hat.

"We'll catch up as we go," he said, heading for the door, causing Bertie to drop the magazine and scramble to his feet. "Too much time wasted already."

As the hansom's metal wheels rattled over cobblestones, Sir Hugh finally felt comfortable enough to enlighten Bertie.

"Damned inconvenient," he said. "I had not even started to dress for dinner last night – good thing too, it turns out – when I was summoned to the front desk. A telegraph from my wife. She had been trying to catch up with me for two or three days."

"Nothing serious, I hope?" said Bertie.

Sir Hugh shook his head. "Not as serious as first seemed," he said. "My wife's father was en route to Poland when he suffered a heart attack. Not too far from here, at Francfort-auf-der-Oder, about two and a half hours by railway. He was taken off the train and placed in the Unterkirche hospital there. Beautiful building. It dates from 1525. Was formerly a Franciscan monastery."

"And your father-in-law?"

"Right! Damn good thing we were here in Berlin, I must say. Wouldn't do for my wife's father to pass over as well as my own father."

"He is all right then?" ventured Bertie.

"What? Yes, thank heavens. I dashed off there to see him and he was sitting up in bed complaining about the food." He paused and looked out at the passing scenery for a moment. "Sorry to leave you like that, Hawkins. Not my usual way of doing things but couldn't be helped. I knew you'd be all right. Damned inconvenient though."

They continued in silence for some time.

"Do we know whereabouts on Kessel-strasse this Benz fellow is located?"

Bertie shook his head. "No, Sir Hugh. It was by the merest chance that I even found out what street he is on. It seems we were lucky."

"What do you mean?"

"His factory, or manufacturing plant, or whatever, is in Mannheim."

"Mannheim!" Sir Hugh stared at Bertie. "But that's the other side of Germany. We could have crossed to Calais and come across France; saved a couple of days!"

"Except that we knew that Benz himself was in Berlin, because of your father and Cedric Bromley's visits here," said Bertie. "Mannheim would not have helped."

Sir Hugh grunted.

Once over the Weidendam Bridge, from Friedrichs-strasse the cab turned up Chaussee-strasse. It didn't take long to get to Kessel-strasse, on the left. Sir Hugh banged on the trapdoor. The driver opened it and looked down inquisitively.

"Lasst mich an der Ecke der Strasse aussteigen," said Sir Hugh.

The hansom pulled over to the side and stopped. They both got out and Sir Hugh paid the man.

"I told him to drop us off at the corner," said Sir Hugh. "It is not too long a street. I thought we'd stand a better chance of finding the place if we walked and studied the buildings."

"If you take one side, I could take the other," suggested Bertie. "That way we shouldn't miss it."

It was a mixture of residences and commercial buildings. The road, at the far end, led into the gardens of the Museum of Natural History. Partway down on the right a short avenue led into the big Exercier-Platz der Artillerie. At the corner of that avenue and Kessel-strasse was a brick two-storey house fronting onto the street. When he reached this, Sir Hugh called out to Bertie and with his cane tapped a small brass plate, one of several affixed to the side of the front entrance.

"I think we have found our Mr. Benz," he said, as Bertie joined him.

The brass plate was engraved:

Benz & Company Rheinische Gasmotoren-Fabrik
Mannheim und Berlin
Benz Patent Motorwagen

Bertie and Sir Hugh followed the signs from the front entrance to a ground floor office located at the back of the house. It was next to the office of a lawyer. The door was open and they went in.

"Forgive my humble office space, gentlemen," said Benz, rising as they entered. "It is, I keep telling myself, only temporary . . . though I have been here almost two years now." He smiled, ruefully.

Karl Friedrich Benz was a serious young man with a large, bushy mustache and a wispy beard hiding a receding chin. His hair was parted neatly on the left hand side of his head and his eyes focused squarely on whomever he addressed. He was smartly dressed and well mannered and Bertie liked him immediately. His English was good and he seemed to enjoy speaking it. He was in his mid-forties and Bertie had heard – from Madeline Fletcher – that he was considered by the ladies to be "quite handsome".

They introduced themselves and Benz waved them to two chairs in front of his desk and reseated himself as they sat. Bertie looked about him. There were two tall, wooden, filing cabinets in evidence, along with several shelves of books, manuals, blueprints, and bric-a-brac. The desk behind which Benz had been sitting was a well-worn wooden affair covered by sheets of notepaper, rough sketches, pencils and a ruler. Around the dingy walls of the office were a number of framed prints and photographs. The largest of these was an artist's rendering of Cugnot's steam-propelled road vehicle, generally accepted to have been the first "horseless carriage". A lumbering three-wheeled tractor, it was built in 1769 for the French army. Close beside it was another artist's idea of Robert Anderson's electric carriage of 1835, sketched in its homeland of Scotland. However, Bertie's eyes were drawn to an illustration which he recognized as having been clipped from the English *Illustrated London News*. It was of Edward Butler's Petrol Cycle.

"And how may I help you, gentlemen?" Benz sat back and steepled his fingers.

"You immediately addressed us in English," said Bertie. "How did you know . . ?"

Benz smiled. "Forgive me, but your sartorial elegance," he was obviously speaking more to Sir Hugh, Bertie realized, "speaks of Bond Street, if I am not mistaken." He shook his head slightly. "I must apologize. It's a little game I play with myself. You can see how few visitors I receive here!" There was a trace of bitterness in his voice.

"What brought you here from Mannheim, if I may ask?" Sir Hugh removed his top hat and placed it on a corner of the desk, having ascertained that it was a clean spot.

"To be blunt, sir, I need to find financial support. Investors are to be found in Berlin; very few in Mannheim."

Sir Hugh nodded understandingly.

Benz continued. "Ardsley. Ardsley? That name is not unfamiliar to me."

"You are connecting it with my father, if I am not mistaken," said Sir Hugh. "Colonel Sir

Dennis Ardsley. You have heard, I presume, of his demise?"

"Yes. Very recently," said Benz. "Is that correct that he was murdered?"

"I must let my associate take up the tale on that issue." Sir Hugh indicated Bertie, who suddenly found Karl Benz's bright eyes focused on him.

"Yes." Bertie sat forward on the edge of his chair. He went on to describe the events leading up to the colonel's death, and the evidence that it was murder. He explained how the colonel had passed on his gold watch to his granddaughter – though he did not go into the details of her marriage problems – and of the subsequent discovery of the note in the back of it.

"Yes. That was written by me," said Benz. "It was to be delivered, with the gold, to Edward Butler. Colonel Ardsley was personally taking care of that exchange."

"Did you not hear of the death – murder, again, I am sorry to say – of Mr. Butler?"

"What?" Benz came to his feet. "When did this happen? What about our agreement? My gold?"

Bertie held up his hand to try to soothe the man. "Yes, Mr. Benz. *Herr* Benz. We are working on all of that. Scotland Yard . . ."

"Scotland Yard is in on this?"

"Oh, yes," put in Sir Hugh. "We are right on top of all this. Mr. Hawkins, here, is a private enquiry agent who is working closely with the Yard." To Bertie he said, "What's the fellow's name?"

"Moss. Inspector Moss, sir."

"Right! Inspector Moss is on top of all this, Herr Benz, have no fear."

"Then you have my gold safe?" Benz breathed a sigh of relief and sat down again.

"Actually, no, sir," said Bertie.

"No?" He was on his feet again.

Bertie looked to Sir Hugh for guidance.

"Now calm yourself, Herr Benz," he said. "Let us examine this piece by piece. This is why Mr. Hawkins and I have come all this way to see you; to sort out what is the present status and what can be done about it."

There was a moment's silence and then, reluctantly, Benz sat down again. He ran his fingers through his hair. When he spoke, it was quietly and obviously with some effort at calm.

"You must understand, gentlemen, that I am in a very, er, *unsicher?. . . schwankend?. . .* 'precarious' position. Financially I am on the edge of the knife, as it were. My motorwagen has proven itself but is in desperate need of a more efficient, more reliable carburetor for the engine. The banks at Mannheim had demanded that my enterprise be incorporated due to the, to them, high production costs necessary for my endeavors. I was therefore forced to improvise an association with an acquaintance, Herr Emil Bühler and his brother, becoming the joint-stock company *Gasmotoren Fabrik Mannheim*. Due to various disagreements, I subsequently withdrew from that corporation and formed a new company with Max Rose; *Benz & Company Rheinische Gasmotoren-Fabrik*. This progressed well, giving me the opportunity to work more freely in designing the vehicle."

"Did you also design the engine for this contraption?" asked Sir Hugh.

Benz nodded. "Indeed I did. A four-stroke engine of my own design, with a very advanced coil ignition and evaporative cooling. Power is transmitted to the rear axle by way of two roller chains . . ."

"We really don't need the technical aspects, I suspect," said Sir Hugh. Bertie agreed.

"Nonetheless, you must know that the smooth running of the engine was dependent upon a spray of Benzoline or petroleum product carbureted with air. Otto – Nikolaus August Otto – has been working with Gottlieb Daimler in Stuttgart and is close to perfecting a similar model, also a four-stroke cycle. They tried to patent theirs but, unfortunately for them, I had already obtained the patent on my design."

Sir Hugh murmured appreciation of Benz's obvious business acumen.

"Would you continue regarding the gold you mentioned and the note you sent, please?" asked Bertie.

"Of course." Benz reached into his desk drawer and produced a cigarette box, which he opened and offered to his two visitors. They both declined but Benz himself took one and lit it. He settled back in his chair, drawing on the cigarette seemingly to steady his nerves. "I had learned of your Mr. Butler's work firstly through articles in journals and magazines, and then through talking with my old friend Colonel Sir Dennis Ardsley – your late father, sir. He and I became acquainted when he was in Berlin about the same time that I first arrived. We both stayed at the Reichshof."

"That's where we are staying," put in Bertie.

"A very fine hotel," continued Benz. "Well, the colonel and I became good friends and he offered to act as a go-between when I expressed a desire to communicate with Butler. That he did, and subsequently it worked well in establishing a business relationship between Butler and myself."

"Yet I understand Butler had no desire to sell his plans to you," said Sir Hugh.

"Initially no. That was certainly the case. He hoped – as well he should – that he might proceed with his own Butler Petrol Cycle and establish it in England. But," he waved away a cloud of smoke, "the British authorities apparently are not very far-sighted when it comes to this exciting new form of transportation."

"I must agree, that does seem to be the case," murmured Sir Hugh.

"Butler finally conceded that it might be better to let me have access to the details of his carburetor after all; that there would at least be a chance for automobile development."

"So the money – the gold – was to pay for his plans?" asked Bertie.

Benz nodded. "Indeed. We had come to an agreement. I wrote a note – the one you have – to that effect and sent it, by way of the colonel, together with one hundred gold marks."

"That is a fair amount of money," observed Sir Hugh.

"Indeed it is, hence my apprehension at what may have become of it." Benz stubbed out his cigarette in an ashtray on the desk. "It represents almost the sum total of investments we have obtained to date."

"To get this absolutely clear," said Bertie. "You gave both the note *and* the gold coins to Colonel Ardsley?"

"I did."

"Was the colonel's valet, Mr. Bromley, present?"

Benz thought for a moment. "Yes. Yes, I believe he was."

"And did he handle the money or did the colonel?" persisted Bertie.

"Oh, the colonel. He was adamant about that. He felt that it was placed in his trust and he took that very seriously."

"Yes, he would," said Sir Hugh.

"Then we can certainly understand your concern," said Bertie. "Believe me, Herr Benz, we will do all in our power to track down that money and return it to you."

"It would be far better to let me have Mr. Butler's plans," replied Benz. "I did, after all, have at least an understanding on that score. Might I ask the disposition of the plans now that Mr. Butler has been murdered?"

Bertie tugged at his mustache. "There have been attempts to steal the plans, by persons as yet unknown to us, and Mrs. Butler does not know where they are."

"You mean, the plans are lost?" Benz's eyes opened wide.

"I think we can use the word 'mislaid'," put in Sir Hugh.

"Yes," added Bertie. "I am sure that Inspector Moss will be able to locate them."

"How do you know that they have not already been stolen?"

"Because whoever tried to get them, in addition to murdering Edward Butler also kidnapped his son to hold for ransom for those plans," Bertie explained.

"Oh, no! I am truly sorry to hear that."

"May I ask," said Sir Hugh, "Why you sent gold rather than notes? It would surely have been easier to transport and exchange paper money, would it not?"

Benz shook his head. "Not really, Sir Hugh. Paper money issued by the Reichsbank, or even the Reichskassenschein, is not, I am sorry to say, as *reliable* as it might be. Far better – especially on an international exchange such as this – to rely on pure gold."

Sir Hugh looked at Bertie. "Well then, Mr. Hawkins, it seems our job – or more specifically *your* job – is to return to England and track down that money and find those plans." He turned back to Benz. "Now that we know the details, we will keep you apprised of the situation, sir, and will see to it that the plans come to you as soon as they are located."

"And the gold?"

"Will, of course, then belong to the widow."

"And hopefully she will have her son back," said Bertie. He prayed that Inspector Moss had made headway while they were away.

Benz wearily got to his feet. "Would you gentlemen be interested in seeing my vehicle?" he asked.

"You have it here?"

"In the coach house at the rear of this building. It was necessary to have an example of the Motorwagen on hand for potential investors to see."

"I understand it has become a bit of a tourist attraction," said Bertie, also getting to his feet.

"What do you mean?" asked Sir Hugh, as Benz led them out of the office and towards the rear of the building.

"I met a lady at the hotel – the one who gave me Herr Benz's address – and she told me of having been here."

"Ah, yes!" Benz held the door open for them. "A good friend of mine, an older gentleman, takes small groups around Berlin to see the city. He did stop by here with three ladies and a gentleman. But that is not a regular occurrence. If it were, I might charge an admission fee!"

They all laughed.

Chapter Twenty-Two

Sir Hugh Ardsley decided to make a stop in Paris on his way home, to do some shopping for his wife and daughter, but Bertie felt the need to hurry back directly. There was a kidnapped boy to find and two murders to solve, not to mention locating the missing gold.

The railway delivered him safely to Ostende, the second port of the kingdom of Belgium and that country's favorite and most fashionable seaside resort. Bertie made out the brightly colored tin roofs coming into sight as his tired eyes strained to see ahead of the steaming engine. After ensuring that his luggage would be transferred safely, he found that he had two hours before his cross-Channel boat left. He decided to lunch in style; after all, Sir Hugh was paying for everything.

He took a cab to the seafront and decided to eat in the new seven-storey *Les Grand Hôtels de la Digue,* built just six years ago. A brochure Bertie picked up at the railway station said that the hotel was in the Neo-France Renaissance style and was the first Ostende hotel to have a hydraulic lift. The white-faced building was immense, with two matching towers on the corners of the main section and a slightly smaller hotel abutting on one side. Souvenir shops spread along the ground floor, opening onto the sidewalk. A bright striped awning stretched across the entire front. Across the road, a ramp with steps sloped down to the sand, where stood a line of brightly painted bathing machines. The *digue*, or promenade, stretched for almost two miles along the shoreline of the North Sea, with bathing machines scattered liberally along the length of the beach. The sands were crowded, it being a fine June day, with families settled for a full day of pleasure. Sea bathing at the resort was considered unsurpassed.

Bertie settled in the hotel dining room and ordered from the extensive menu. The only thing that detracted from his complete pleasure was that the service was unbelievably slow and he ended having to forego his coffee in order to be sure of making the paddle-wheeled ferry.

The white and green funnel of the ship – *so very much smaller than that twin-hulled monstrosity that had taken us there,* thought Bertie – puffed out grey smoke that quickly dissipated in the light breeze blowing off the Dover shore. Bertie tried to be patient as he waited in the press of passengers and watched the captain slow the vessel and bring it smoothly and carefully alongside the dock. The gangway was quickly in place and soon Bertie was borne along with the crowd that surged forward towards dry land.

In no time Bertie was watching his bags being loaded onto a cart and transported to the railway platform of the South Eastern & Chatham Railway. The dark green engine and its line of carriages stood getting up steam as Bertie climbed aboard one of the First Class carriages. He settled into a corner seat and gave a great sigh of relief and satisfaction. He was back in England having survived his first excursion to the Continent.

The lush green fields of Kent opened up when the train emerged from the long tunnel after passing Kearsney, and steamed on towards Canterbury, where it stopped briefly. From there it was on to Chatham, Rochester, and Gravesend. He passed acres of hop fields with their attendant oast houses. The crop would be harvested in September, descended upon by an army of thousands of hop-pickers – men, women and children – from London and surrounding areas, plus some who came across the Channel just for the picking. Bertie could see the lines of tall poles and wires strung across for the hops and could imagine, from a visit in his youth, the men balanced on tall stilts reaching up for the hops on the very top.

Eventually the train steamed into Charing Cross Station and Bertie was able to get up, stretch, and descend from the carriage. He made his way to the baggage car and claimed his bags, getting a porter to take them out and hail him a cab. Within half an hour he had arrived home at Penny Court.

Bertie stood in the middle of the room looking about him at the mess of books and papers strewn about the floor. Nellie was at his side and Isobel hovered in the doorway. They had had an emotional reunion and then Nellie had broken the news that just two nights before Bertie got back, their home had been broken into and the drawing room ransacked.

"I slept through it but poor Isobel heard a noise and came to investigate," said Nellie.

Bertie looked towards the maid, who was nursing one arm in a makeshift sling and trying to wipe her nose on it.

"I 'eard a noise, Mr. 'awkins. Didn't know what it was. Thought maybe Mrs. 'awkins couldn't sleep or something. So I comes down the back stairs and suddenly this man leaps out of the drawing room and knocks me clean down the apples and pears!" She sniffed.

"We thought she'd broken her arm," explained Nellie. "But thankfully it was just a sprained wrist."

"Don't 'alf 'urt!"

"I left everything as I found it, so that you could investigate."

"Good. Thank you, Nell. And I'm really sorry you had to suffer, Isobel."

"'s all right." She blushed and looked down at her feet.

"Now then," said Bertie, looking about him. "Do you know if anything was stolen? Goodness knows we don't have much of anything. It's not as though Penny Court is Mayfair!"

"Isobel and I had a quick look around," said Nellie. "We tried not to move anything; just looked. But we couldn't see anything missing. Anything noticeable, that is."

"Well, I can see one thing," said Bertie. He crossed to the open desk against the far wall. "I had been looking at some drawings here before I left. Just one or two pages I took out of the *Illustrated London News*. I distinctly remember leaving them spread out on top of the desk." He tugged at his mustache. "They are gone."

"Were they important? Or valuable?"

"Neither," said Bertie. "As I said, I had simply removed them from the magazine. They were part of an article and showed details of Mr. Butler's Petrol Cycle, which is why I detached them." He thought for a moment and then looked at Nellie, the beginnings of a smile on his face.

"What? What is it?"

"Just back from my trip and I am plunged deep into the case once again," he said. "This, Nell my dear, is all tied-in with the Butler murder and kidnapping case."

His wife and his maid stood looking at him, waiting for him to explain himself.

"And the conclusion I can immediately draw," he said, brightly, "is that this burglary, or attempted burglary, was carried out by what they call an 'underling'; not by the head man."

The two women were obviously impressed and awaited further explanation.

"Whoever came here was looking – still looking, I think we can say – for Edward Butler's plans. They must have thought that I'd acquired them and brought them home for safekeeping. But . . ." He paused for dramatic effect. "They took what they thought to be the plans but what, in fact, were no more than pages torn from a magazine. If it had been our prime suspect, he would have known immediately that they were magazine pages, but his 'hired underling' obviously wasn't sure so he took them to be on the safe side."

"And just who is your prime suspect?" asked Nellie. Isobel was at her elbow, mouth agape.

Bertie shrugged. "We cannot yet be certain but, to my mind, all signs so far point towards our Mr. Lawson as the mastermind."

There came a ring at the front door bell and, after a nod from Nellie, Isobel scampered off to answer it. She returned with Inspector Moss in tow.

"Thought I'd swing past and welcome you home, Bertram. I had it in my notebook that you would be back today. I . . . what? What's going on here?"

"Mr. 'awkins says as 'ow Mr. Lawson paid a visit," enthused Isobel.

"No! That's not what I said," protested Bertie.

"Isobel! I think perhaps you and I had better retire to the kitchen and leave the gentlemen to take care of this. Come along!"

Isobel scurried off ahead of her mistress who, with a quick glance at Bertie and a nod to the inspector, followed after the maid and left the room.

"Good of you to come along, Campbell," said Bertie. "As you can see, we had a visitor while I was away." He went on to give his thoughts on what had taken place. The policeman nodded soberly and produced his notebook.

"I would agree with your thinking, Bertram. And also agree that the finger seems to be pointing more and more in the direction of friend Lawson. Though we are far from having any positive connection, of course."

"Agreed."

"One note of interest concerning that gentleman," continued Moss. "It seems he recently acquired the Humber Bicycle Company and also – now hear this – the exclusive British rights to manufacture the De Dion-Bouton motor vehicle." He pronounced the words very carefully. "Apparently they are a young French automobile company."

" Here! Toss those books on the floor with the rest – I'll have Isobel tidy up later – and sit down, Campbell. That is most interesting. So Mr. Lawson is most definitely in the market for automobile parts . . . and plans? I need to catch up on what you have been up to, Campbell, and then I'll give you my news."

"I did speak more with Mr. Bromley, but he seems more concerned with finding future employment than anything else," said the inspector. "I found out, at his club, that his tab is in arrears and that he has stalled efforts to get him to pay it. He seems to have a bit of a reputation where the horses are concerned. Not too successful at picking winners, it seems. However, he does seem very much saddened about the passing of his old employer, I'll give him that. Otherwise I'd class him as uncooperative."

"Pretty much what I decided, when I spoke with him," agreed Bertie. "How is Mrs. Butler? Any development on the kidnapping?"

Moss sighed and scratched the top of his head. "I've had a man watching Lawson's warehouse – the one you paid a visit to before you went away – but there doesna' seem to be any great activity there, though we have seen Squire coming and going a number of times. The main point is that Mrs. Butler has received another letter, this time giving her one more week to produce the plans."

"Otherwise . . . ?"

Moss shrugged. "We can only guess. They have that wee lad and they can do what they like but my bet is that, since he's their only bargaining piece, they willna' do anything to harm him."

"I hope you're right."

Bertie went on to tell the policeman the details of his trip to Germany and his meeting with Karl Benz.

"So there is definitely an amount of gold that is missing," Moss said, making a note in his book. "And it was in the care of the old man himself, you say?"

"That's right," agreed Bertie. "So it would seem likely that it disappeared somewhere between Dover and Victoria Station."

It had been late when Bertie had arrived home and now it was completely dark outside. He yawned and got to his feet. "You are going to have to excuse me, Campbell. There's a lot to go over, but it's been a very long day and travel can be very tiring."

"Of course," said the inspector, putting away his notebook and pencil and getting to his feet. "I'm sure all this foreign moving about and hobnobbing with baronets and German men of science has to take a lot out of you!" He moved towards the door. "No need to show me out, Bertram. You need your rest. We'll be in touch."

Much later that evening, Bertie crouched outside the big wrought-iron gates to Lawson's warehouse. It seemed only yesterday that he'd been there before, ending with his ignominious descent into the rain barrel and then a hasty exit and intimate acquaintance with the guard dog. This time he had his brother-in-law with him and had a good idea of the layout of the place.

"What's the plan?" asked Arnold in a hoarse whisper.

Bertie had been shown the latest letter from the kidnapper and the deadline given was now only two days away. He had decided to act, to either rescue the boy or to force the kidnapper's hand, if indeed the kidnapper was Harry Lawson. He really had no plan, other than to somehow get into the building and search it for the boy, but there was no need to let Arnold know that, he thought.

"First things first, Arnold," he said. "We need to get inside these gates."

"How did you do it last time?"

"I managed to slip between them; there was just enough room if I . . . Oh!"

"What?" Arnold's voice came out as a squeak.

"Don't worry," assured Bertie. "It's just that I see they must have used these gates since I was last here. The chain is really tight now and there's no way to squeeze through."

"Oh!" Arnold gave a sigh that, to Bertie, sounded like one of relief.

"Come on, Arnold," he said. "We have to get in there. Let's have a look around."

They moved away from the gates and along Emmett Street, beside the high brick wall that stretched in both directions away from the entrance. There was no obvious way in. They reached the end of the wall in one direction, where it met up with a tall iron-railing fence to the next-door warehouse. Hand-painted signs proclaimed that to be for the storage of boats, carts, wagons, and building materials. They retraced their steps and followed the wall on the other side of the gates. Once again it finished by meeting up with the perimeter fence of the next warehouse.

"Now what, Bertie?" asked Arnold.

"Ssh! Wait a minute." Bertie looked at the next-door fence. It was high – too high to climb – and of wood rather than metal. Bertie moved along it a short way and then stopped. "Here, Arnold. Give me a hand."

The top of one of the wooden palings was broken, probably from a falling tree limb at some time, thought Bertie. There was in fact a large cedar tree on the far side, not far from the fence; too far away, however, to be of any immediate help. Bertie studied the broken top of the fence.

"If I stand on your shoulders, Arnold, I bet I could reach that fence top where it's broken and pull myself up and over it."

"But we want to be at Lawson's. That's not this one."

"You are quite correct," agreed Bertie. "However, it could well be that getting over from this warehouse into Lawson's might be much simpler than trying to get into Lawson's from outside. I think it's worth a try."

Climbing up onto Arnold's broad shoulders proved to be trickier than it had at first seemed, mainly because the big man turned out to be extremely ticklish. Bertie would be almost on his shoulders when Arnold would dissolve into laughter and shake his partner off and back onto the ground. But with threats from Bertie and by Arnold holding his breath at the necessary time, they managed to get Bertie up and clinging to the top of the fence, with Arnold supporting his feet. It took only a little wriggling and tugging for Bertie to get over the top and he let himself drop down on the far side.

"Are you there, Bertie?" came Arnold's loud stage whisper.

"Yes, of course I am!" called Bertie. "Now, keep quiet. Go back to those gates and see if you can see anything from there. I think it looks good for getting over this dividing fence."

"Watch out for any guard dogs," said Arnold, as he set off back to the gates.

"Thanks a lot!" muttered Bertie.

In fact Bertie found it relatively easy to pass from one warehouse property to the next. The smaller fence between the two had obviously been damaged many times, probably by wagons turning and goods being loaded and unloaded. He was soon on the side of Lawson's building and moved up to the inside of the gates.

"All right, Arnold. I'm here," he said.

"Oh!" Arnold jumped and let out a yelp.

"Ssh!" hissed Bertie. "Now listen. I'm going to try to get into the building. I don't think there's anyone in there – no lights that we can see – so I should be all right once inside."

"What about the dog?" asked Arnold.

Bertie smiled, though realizing that his brother-in-law couldn't see his expression in the dark. "Don't worry about him," he said, patting his pocket. "I brought a pork chop with me, to throw down for him if I have to."

"Does Nell know?"

Bertie ignored the question. "Now all you have to do is to keep watch from here, Arnold. If anyone comes, then toss a pebble against the windows . . ."

"Which one?"

"I don't know! Just toss pebbles against as many windows as you can and I'll try to keep an ear open for anything. Now, let's get on with this."

"Bertie?" But Bertie had already gone.

Chapter Twenty-Three

Getting inside the warehouse proved much easier than Bertie had expected. The sliding door at the loading dock was not locked and he was able to slip inside with only minor squeaking from the door. Through Inspector Moss, he had borrowed a police bulls-eye lantern and now carefully opened the front of it and struck a Lucifer to light the wick. It gave a strong, narrow beam that meant he could move about easily without the light spilling out and illuminating the windows.

The room he found himself in was large, extending the full width of the building. It was untidily piled with empty wooden boxes and crates. Bits and pieces of machinery, unrecognizable by Bertie, lay in no particular order. He did recognize five or six bicycles, complete and incomplete, in one corner of the room. Off to one side was a low-lying wagon-bed on small wheels, probably used for moving items about the warehouse. In the far left corner was a wooden stairway going up to the next floor. There were large sliding doors to other sections of the warehouse at both ends of the room he was in; all of them closed. In the center of the ceiling above was an open trapdoor with a chain hoist hanging down through it.

Bertie moved across to the sliding door on his left and eased it open. It slid easily, on well-oiled runners. Shining the light inside, Bertie saw a number of machines; a metal lathe, band saw, and a drill press being the only ones that he recognized. He turned and walked across to the door on the opposite side. This opened into a large room containing drafting boards, desks, blackboards and easels, and numerous filing cabinets and cupboards. Beyond that was yet another door; this a regular-sized one.

Bertie moved back to the bottom of the stairway and carefully started to climb. As his head came above the level of the next floor, he brought up the lamp and shone it around. He was in another large room, again with a number of smaller empty boxes randomly lying about. He saw that the chain hoist was suspended from the roof beam above the trapdoor. To either side of him he could make out passageways, disappearing into the darkness.

Carefully and as quietly as he could, Bertie climbed up the last few steps onto the floor and advanced in the direction of the window he had seen lighted on his previous visit. *It was obviously down this passageway*, he thought. Peering ahead, he could see no sign of any lights this time; all appeared in darkness. He moved slowly along the passage. The room he had seen lighted would be the last one on the right, he reasoned, picturing the outside of the building as he had last encountered it.

When he got to the door, Bertie carefully turned the handle and eased the door open. It was a small room, and seemed to be an office. There was nothing unusual about it that he could see, as he slowly swung the lantern light around. There was a pewter plate resting on the desk with what looked like the remains of a sandwich on it. His light briefly flashed over the window. The warehouse was on a back road and there had never been any traffic along the road when he'd been there so he was not too concerned about that.

As he stood looking around at the desk and wooden filing cabinets, he couldn't help but notice an obnoxious smell. He sniffed deeply and then regretted doing so. He wondered where the smell came from and slowly moved farther into the room. He looked behind and under the desk, alongside the filing cabinet, even into the empty wastepaper basket. And then he saw an old metal bucket standing on the floor in a far corner of the room. As he approached it he knew it was the source of the mephitic odor. Peering inside, he saw that the bucket was half full of human excrement; it had been used as a privy and had not been emptied. Backing away rapidly, Bertie wondered what that could mean. Surely there was a proper privy either inside or just outside the building? Or did the person who used the office have some physical problem that necessitated immediate relief? But if that was the case, surely a regular emptying of the bucket would be in order.

Bertie retraced his steps along the passageway. As he neared the end of it, and approached the staircase, he heard someone entering the building below. Someone big and heavy started up the stairs and Bertie looked around frantically for some sort of weapon. He hadn't expected to meet anyone and least of all to have to defend himself. He saw a small crowbar leaning against the wall, alongside an opened wooden crate, and moved forward to get it.

As Bertie crouched, with crowbar in hand, a large bald head appeared, attached to the man coming up the stairs.

"Arnold!" Bertie hissed. "What the devil are you doing here? You gave me a proper start and no mistake!"

"You all right, Bertie?"

"Yes, of course I'm all right."

"Only, I saw your signal and came as fast as I could."

"You saw my signal? What are you talking about?"

"You flashed your light on the window. I thought you must be calling for help."

Bertie gave a great sigh. "I'm sorry, Arnold. You're right. The light did flash across the window but I didn't think it would matter. That was good of you."

"Did you find what you were looking for? Is the boy here?"

"No." Bertie shook his head. "No, he's not here. But there's evidence that he's been in this place; probably kept here for a while but now moved somewhere else."

"Where would that be, Bertie?"

"Ah! That I don't know, Arnold. Looks like we're back to square one."

Inspector Moss hurried along Paternoster Row. He glanced up, as he always did at this spot on the route, at the huge dome of St. Paul's Cathedral, dwarfing all about it. An Anglican cathedral, designed by the famous Sir Christopher Wren, it was built on Ludgate Hill, the highest point of the City of London. The building dated from the seventeenth century and was actually the fifth cathedral to be built on that site since the first one made its appearance in 604 A.D.

The inspector looked on the cathedral as the true emblem of London; more so than Westminster Abbey or the Houses of Parliament, or the relatively recent Nelson's Column. He didn't really know why he felt that way. He had certainly never stopped to examine his thoughts and feelings but he just found something very satisfying and comforting about the building. Besides, he'd once been caned at school for not remembering who it was who designed it.

Penny Court was to the north of the great building and the inspector had also come to find that particular little house, at number twenty-seven, to be satisfying and comforting. Not that he would ever say as much to Bertram or Nellie, of course.

Campbell Moss had never married. As a young man, growing up just outside Glasgow in his native Scotland, he had had a brief flirtation with the daughter of the Kirk's minister but that nonsense had been swiftly beaten out of him. Ruefully he considered the fact that most of his major lessons in life had been endorsed by sharp emphasis on his posterior. He still found it uncomfortable to sit for long periods at his Scotland Yard desk.

"Campbell! How nice to see you." Nellie greeted him warmly, as usual, as she opened the door. He went inside, automatically finding his way down to the kitchen where Bertie sat at his usual place at the kitchen table.

"Ah! The very man I wanted to see," said Bertie. "Arnold, make way for Scotland Yard."

Arnold, without taking his eyes off his inevitable newspaper, slid across to another chair so that the policeman could sit beside Bertie.

"I want to thank you for letting me know about the evidence in Lawson's warehouse," said Moss, sitting down and stretching his long legs under the table. Isobel came and put a steaming cup of tea in front of him. "Of course, we've no real hard evidence that the boy was there, but from what you say it seems pretty certain to me."

"And to me," agreed Bertie. "The big question is, where is he now?"

"Here's an interesting item," said Arnold, to no one in particular.

"Not now, Arnold," said Nellie, who was half listening to the conversation between Bertie and Campbell, while cleaning the silverware. Isobel regained her seat opposite Nellie and took up the other polishing cloth.

"No, this is something you want to know," said her brother.

She sighed. "All right."

They all looked at the big man, who held the newspaper up in front of his face so that he couldn't see the eyes focused on him. He began to read.

"*Mr. Lawson's acquisition of the De* . . . De-Dee . . ."

"De Dion-Bouton," suggested Bertie.

"What he said," continued Arnold. "*Mr. Lawson's acquisition of the 'whatever' manufacturing rights opens the doors for employment at Mr. Lawson's factory near Finsbury Market.*" He lowered the paper. "Is that the Lawson I think it is and, if so, did you know that he had a factory near Finsbury Market, Bertie?"

Bertie and the inspector both spoke together. "No!"

"Well spotted, Arnold," said Nellie.

"Yes," agreed Bertie. "What else does it say, Arnold?"

"Just talks about starting to build these Froggy vehicles," he said. "Nothing more about the factory."

Moss had out his little blue notebook and was writing feverishly. "Near Finsbury Market. Does it give an address?"

Arnold ran his finger down the article, finally stopping near the end of it. "Sun Street, it says. "Off Bishopsgate."

"That's not too far from his warehouse," said Bertie, excitedly. "I guess you'd go up the Minories and then Houndsditch."

"I'll get on it at the yard and see what's what."

"Do you think he might have moved the boy there?" asked Nellie.

"We won't know until we look!"

"But how many places does he have?" asked Arnold. "Do we have to look in all of them?"

There was a long silence.

"Yeah!" It was Isobel who spoke, with a wide grin on her face.

"You know, she's right," said Bertie. "If we're to find that boy, yes, we do need to look in every possible place."

"Then let's get on it," said the inspector pushing away the cup of tea, with some reluctance, and getting to his feet again. "I can get the boys at the Yard and see what other properties our Mr. Lawson might own and then we'll systematically go through them all. But we'll start with this one."

Bertie got up and Arnold scrambled to his feet as well.

"Come on Arnold," said Bertie. "We may well have to split up to do this. We'll need every one of us eventually."

"What about me?" asked Nellie.

"And . . ." Isobel started to say, but Nellie gave her a look that silenced her right away.

"We'll keep you in reserve," said Bertie to his wife. "If we need more eyes on places as we progress, I'll definitely call on you."

The Lawson factory on Sun Street was a large, three-storey, brick building with a slate roof. The windows along the sides looked as though they had never been cleaned throughout the life of the building, and a long length of battered guttering hung down from the west side of the roof. But for all that Bertie, Arnold, and the inspector found it very busy. A line of men stretched from the front doors of the building almost to the gates leading out onto Sun Street. Obviously word of possible employment had been picked up by many of London's great unemployed. There was some jostling and pushing but generally the queue kept in order. The trio of Scotland Yard Policeman and Penny Court Enquirers stood at the entrance gates and surveyed the scene.

"I can't see that he'd have the child here. Not with all of this going on," said the inspector.

"I don't know." Bertie tugged at his mustache. "This could be a very good distraction."

"Well, where would he keep the boy?"

"The top floor, I would imagine." Bertie pointed. "Look, there's a wooden outside stairway up the far side of the building. It has landings at the different levels. I wouldn't mind betting that if I was to get up that, up to the top floor, and then get inside . . ."

"How are you going to do that, Bertie?" asked Arnold. "With all this stuff going on here, how would you even get to the stairs?"

"My thoughts too," added Moss.

Bertie studied the scene and then smiled. "You know, I think with all this 'stuff' going on, as you put it, Arnold, I should find it easy to slip by and climb up."

"We could make a diversion!" said the inspector eagerly, now smiling. "Me and Arnold could join the end of the line and then start a fight . . ."

"A fight?" Arnold sounded uncertain, even though he towered over the tall policeman.

"Just a pretend one," said Bertie. "More noise than anything."

"Right!" said the inspector.

To Bertie, slipping past the crowd and ducking around the corner of the building, it sounded a very phony disagreement. Arnold sounded as though he was reading lines from a play, while inspector Moss did more growling and shouting threats than anything else, but eventually the policeman swung a dangerous looking punch that completely missed Arnold but somehow caused the big man to lose his footing and fall to the ground. That was enough for many in the queue to gather around and cheer them on and Bertie felt safe running across to the bottom of the stairs and starting to climb.

As he climbed, the shouting died down and it seemed that any excitement was quickly over, but it had been enough to distract everyone from Bertie's early actions. He climbed on upwards, his face grim with determination.

At the top floor landing, Bertie tried the door. It was not locked, presumably because the stairs had to be available for exit in case of fire. He turned the handle and tried to ease open the door but apparently it had been many years since it had been asked to move. It opened no more than six inches and then stuck. Bertie tugged and pulled but it wouldn't move. He put his ear to the narrow opening and listened. Not a sound.

With grim determination, Bertie grasped the door handle with both hands and raised his foot to the door jamb at the same level. Then he heaved backwards, lifting the other leg as well so that he had both feet braced against the door frame as he heaved on the door itself. For a long moment nothing happened, as he strained and pulled. Then, slowly, the door started to move open but with a loud, screeching noise that echoed off the rooftops all around the building. Bertie dropped his legs and stopped pulling. The ear-splitting noise ceased and he listened to see if there was any response from inside the building. All remained quiet. The door was now just far enough ajar to allow him to squeeze through, which he did.

Bertie found himself in a dim corridor running alongside the outer wall of the building. There were no lights, the only illumination coming through the begrimed windows at periodic intervals along the wall. He stood there wondering which way to go. Suddenly his mind was made up for him. To his right, a short distance along the passageway, a door opened and gaslight streamed into the dim hallway. A dark-haired man emerged, facing back into the room and addressing someone inside.

"You get that food down yer and stop belly-aching, kid, if yer knows what's good for yer. I ain't afraid to take me belt off to yer, yer know!"

He turned away, ready to close the door, when he saw Bertie. Bertie immediately recognized the pock-marked face of Thomas Squire, and started towards him at a run. Squire slammed the door and turned to face Bertie. A high-pitched wailing started issuing from inside the room.

"Who have you got in there, Squire?" demanded Bertie, sliding to a halt in front of the man.

Squire immediately brought his fists up in a pugilistic stance. Bertie took a step back.

"That's Edward Butler's boy Eric, isn't it?"

"What's it to you?" sneered Squire. "I ain't saying 'oo it is."

"You kidnapped the child," persisted Bertie. "And murdered his father. You'll hang for that, you know."

"I don't know what you're talking about. 'oo the 'ell are you anyway? You ain't no copper."

"No. No, I'm not a policeman. But there's a Scotland Yard inspector downstairs. You are caught, Mr. Squire. And there's no getting away."

"Oh, no?"

Squire suddenly lunged forward, swinging his fists. A punch landed on Bertie's shoulder, sending him spinning against the wall and then sliding to the floor. Squire jumped over him, kicking at Bertie as he went. His foot caught the same shoulder and Bertie cried out in pain. Squire ran for the partially opened outer door and tried to fling it wide, but it was still locked firmly in position.

"Devil take you!" Squire shouted, and kicked hard at the door. It gave another inch or so, enough for the man to squeeze through and Bertie heard his feet pounding away down the stairs.

With one hand on his shoulder, and wincing at the pain, Bertie got to his feet and moved to the door. Sliding through himself, he looked over the side and saw Arnold and the inspector advancing on the bottom of the stairs. Squire was still running down them.

"Get him!" Bertie shouted down to his friends. "I've got the boy up here."

Chapter Twenty-Four

"I got the boy back to his mother," said Bertie. "She was so delighted to have him safe, it quite brought a tear to my eye." He sat with Inspector Moss in the inspector's office at Scotland Yard.

"We're holding Squire at H Division in Whitechapel," said the policeman. "He's squealing! He claims it was all Lawson's doing and he was just being paid to do the dirty work."

"Not a big surprise, I suppose," said Bertie.

"He admits to being the one who abducted the boy for Lawson but denies knowing anything about Butler's murder. Says that wasna' part of Lawson's plan and he doesna' know how it could have happened."

"So what was the plan?"

"According to Squire, it seems Lawson knew he was getting the deal with De Dion-Bouton and knew that he could well use Butler's carburetor when he started producing the vehicles. So he planned to hold the boy for ransom in order to get the plans. Leastways, that's Squire's version of it."

"And Lawson himself?" asked Bertie.

The inspector shook his head. "We canna' find the man. He seems to have done a bunk. I thought he'd be at the factory interviewing all those men who had gone there looking for work, but he'd left that up to a manager. Fellow by the name of Tattersall. No record."

"Did this Tattersall say where Lawson is?"

Moss sighed. "I don't know how the man became a manager, if that's what he truly is! He could write down names and knew his numbers but that was about it, I think. He had no idea where Lawson might be or when he'd be back . . . if ever. I've got a bulletin out to all stations and to the ports. He could do a bunk to the Continent, I suppose."

"He might try travelling to the De Dion-Bouton people, wherever they are," said Bertie.

"Aye! I know." Another sigh from the inspector. "We'll want him for questioning on the murder of Butler, though we're keeping Mr. Squire for that right now. At the very least Lawson is wanted as accessory for kidnapping and murder. One of the two of them killed Butler, I'm sure."

"We still have the two mysteries," said Bertie. Inspector Moss cocked an eyebrow. "Where are the plans and where is the gold?"

"That's true enough. Any ideas, Bertram?"

"I did have one regarding the plans," said Bertie. "I'm sending Arnold off to check on something for me. It may lead to what we want."

Inspector Moss chuckled to himself. "So you're not going to tell me, are you?"

Bertie smiled. "I may be completely wrong," he said. "I don't want to make a fool of myself."

The bar at *The Printer's Imp* was busy but Bertie and Taffy had managed to get a table. Bertie took pleasure in paying for the drinks, since Taffy had paid the last time they were there, when Bertie was newly out of work.

"You must be doing all right then, is it?" said Taffy, sipping his Newcastle Brown and leaving a line of foam on his mustache.

"So far so good." Bertie took a drink from his pint of Black Eagle porter. "I've managed to keep busy . . . and out of Nellie's hair!"

"Thank you for the details of finding the kidnapper. I appreciate that. We got it into the last edition."

"You're very welcome, Taffy. But we are still working on the murders. Inspector Moss thinks he's got Butler's murderer – Thomas Squire; the same man who kidnapped the boy – but I'm not comfortable with that."

"Oh?" Taffy licked the foam from his mustache.

"Squire just doesn't seem the type," said Bertie.

Taffy chuckled. "And what is 'the type', Bertie? You know as well as I do that murderers come in all shapes and sizes and the most unlikely people do the deed."

"Oh yes, of course I know that," protested Bertie. "But I don't know about this . . . perhaps I'm picking up Arnold's intuition thing!" He sipped his drink. "I would put my money on Lawson. He could have killed Butler while Squire was nabbing the boy and Squire wouldn't even have known about it. Butler was garroted so there would have been no blood on Lawson's hands."

"And you think he killed the colonel as well? What's the connection there then, boy?"

"No." Bertie shook his head. "No, I do think there's a connection between the two murders but I don't think Lawson is it. It's very frustrating! There is a connection, I'm sure, but Lawson isn't it."

"And yet you think Lawson killed Butler?"

Bertie stared into his drink for a moment. "He seems the most likely so far. But I may be quite wrong on it."

"Bertie!"

Bertie and Taffy turned around at the shout. Arnold was to be seen making his way through the crowd towards their table. He waved to them and then almost knocked a drink out of a man's hands. The man, whom Taffy knew worked at the nearest knackers' yard, came to his feet, his hand already made into a fist, but then he saw how tall Arnold was and sat down again. Arnold patted his shoulder, apologized, and moved on.

"Arnold! What are you doing here?" asked Bertie.

"Nell sent me to find you," said Arnold. He nodded to Taffy and then studied what they were drinking. "What's that you've got then, Bertie? Porter?"

"Black Eagle," said Bertie. He sighed and, reaching into his pocket, pulled out a coin and gave it to Arnold. "What did Nellie want?"

"Oh! Just let me get myself a drink and then I'll tell you." And Arnold was off towards the bar, moving much faster than when he had first come in.

"Smarter than he looks," murmured Bertie.

"Oh?"

"Yes. If Nellie sent him here after me, it was to fetch me home, for whatever reason. But if Arnold had said that right away, he knew he wouldn't have been allowed to go and get a drink."

"Ah!" Taffy nodded appreciatively and sipped his ale.

When Arnold was back and seated – Bertie noted that his brother-in-law had not volunteered any change from the price of his drink – he beamed at the Welshman.

"How are you this fine day, Mr. Lloyd?"

"I am well, thank you, boy."

"Come on, Arnold," said Bertie. "Why did Nellie send you here after me? Does she want me home?"

Arnold took a long drink, wiped his mouth with the back of his hand, and returned the tankard to the table. "Ah, that's good! Yes, Bertie. She wants you to get back home. We have a visitor."

"A visitor?"

"It's that young woman who was nearly killed. The one that fell into the river."

"Emily Ardsley?"

"The very one."

Bertie began to get angry. "Now see here, Arnold. If Miss Ardsley came all the way to Penny Court it must be for something important. Instead of lollygagging about and spending my money on ale, you might have said she was there the moment you came in."

Arnold looked suitably crestfallen. "I'm sorry, Bertie. You are right, of course. I don't know what came over me." He pushed his tankard away.

"Oh, go on and get that down you," said Bertie. "Did you walk here or come by cab?"

"I walked."

"Then we'd better take a cab back, you've already been taking too long." He turned to Taffy. "I'm sorry, Taffy, but this may be something to do with the colonel's death, or who knows what. I'll have to get back . . . just as soon as Arnold, here, gets outside that porter!" He stood up.

Arnold gulped down his ale and also came to his feet.

"Don't worry, Bertie, my boy. We can talk another day." Taffy waved them away and went back to sipping his own drink.

Nellie and Emily were sitting chatting in the drawing room, each with a cup of tea. Isobel led Bertie and Arnold into the room and then managed to hover by the door without actually leaving the room.

"Miss Ardsley! So very nice to see you again," said Bertie.

"I was just saying to Mrs. Hawkins, that I do hope I am not intruding," said Emily.

"Not at all. Not at all. How may I be of service?"

"Miss Ardsley has made a discovery about her grandfather's watch," said Nellie, unable to contain herself. Then, realizing that she should have let Emily speak for herself, she leaned forward and poured tea for her husband and her brother. Arnold found himself a seat close beside Bertie.

"I don't really know whether or not it is important," said Emily. "So I thought I had better come and verify it with the expert."

"Oh, I don't know about that." Bertie felt himself actually blush. He wasn't used to receiving compliments from young ladies.

"I had decided to polish the watch," Emily continued, "and in doing so I opened the back of it – where you so cleverly discovered that piece of paper – and was about to apply my cloth to the inner surface when I noticed something."

"Oh?"

"At first I thought that it was scratched and prepared to rub it hard, but then I saw that there was a pattern to the scratches."

"I'm not sure I follow you, Miss Ardsley," said Bertie.

"Oh dear! I am not good at describing things," she said. She dug into the reticule on her lap. "Which is why I thought it best to bring the watch with me to show you. Here, Mr. Hawkins. See what you think."

Bertie took the watch and looked at it. Arnold leaned forward for a better view. Bertie again admired it's design and the heaviness of the gold, once again conscious of his own old, but trusty, silver watch hanging from his waistcoat. He turned over the gold watch and managed to insert a thumbnail into the crack and pried open the back. This time it opened easily on its hinge and, looking in, Bertie was aware of what looked like minor scratches on the inner surface. He had been unaware of them before, when his attention had been all on the hidden piece of paper. He reached into his pocket and pulled out his spectacles.

"I thought perhaps it was writing," continued Emily. "But then I saw it wasn't letters scratched there."

"No," said Bertie, holding it close and turning to catch the light. "No. It's numbers."

"Numbers?" echoed Nellie and Arnold together.

"Yes. A series of numbers; must be about thirty or forty of them. Very small and very lightly scratched into the surface."

"Engraved, is that?" asked Arnold.

"No." Bertie shook his head. "No, they look as though they have been scratched into the watch back with something sharp. Perhaps a tie-pin, or similar?"

"Into the metal?" Nellie sounded surprised.

"Gold is a very soft metal," explained Bertie. "You can see how the colonel's engraved initials on the front of the watch have worn down and could soon disappear, just from regular handling. No, these numbers have been intentionally scratched into the gold. Very interesting."

"So it's not something you could simply read?" said Emily. "Why would that be?"

"I would guess that it was done by the colonel, your grandfather, at the same time that he hid the paper here. I would further guess that there is a connection between these numbers and what was written on that paper."

"To do with the deal between Butler and Benz?" asked Arnold.

"Precisely." Bertie turned to Emily. "Miss Ardsley, may I keep this watch for a day or so? I promise you I will guard it faithfully, but I will need to work on this . . . this cipher."

"Oh!" Isobel gasped excitedly, and then clamped a hand to her mouth. Nellie frowned at her but did not say anything.

"Why of course, Mr. Hawkins. I thought perhaps you may need to do that. Please take all the time you need. I know it is in good hands." Emily rose, and Bertie and Arnold quickly did the same. "And now I must be getting home. I have done my duty . . . to my grandfather, I believe. He obviously scratched the watch to leave a message, whether to myself or to someone else, we will have to discover. I look forward to learning what you find, Mr. Hawkins."

Arnold stood uncertainly on the short platform at Erith station, watching the train he had arrived on steam off into the distance. He pulled out his notebook and wrote down 12s/0d for the return fare . . . Nell would want to know that. He was only fifteen miles from Charing Cross Station but it seemed like a different world. It was a beautiful day, for a change, and the sun felt good on the top of his bald head. He ran a hand over it as though to be sure it was still fully intact.

Erith was close to Dartford, in Kent, just before the railway line crossed the Cray River, which ran towards the Thames. It was a pleasant little village at the base of a wooded hill. Centerpiece was a picturesque ivy-covered church. Close by the church Arnold discovered *The Ploughman* inn. As if to nudge him, the church clock chimed the noon hour and Arnold headed into the public house.

After a pint of porter and a ploughman's lunch, the big man got down to business. From the innkeeper he got directions and walked the length of the High Street to a stone cottage with a matching stone el-barn attached to it. A small, hand-painted sign on the barn door said *F. P. Shuttleworth Works*. He knocked on the door and went in.

Nellie urged Bertie to decipher the scratched numbers as soon as possible, but he told her he had decided to first share the discovery with Campbell Moss.

"I thought you were working against the police?" said Nellie.

"Not exactly *against* them . . . Well, all right, yes. I suppose that was my original incentive." Bertie paused on his way out the door. "I don't know. I've come to rather like Campbell.

Not the police as a whole," he quickly added. "Just Campbell. And I'm certainly not going to let him see the numbers or anything like that. I just thought I'd let him know that a cipher was there, to make the whole case that much more interesting."

"Sort of, waving it under his nose, then?"

Bertie smiled. "That's a good way of putting it, Nell." He paused a moment longer. "That wouldn't be construed as 'gloating', would it?"

She smiled. "You know very well it would! Now be off with you."

"Ah! Bertram. Good!"

Inspector Moss glanced up briefly and then went back to the papers on his desk. It was almost, thought Bertie, as though he was expected.

"Sit down, Bertram. Make yourself at home."

"Make myself at home in Scotland Yard?" Bertie couldn't help chuckling, thinking of how his original derision of the police had brought him there. "Well, that's very good of you, Campbell." He took a pile of papers from the chair and moved it to the floor, so that he could sit. He placed his bowler hat on top of the pile. "What are you up to?" he asked the inspector.

"Most interesting. Just let me make a note here." Moss scribbled something in the margin of the paper in front of him and then sat back and looked at Bertie, a satisfied smile on his face.

"You look like the cat that got the cream," said Bertie.

"In a way I suppose I am. And the cream was worth waiting for." He reached forward and lifted the top paper from the folder he had been working on. "Now listen to this. Our wanted man, Mr. Harold John Lawson, in his younger days attended St. John's College, Cambridge. He did not graduate. He was asked to leave – if we can put it politely – because of numerous gambling debts he had incurred and, more especially – listen to this, Bertram – for trying to fix the Oxford and Cambridge boat race!"

"What?" Bertram was aghast. The annual boat race between the Oxford University Boat Club and the Cambridge University Boat Club was rowed, on the Thames, between competing eights every spring. The first race had been in 1829 and had then been held annually since 1856. It had become a national tradition. To interfere with it seemed to Bertie to be almost sacrilegious.

"But wait!" Moss held up his hand. "There's more. Mr. Lawson had a fellow conspirator, also at St. John's College, who was also asked to leave." The policeman waited a moment to build the suspense. "That conspirator was none other than our Mr. Cedric Bromley!"

"The colonel's man?"

"The same!"

"Well, I'm . . ."

"Aye! I know." The inspector sat back and looked at Bertie.

After a long while, to digest what the inspector had said, Bertie ventured, "Are they in cahoots, do you think, Campbell? Working together?"

"It would tie together the two murders, would it not?" The inspector stretched, leaning back as far as his chair would allow, tipping it onto its back legs. "Though I'm damned if I can see where it's all leading."

"Well, perhaps I may have stumbled on a clue," said Bertie. "Or rather, had a clue presented to me, by Miss Emily Ardsley."

"The young lady who took the dive off Blackfriars Bridge?"

"The same. She came to my house, bringing with her the gold watch that her grandfather left her."

"Oh?"

"Though if you recall, he didn't just leave it to her, in the usual sense, he *sent* it to her, by post, when she was with Squire."

"And?" The inspector let the chair bang back down onto all four legs.

"I think the colonel sent it to her to protect what was in it."

"You mean that piece of paper? I thought we . . ."

"No!" Bertie couldn't help feeling a trifle smug. "There was something else in it. Nothing tangible, like the piece of paper. There was a message scratched into the inside case."

"Go on." Moss leaned forward across his desk, his attention focused on Bertie.

"To me it looks as though he had taken his tie pin, or something similar, and scratched a message into the soft gold of the case and then popped it in the post to his granddaughter so that no one – or perhaps someone in particular – would not find it."

"Someone like Bromley, you mean."

"That was my thinking."

"When would he have done that?"

"While on the train, or somewhere along his journey back from Germany. And then posted it from a pillar box on a platform at some station the train stopped at on its way to Victoria Station."

"All right, Bertram, so what does it say?'

"Ah!" Bertie tugged at his mustache for a moment, seeing that the other man was hanging on his words. He smiled at the inspector. "We do not know what it says . . . yet, anyway."

"What do you mean, you don't know what it says?" Moss exploded.

"The message is written in code. More precisely, in a cipher. I have yet to decipher it."

"So what's stopping you, Bertram?" The inspector squinted his eyes as he studied his friend. "Do you need the help of Scotland Yard for this?"

"No." Bertie shook his head. "No, I don't think so. I'm something of a puzzle fanatic . . . these new crosswords, and all that type of thing. I think it will be fun finding out what it says."

"Fun?" Inspector Moss came to his feet and started pacing back and forth in the small space behind his desk, scratching the top of his head. "Fun? This is part of a murder investigation, Mr.

Hawkins, if I may remind you. This is no time for
fun!"

"Oh, I don't know," replied Bertie, unfazed.
"The message has to be deciphered so why not have
fun doing it? That's my thought, anyway." He
looked up at the inspector, his eyes twinkling.
"Don't worry, Campbell. I'll let you know what it
says just as soon as I find out. And I promise you
that if I have any difficulty, then – and only then –
I'll let your ubiquitous Scotland Yard in on the
process."

Inspector Moss grumbled and grunted and
sat down again. He glared at Bertie through lowered
eyebrows. "You can press a friendship too far, you
know."

"Indeed I do," replied Bertie amiably. "But
just to soften things, as it were, I thought I'd let you
know that I have managed to locate Mr. Butler's
long lost plans. Those for which, probably, he was
killed."

"What?" The policeman was on his feet
again, this time leaning forward, hands gripping the
edges of his desk, and glaring at Bertie. "You've
found the plans?"

Bertie couldn't help smiling. "Well, it
seemed that Scotland Yard wasn't going to locate
them, so . . ."

Chapter Twenty-Five

Inspector Moss settled himself in what was quickly becoming his usual chair at the Hawkins's dinner table. At Bertie's bidding, he had dropped by after concluding his official affairs for the day at Scotland Yard. He was eager to see the coded message in the gold watch and to hear the details of Bertie's recovery of the plans for the Butler Petrol Cycle.

"I'll show you the watch when we get through Nellie's roast beef, roast potatoes, and Yorkshire pudding," said Bertie, taking the meat platter from Isobel and putting it down on the table in front of himself. He soon displayed his prowess with the carving knife and all was quiet for a few minutes as the plates were distributed by Isobel and everyone helped themselves to the mouthwatering meal.

"So tell me about the plans," said the policeman at last. "You can show me the watch after we've eaten but I confess I can contain myself no longer, Bertram. Where were the Petrol Cycle plans and how did you find them?"

"They were in Kent," piped up Arnold.

"Kent?" The inspector's knife and fork stopped their rapid movement.

"Do you recall those visitor's cards we retrieved from Butler's residence when we first went to view the scene of the crime?" asked Bertie.

"The ones that you somehow 'acquired' while you were there, without telling me?"

"That's neither here nor there," Bertie dismissed. "You do recall them, then?"

"Aye, I do."

"One of them was from a company in Erith, Kent. The Frank B. Shuttleworth company, to be precise."

Inspector Moss nodded, once again busy on his roast beef.

"Well," continued Bertie. "I was looking at the article about Butler's vehicle, in the *Strand Magazine*. It mentioned that the cycle was then being built. Well, it struck me that if it was being built somewhere, then obviously it had to be built from the plans."

"Of course!" The inspector's knife and fork clattered onto his plate. "If it was being built, then the person or people building it *had* to have the plans! Brilliant!" He beamed at Bertie in undisguised admiration. "Now why didn't I – why didn't the Yard – think of that?"

"Because . . ." began Isobel, who had been gathering up plates.

"Isobel, no!" interrupted Nellie. "Let's not go there."

The maid gave a long, audible sigh followed by a sniff, and continued with what she was doing.

"I went back to look at those cards," continued Bertie, "and noticed the one from Frank Shuttleworth, listed as a manufacturer. I then had Arnold pay the company a visit."

"I told them what had happened," said Arnold. "They were building a Petrol Cycle and had been wondering why they weren't getting any further instructions from Mr. Butler. It seems they'd written a letter or two but had no response. Anyway, they let me have the plans to return to Mrs. Butler and said they'd be in touch with her."

"And you've given her the plans?" asked the inspector.

"Not yet," said Bertie. "But I intend to as soon as we clear up the matter of Karl Benz's gold. Then Kate Gildersleeves Butler can decide whether or not to honor his bid and give him the plans, or to take other steps."

The inspector nodded his head in agreement. "That makes sense," he said.

"Speaking of the gold," said Nellie. "I was wondering if the message in the watch might have something to do with that. After all, the colonel scratched the message and it was he who was bringing back the gold."

"What about Bromley?" asked the inspector. "Would the colonel have entrusted him with the money? He did send Bromley on ahead. Perhaps he sent him with the gold, Butler accepted it and then hid it, or put it away safely somewhere."

"Without telling his wife?" asked Nellie. "They were very close, it seemed. She had no knowledge of it."

"So Bromley didn't deliver it but hid it," suggested Arnold.

Bertie shook his head. "No. The man is in debt up to his collar-studs. If he'd got his hands on the gold he would have dipped into it. No, but I do think he may have been working with Lawson to try to get it."

They finished the meal and left the table to sit at ease. Isobel cleared the table and Nellie excused herself to go and help the maid in the kitchen. Bertie went to the bureau and took out Emily's gold watch. He gave it to the inspector and then sat down in the chair next to the policeman. Almost reverently, Inspector Moss opened the back and peered inside.

"Do you see what I've been talking about, Campbell?"

The inspector held it closer. "How the devil did anyone spot these marks in the first place? You could easily miss them."

"Miss Ardsley was giving the piece a polish when she noticed them," said Bertie.

"So what does it say?"

Bertie realized that the inspector couldn't really see the details without spectacles. He pulled out his own, put them on, and took back the watch.

"It's a series of numbers. Thirty-five of them, to be exact: *14.27.7.8.1.23.4.9.5.3.2. 43.5.1.10.6.1.20.4.3.26.3.2.2.4.7.33.8.6.9.2.2.37.3.4.* Now, what do you make of them, Campbell?"

"Ha!" The inspector let out a laugh. "Me and arithmetic never did go together, Bertram. I don't mind telling you that. Nay, I'm afraid you're on your own where this goes. Now, you said you're a puzzle man, if I recall. Well, here's a real puzzle for you."

"He has made a start, haven't you, Bertie?" put in Arnold, who had eased himself into one of the more comfortable chairs.

"Not so much a start, Arnold," said Bertie, his brow furrowed as he studied the numbers. "But I did manage to find a bit of background information."

"Oh?" The inspector loosened his belt a notch, as he had become accustomed to doing after one of Nellie's excellent meals.

"I thought it might be worthwhile to have a look at the colonel's background to see where he might have learned to do ciphers."

"The military, I presume," said the inspector.

"Correct. But where and why?"

"For sending dispatches!" said Arnold darkly.

"Probably," agreed Bertie. "Though this doesn't look like any code or cipher used in India when the colonel was there."

"How do you know that?" asked the inspector.

"My good friend the editor of *The Morning Post*. Obviously he doesn't know every type of code and cipher used by the army, especially those in India and elsewhere, but he does have contacts and can make a lot of assumptions that we – that I – can't make."

"So where does all that lead us?" asked Moss.

"It seems that our Colonel Sir Dennis Nigel Ardsley, before he retired from the army in 1879, had befriended a young lieutenant serving in the 13th Hussars, named Robert Baden-Powell. 'B-P', as he was known, had enhanced and honed his military scouting skills amidst the Zulu in the Natal province of South Africa, where his regiment had been posted, and where he was Mentioned in Despatches."

"What's that? 'Mentioned in Despatches'," asked Arnold.

"It's a military award for special service. A 'despatch' is an official report from a senior commander. "

"Oh."

"You were saying . . . Robert Baden-Something?" said the inspector. "B.P.?"

"Baden-Powell. Yes. Apparently the man had a bee in his bonnet about teaching what he had learned from military scouts to young men and boys at home. A sort of big brotherhood organization. Not that I think it would ever catch on."

"What's all that got to do with codes?" asked Arnold.

"Everything . . . I think," said Bertie, stroking his mustache. "I think that what we have here, in this watch, is a cipher that Colonel Ardsley may well have picked up from Lieutenant Baden-Powell."

"So what does it say?" persisted Arnold.

Bertie again raised the gold watch and its scratches and scrutinized everything through his small-lens spectacles. He was dying to load up his pipe and smoke a little Gallagher's Honeydew, but felt some sort of obligation to first try to further explain the colonel's hidden message.

"It has to be something fairly simple," he said, "because the colonel was traveling home – might well have been on the train when he did it – and would not therefore have had access to any special books or mechanical devices for code work. Most codes are too complicated to carry around in your head, so it *had* to be relatively simple."

"I'm glad you said 'relatively'," said the inspector. "It makes no sense to me; none at all."

"Well, I've looked all over the watch, using a magnifying glass, and there doesn't seem to be anything else. I've made a note of these numbers, trying to copy them down exactly as they are. I think, then, that I'll return the watch to Miss Ardsley and perhaps have a word with Sir Hugh, to see if he has any ideas." He replaced the watch in the bureau drawer and finally reached for his pipe and tobacco. "I'll let you know what I find."

The Ardsleys greeted Bertie and even, he thought, seemed pleased to see him. Soon he, Emily, Sir Hugh, Lady Claire, and the Pekinese dog were all seated in the conservatory.

"Hunter, have Marcia bring us some refreshments," said Lady Ardsley. With a lift of his beak of a nose, and the slightest inclination of his head, the footman departed.

"Thank you for returning the watch, Mr. Hawkins," said Emily. "You could have kept it longer if necessary, you know."

"Thank you, Miss Ardsley, yes. Very good of you. But I got all I needed from it." Bertie turned to Sir Hugh, withdrawing a folded sheet of paper from his pocket. "I copied down the numbers scratched inside the watch. Sir Hugh, perhaps you'd care to look at these?"

Sir Hugh popped his monocle into his eye and studied the lines of numbers. "What am I supposed to be seeing?" he asked, looking up again at Bertie.

"These are the numbers scratched into the watch case. I just wondered if they meant anything to you, my lord. I just thought it was worth asking."

"No." He shook his head and handed back the paper. "No, they don't mean a thing. What do you, yourself, make of them, Hawkins? You are the enquiry agent, after all."

"Ah, yes," said Bertie, looking down at the figures.

"They do kind of remind me of the old book code though." Sir Hugh dropped his monocle into his waistcoat pocket and settled back in his chair.

There was a tap at the door and then a maid entered bearing a large silver platter with tea for everyone. It took a few minutes for the cups and saucers to be passed around and the tiny cakes and sandwiches to be offered. Finally the maid retired.

"The old book code, you said?" Bertie looked enquiringly at Sir Hugh. "I'm afraid I am not familiar with that."

"Well, I wouldn't say that I am 'familiar' with it," admitted Sir Hugh. "All I know is that a string of figures indicates words and letters in a book. Page numbers and things like that, you know."

"I see," said Bertie, looking even harder at the list. "Now what book would that be?"

"Heavens man, I don't know!" Sir Hugh helped himself to lumps of sugar and then stirred his tea vigorously.

"Didn't they use the Bible for that?" asked Emily.

"You also know of this, Miss Ardsley?" asked Bertie.

She smiled and dimpled, shaking her head slightly. "Not really, Mr. Hawkins. Like my father, I am not familiar with it but it's something of which I've heard. Probably from my grandfather. He would often tell me fascinating bits and pieces of information. I could never remember it all."

"But you think it involved the Bible?"

She shrugged and her brow creased as she put her mind to it. "As I recall, it involved the two people – the one sending the message and the one receiving it – using the same book. Therefore it was often the Bible, since they would both have easy access to one even if they were miles apart."

Bertie looked again at the figures on the paper. He shook his head. "I'm afraid I see nothing that would indicate the Bible. No references to

Books or Chapters or Verses or anything. Not that I can recognize, that is."

"It wouldn't *have* to be the Bible," put in Lady Ardsley, as she broke off pieces of biscuit and fed them to the dog in her lap. "Would it?" she asked her daughter.

"I don't think so, mother. I think it could be done with any book so long as they both had the same one." She turned to Bertie. "May I see your list, Mr. Hawkins?"

He handed it to her and then busied himself with tea and a biscuit. Emily Ardsley, meanwhile, opened the back of the watch and then sat studying the scratching and comparing it to what Bertie had written down.

"Did I get them all right, Miss Ardsley?" he asked. "I did check them a number of times but, you never know . . ."

"Actually," she said slowly, "I do believe there is one that you might look at more closely."

"Oh?"

"The very first one," she said. She passed both watch and paper to Bertie. "Or perhaps I should say the first two. You have two numbers written down – 14 and 27 – but I'm not certain there's a dot after the first one, in the watch. It looks to me as though that's all one number – 1427. Do you see what I mean?"

Bertie took his time studying them. Sir Hugh got up from his chair and went through to the next room. He returned shortly with a magnifying glass.

"Here, Hawkins. This is a powerful glass. Got it for my butterfly collection . . . but then stopped collecting the blighters."

Bertie took the glass and studied the watch scratches. Slowly he nodded his head, eventually looking up and around at the three of them. "I do believe you are correct, Miss Ardsley. Your eyes are younger than mine but still, it was foolish of me to miss that. Yes, there is no mark between those numbers so it must be fourteen hundred and twenty-seven." He sat several minutes longer looking at the figures. "There are, then, thirty-four numbers all together. If we separate that first one, as the only four-digit number, then that leaves thirty-three characters."

"Three sets of eleven or, more likely, eleven sets of three," mused Sir Hugh. "Page, paragraph and word, or some such combination."

"I think you may well be right." Bertie nodded. "But again, from what book?"

They puzzled over it for some time before deciding to let it rest for a while. They finished their refreshment and Bertie told them of the search for, and the finding of, the kidnapped boy.

"Well done, Hawkins," enthused Sir Hugh. "I can see you are cut out for this type of pursuit."

"Thank you, my lord."

Sometime later Bertie was preparing to leave. He had looked at Sir Hugh's truncated butterfly collection, had admired the Pekinese, and given his views on the possible future of the automobile. He received his bowler hat, gloves and cane from the stone-faced Hunter and was about to take his leave, when Emily came rushing in from the hallway.

"Mr. Hawkins! I do believe I might have solved the conundrum," she cried.

Chapter Twenty-Six

"What conundrum is that, my dear?" asked Lady Ardsley.

"The book! Which book grandfather used for his code."

"Really?" Bertie felt excitement course through his body. Sir Hugh came to stand beside him to see what Emily had to say.

"I was putting away grandfather's watch. As you know, father, I keep it in a velvet bag and set it on top of grandfather's copy of his Berlin Treaty."

"That massive thing he insisted on carrying everywhere he went?" said Lady Ardsley, sounding slightly exasperated, thought Bertie.

"He was justly proud of it," put in Sir Hugh.

"It passed through my head that it was always referred to as a 1,458-page tome," went on Emily. "Then I thought of that first number that he had scratched: 1427."

"Of course!" cried Bertie, interrupting her in his excitement. "How many books have 1,427 pages or more? And the colonel would have had the treaty with him on his journey home. That first number is the clue, both to the book and to the page of the book that he used. Oh, well done, Miss Ardsley!"

She blushed and lowered her eyes, but was obviously excited.

"Well done," echoed Sir Hugh. He turned to the butler who still hovered in the background. "Hunter. Take Mr. Hawkins' things again. He's not leaving right away. Right, Bertram? Oh, and Hunter, when you've done that, go with Miss Emily and carry down a large book for her. Bring it to the library."

They were soon all gathered in the library, with the massive Berlin Treaty on a lectern. The others gave way to Bertie, who opened the book near its end.

"Here we are," he said. "Page one thousand four hundred and twenty-seven. My word! Just glancing down it looks like a lot of legal terms."

"Is page 1,427 correct?" asked Lady Ardsley. "I mean, could not those first numbers in each group be different page numbers?"

"I think not, Lady Ardsley," said Bertie. "Otherwise why give that one particular page to start with? No, I think the sets of three are for lines, words in those lines, and then letters in those words."

"So each set of three is just one letter?" asked Emily. "I thought each would lead to a whole word and then we'd get a long message?"

"That thought had crossed my mind," said Sir Hugh.

Bertie shook his head. "I don't think that's the case here," he said. "I could see how that could be done, but then – if all were on one page – it would only need two numbers in each set: one for the line and the second for the word."

"My head is spinning," said Lady Ardsley.

"Let's just try it," said Bertie. "If it doesn't work, then we'll think further on it."

"Agreed," grunted Sir Hugh. "Emily, take a piece of paper and write down the pertinent material as Mr. Hawkins finds it."

"Yes, Papa."

"Would you, then, Sir Hugh, be kind enough to call out the sets of numbers and I will find them on the page?" said Bertie.

Sir Hugh adjusted his monocle, peered at the numbers and called off the first set. "Seven, eight, one."

Bertie counted down lines from the top of the page. "Seven lines down. The eighth word – hmm! *The*. That's simple enough. So the first letter of that, and of our message, is *T*."

"Got it," said Emily.

"Next, 23,4,9," said Sir Hugh.

"Line 23," Bertie again counted down. "Word four, ninth letter is *R*."

"This is rather fun!" said Lady Ardsley, rocking the Pekinese in her arms.

"5, 3, 2."

"The letter is *A*."

So they continued to the end.

"So what do we have?" They all turned to Emily.

"*T.R.A.N.T.S.F.O.L.L.Y,*" she read. "That's 'Trant's Folly' is it not?"

"Trant's Folly, by Jove!" exclaimed Sir Hugh. "It's been a long time since I heard that name."

"Never heard of it!" exclaimed Inspector Moss, when told of Trant's Folly.

"Well, I'm not altogether surprised," responded Bertie. "Apparently it's on private land – land belonging to the fourth Earl of Egremont, as it happens – and is a place the colonel used to take Sir Hugh when he was a child. It seems it's built like an ancient ruin and is on an eyot in the middle of an artificial lake on the Earl's property."

"What's an eyot?" asked Arnold.

"It's an island."

"So why don't they say 'island'?"

Bertie ignored him. "A lot of rich landowners built what they term 'follies', especially last century and early this century. They have no real purpose; they're just ornamental. This one apparently looks somewhat like a half-ruined section of a castle."

"Barmy!" muttered Arnold.

"So where is this ruined castle located?" asked the inspector.

"Near Horsham . . . which is on the London, Chatham, and Dover Line *coming up from Brighton*," said Bertie triumphantly. "The colonel could have hopped off the train there, done whatever he had to do with the gold at the folly, and then got back on the next train continuing up to Victoria Station. It's about thirty miles from London and less than twenty from Brighton."

"Got off and hid the gold, you mean?" asked Nellie.

They were once again all gathered in the kitchen at 27 Penny Court; sitting around the kitchen table with hot cups of cocoa in front of them. Bertie had brought them up to date with what had transpired at the Ardsleys.

"Cor! Buried treasure!" exclaimed Isobel.

"Now don't you go getting too comfortable, my girl," said Nellie. "There's fires to be lit in the bedrooms and hot water bottles to be filled."

The maid grimaced and buried her face in her cocoa cup.

"So what's the plan?" asked the inspector. "When do we go and search the place?"

"Strike while the iron's hot," said Nellie.

"I agree," said Bertie. "In fact, I have arranged for us to go there tomorrow – early morning train out of Victoria. Miss Ardsley was very keen to accompany us and I didn't have the heart to refuse her. Besides, she's our link, as it were, to going onto the Earl of Egremont's property. She will meet us at Horsham station."

"So who is going?" asked Nellie. "I can't. I have the shopping to do tomorrow. Isobel and I have to go to Covent Garden early in the morning."

"I'm ready," said Arnold.

"Well, that's pretty much as I thought," said Bertie. "It will be Campbell, Arnold and myself, with Emily Ardsley."

"We'd better prepare a hamper for you," said Nellie, getting to her feet. "Come on, Isobel. Before you do the bedrooms you can help me get together something for them."

It was an overcast morning, with a drizzle of rain. The temperature was not so cold that there was any need for heavy coats, but umbrellas were definitely in order. Bertie, the inspector, and Arnold, carrying the picnic hamper, got off the train and found Emily Ardsley awaiting them in the station's cramped waiting room.

"My father found out that the earl is away somewhere on the Yorkshire moors right now," said Emily. "So we have no need to fear interruptions."

"But it is all right for us to go there?" asked Moss.

"Oh, yes." Emily nodded and smiled brightly. "The Ardsleys have been friendly with the Egremonts for years. We haven't seen anything of each other for a while, but there will certainly be no problems with us going to the folly."

There was a lone carriage waiting outside the station. They commissioned it and set off along the road through the little market town of Horsham. On the far side they left the banks of the River Arun and took the road to Rusper Nunnery.

"The Nunnery is the Egremont family seat," explained Emily. "Back a few centuries – before the end of the twelfth century, I think it was – it was the Benedictine Nunnery of St. Mary Magdalene of

Rusper. There was some scandal with the prioress and a bishop in the fifteenth century, and the residents were eventually turned out of the building. That's when it came into the hands of the earls of Egremont."

"Fascinating," said the inspector, drily, looking out of the carriage window at the passing scenery. "Has anyone thought about how we're to get out to this island?"

"We will have the driver let us off by the boathouse," responded Emily. "There should be at least two or more rowboats there, which we can use."

That sounded promising to Bertie, but the boathouse was not all that he pictured. The roof was bowed downward with age and covered in moss; there were planks missing from the sides of the building, allowing glimpses of the lake water through it.

"Should we tell the carriage to wait?" asked Arnold, looking doubtfully at the structure.

"No." Bertie made the decision and waved off the coachman. The four of them stood, under umbrellas, studying the decrepit structure as the horse's hooves faded away behind them.

"Well, let's do what we came for," said Bertie, leading the way.

One of the two doors into the boathouse had sagged on its hinges to the point where it was immoveable. The other opened partway, under protest. They squeezed inside.

"Well, at least we are out of the rain," said Arnold, looking up. "I think all that moss on the roof is keeping it waterproof."

"There are the boats!" Emily pointed to two rowboats, a punt, and a canoe up on racks on the side of the building. A third rowboat was just visible, through the murky waters, as it sat on the shallow lake bottom with only the top of its seat above water.

"We won't be needing that one," murmured the inspector.

"It's shallow here," said Emily, "but then drops off quickly once you clear this little inlet where the boathouse is situated."

Bertie moved across and studied the craft on their shelves. There were oars standing stacked in a corner and three canoe paddles hung on the wall. "Do you think any of them are still watertight?" he asked, of no one in particular.

"Well, something has been out recently," said the inspector, pointing. "See? There had been something else sitting on this shelf that has been taken away."

"Perhaps the one down under water," suggested Arnold.

"Let's try the bottom rowboat," said Bertie, moving forward to it and up to the bow. "Arnold, put down that hamper and get the stern of this. We can swing it over and into the water."

With the inspector's help, they soon had the boat in the water. There were no obvious leaks.

"Put the hamper in the stern," said Bertie. "Campbell and I will row. Arnold and Miss Ardsley can sit on the seat; perhaps you'd take the tiller lines, Miss Ardsley?"

As the loaded rowboat emerged from the shelter of the boathouse, the rain tapered off and the sun broke out, fighting its way through ragged grey clouds that only a short while before had seemed to hang down to treetop height.

"Oh! I see the castle," gasped Arnold.

Both rowers paused and looked over their shoulders. Out near the center of the lake was the island. It was not large and seemed to be covered with low trees and lots of bushes. Pushing up through the shrubbery was what looked like an ancient, crenellated, stone tower attached to a section of wall that came out of nowhere and dropped off into ruin after a very short length. There had once been – or such was the appearance given – a narrower pinnacle that thrust up from the top of the tower, but that now lay on the ground as though struck down by ancient cannon fire.

"Very impressive," said the inspector.

"It looks like part of an ancient castle," agreed Bertie. "Though one wonders where the rest of it would have stood, since it's on such a small island."

"Such is the nature of a folly," laughed Emily.

The two men returned to rowing and the island tower slowly grew closer.

"With the small size of the island, it shouldn't take a lot of searching to find what we want," said Bertie, between pulls of the oars. "Do you think it will be in the ruins themselves, or might the colonel have buried the gold somewhere?"

"That's a terrible thought," grunted the inspector. "We'd have to dig up the whole island."

"Or just look to see where it had been recently dug," put in Arnold.

"Good point, Arnold," said Bertie. His brother-in-law grinned.

Nearly half an hour later they were bobbing on the surface of the lake, just off the bank of the island closest to the ruin.

"There used to be a dock," said Emily. "It may have fallen in but we should be able to espy some evidence of it."

"There's another old boat," said Arnold, pointing off to one side. "Look! Stuck in the bushes there and half sunk. Probably got left behind by the people last out here."

"There's the dock!" cried Emily. "Or what remains of it. See it?"

"I've got it," grunted the inspector. "Pull gently, Bertram. You steer us in, Miss Ardsley."

Within a few minutes they were all safely ashore, the boat's painter tied to a stick of dock and the hamper sitting safely on the grass. Bertie pulled out his pocket watch and studied it.

"What do you think? Shall we have lunch first and then spend a pleasant afternoon scouring the ruins, or shall we . . ."

"Oh, let's look first!" cried Emily, excitedly. "We've been waiting for this. I have a feeling we will find the gold quickly and then we can eat to celebrate."

"That's fine with me," said Bertie.

"And me," echoed the inspector.

They didn't ask Arnold, though he looked longingly at the picnic hamper.

It was a good two hours later that they gathered again by the remains of the dock, their search having revealed nothing. Arnold had a line of dirt across his forehead and over the top of his bald head. The inspector's bowler hat had disappeared and his thin grey hair was in disarray. Bertie had taken off his coat and his waistcoat and rolled up his shirt sleeves. Emily, although she retained her femininity, was flushed and her hair had fallen down on one side.

"Nothing!" Inspector Moss spat out the word.

"Are we sure it's here?" asked Arnold.

"No," said Bertie. "We are not. But it's the clue that the colonel left. Everything seems to point to it being here."

"I think we need to replenish our strength," said Emily. "Why don't we have some lunch and discuss it?"

They found a spot under the trees where the grass was not too wet, and emptied the hamper of pork pie, hard-boiled eggs, fresh carrots, bread, cheese, a crumble-crusted apple pie, and a bottle of wine.

"We must drink a toast to Nellie," said the inspector. "This is delightful."

Three-quarters of an hour later they were sitting back digesting their meal, when Bertie suddenly sprang up.

"Did anyone examine the top of that pinnacle that supposedly came down off the main tower?" he asked. There was silence, though they each shook their head. "If it were me hiding the gold," he continued, "I would put it somewhere 'special'; somewhere notable." He turned and started off towards the ruin.

"Wait!"

As though in complete agreement, the rest of them jumped up and followed him as he made his way to the narrow stone column lying half sunk into the ground beside the main structure.

"The very pinnacle, I think," Bertie said. He moved to the slate-covered top of the section and gasped. "Look!"

It was obvious that some of the slates had been moved or broken away, revealing a hollow section inside. It was empty.

"I think I may have that which you seek."

A voice came to them across the grass and brush, apparently coming from the direction of the surface of the lake. They all turned and rushed to the lakeside. Sitting in their boat, several yards off shore, was Cedric Bromley. He held up a dark blue canvas bag and shook it. They could distinctly hear the sound of coins rattling inside it.

"Bromley!" Bertie and the inspector spoke together.

"Cedric!" Emily's voice was plaintive.

"Sorry, Miss Ardsley. But we must all get our just rewards. Thank you for telling me of this folly."

"You told him?" Inspector Moss was incredulous.

"I had no reason not to," she said, defensively. She turned to Bertie. "Cedric called at the house shortly after you had gone, Mr. Hawkins. I was still excited about our – about your – discovery. I blurted it all out, I must admit. I had no idea . . ."

"No. No, of course you didn't," said Bertie.

"I've been stuck on this blasted island since shortly after dawn," said Bromley. "The boat I took started taking on water before I was halfway here. I'm lucky I made it. Thank you for bringing me a replacement."

"You murdered the colonel!" Bertie moved to the very edge of the dock as he made the accusation.

"Oh, yes. The old fool had been getting too full of himself; ordering me here, there and everywhere. Then, just when I thought I could get my hands on the money, I found that the wretched man had stopped on his way home and hid Benz's gold. I think he was getting suspicious of me. I didn't set out to kill him when I went to meet him at Victoria Station but he had to struggle, blast him."

"And what about Edward Butler?" demanded the inspector, joining Bertie at the water's edge.

Bromley nodded. "Oh, yes. Him too. It gets easier after the first one, you know. I figured if I couldn't have the gold then I'd get the plans and sell them. There were others besides Benz who would pay for them." He looked about him and then dipped the oars into the water. "Well, I can't sit here, pleasant as it may be. By the time you get off the island – if indeed you do – I'll be somewhere in Europe. You'll never find me. *Au revoir* . . . or I should say, Goodbye."

As he applied himself to the oars, Bertie heard a shout from behind. Arnold came running, very fast, across the patch of grass and launched himself off the end of the crumbling dock. He hit the water and started swimming strongly toward Bromley's boat. Bromley pulled vigorously on the oars but, in a panic, slipped and one of them came out of the rowlock. As he struggled to get it back in position, Arnold reached him and tried to pull himself up over the side of the boat. The vessel rolled sideways and Bromley pitched into the water.

"Amazing!" Inspector Moss's mouth hung open.

Bertie shrugged. "Not really," he said. "Not if you knew Arnold like I do. He idolizes Captain Matthew Webb – you know, the man who swam across the English Channel a few years back? Arnold is reading his book on the art of swimming. I must presume it is paying off."

Bromley was spluttering and crying that he couldn't swim. Arnold had his arm locked about the other man's neck and now started drawing him back towards the bank.

The inspector dug into his coat pocket and produced a pair of handcuffs. "Never know when you may need the derbies," he said grimly.

Chapter Twenty-Seven

"I can never thank you enough, Mr. Hawkins," said Kate Butler. She wore first mourning, sitting in a black dress of watered-silk edged with black crepe, a black cap on her head. "I will accept Mr. Benz's generous offer. The money will be needed to give Eric a proper education; something that Edward was insistent upon."

She looked across the room at her young son, neatly dressed in jacket and waistcoat, buttoned to the neck, with knickerbockers, stockings, and boots buttoned to the ankles. Bertie followed her gaze and thought that the boy looked none the worse for having gone through the kidnapping inflicted upon him.

"He's a fine boy," he said. "I'm sure he will do his father proud."

"I understand that Sir Hugh Ardsley has offered to personally deliver Edward's plans to Mr. Benz," Kate continued. "That is extraordinarily kind of him. He said that he wants there to be no more mishaps in the exchange. Sir Hugh will then bring back to me the balance of the payment."

"A most satisfactory conclusion all around," said Bertie.

"I know that there was not any sort of formal agreement between us, Mr. Hawkins, but I will be wanting to pay you – your Penny Court Enquirers – for all that you have done in bringing my husband's killer to justice." Kate's big green eyes were turned to look directly at him.

Bertie always felt uncomfortable when it came to discussing money, especially so with a recently bereaved widow. He mumbled something indistinct and got to his feet, claiming that he had to meet with "the inspector from Scotland Yard".

"Oh, by the way, Mrs. Butler," he said, turning at the door. "I understand that young Eric did identify Thomas Squire as the man who abducted him?"

"Yes, he did."

"It seems there was no direct connection between the murder of your husband and the kidnapping of your son. While Squire was upstairs taking the boy, unknown to him Cedric Bromley was in your husband's study, murdering him and trying to locate the plans. Extraordinary!"

"And have they not been able to link Mr. Squire and Mr. Lawson?" asked Kate.

Bertie shook his head. "No. It would seem that Lawson is too smart for that. Squire was in his employ; no question. And Squire insists he took your son on Lawson's instructions. But until we can apprehend Lawson, Thomas Squire must carry the full blame for the kidnapping. There was also some link between Bromley and Lawson in years gone by

– two rotten apples from the same barrel, one might say – but no connection, that we have found so far, between the two actions." Bertie paused a moment, and sighed. "Good day to you, Mrs. Butler."

It was one of Nellie's usual excellent dinners but was treated like a special celebration. The air was one of festivity. Inspector Moss sat all evening with a wide smile on his usually somber face. Arnold, with an occasional quizzical look about him, spent most of his time beaming silently at one and all, and Bertie basked in a glory that only he could fully appreciate.

"The Penny Court Enquirers have fully justified their existence, I think we can say," he said, carving the big leg of lamb and watching as Nellie passed the loaded plates around to their guests.

"As good as anything Tommy Turnbull could've done!" proclaimed Isobel. Nellie let her contribute. In fact, Isobel had been given a seat at the end of the table, next to Arnold, where she could sit after serving everyone else.

"I do believe I should not be here encouraging you people," said the inspector, helping himself liberally to mint sauce. "I hope word never gets back to the Chief Inspector."

"It won't through any of us," said Nellie, with a smile.

"Am I to understand, Bertram," the policeman continued, "that you started this enterprise through frustration at the regular police methods and procedures?"

"That is correct, Campbell. And I think I have proved my point!"

"Well, I have to thank you for allowing our bumbling, stumbling officers of the law to take the credit for capturing Mr. Bromley."

Bertie waved a dismissive hand, still holding the carving knife. "We are not in it for the glory," he said, magnanimously. "We are in it for the thrill of the chase."

"And to show up the police," said Arnold, spearing a beetroot and depositing it on his plate.

"Now, Arnold!" said Nellie.

Inspector Moss merely smiled. "You are nay baiting me today, Arnold," he said. He grew serious for a moment. "But I do have to report that our Mr. Lawson seems to have gone to earth. There's neither hide nor hair of him anywhere . . . according to the police force. But I dina' doubt he will show his face at some time."

"He has businesses to run," said Bertie. "He will have to."

"Aye, that's what we're counting on." The inspector filled his mouth with lamb and chewed contentedly for a few moments. Then he looked at Bertie. "If I may make so bold, Bertram, how is this new enterprise of yours doing financially? Oh, I know it's none of my business, and not a subject I should be mentioning, but I do rather want to see you continue . . . if I may be so bold."

"You just want Nellie's dinners to continue," said Bertie, laughing.

"Actually we are doing very well for a brand new business," said Nellie. "Mrs. Butler has shown wonderful appreciation of our services, as has Sir Hugh. The Penny Court Enquirers solved the mystery of the missing woman, rescued a kidnapped child, and solved two murders. Not bad for amateurs, I would say."

There were murmurs of agreement all around. Bertie, who had sat down to eat his own dinner, now stood up again. He spread his jacket and displayed his waistcoat. Across the front of it hung a solid gold watch chain in place of his old silver one.

"Miss Emily Ardsley, bless her young heart, saw fit to entrust me with her grandfather's gold watch, in appreciation of what we have managed to do," he said. They all noticed a slight catch in Bertie's voice as he said this, but no one commented. "I am honored to be so entrusted and I deem it as a sign that we are meant to continue our work."

"Just don't get underfoot with Scotland Yard," muttered the inspector, *soto voce*. They all laughed. He then looked directly at Bertie. "So what's the next step, Bertram?"

Arnold reached down and pulled up a newspaper that he had been holding on his lap. "Funny you should ask," he said. "Bertie, did you see this? Headlines in this afternoon's newspaper?"

RAYMOND BUCKLAND is a prolific prize-winning author of both fiction and non-fiction. His books have been translated into seventeen foreign languages. Born and raised in England, he is fascinated by the Victorian age and loves to set his mysteries in that era.

Visit www.raymondbucklandbooks.com